O9-BUB-364

Kissing Mr. Right

THE CACTUS WREN
BOOK EXCHANGE
56336 29 PALMS HWY.
YUCCA VALLEY, CA 92284
(760) 365-6652

ALSO BY MICHELLE MAJOR

Still the One

Her Accidental Engagement

A Brevia Beginning

A Kiss on Crimson Ranch

A Second Chance at Crimson Ranch

The Taming of Delany Fortune (The Fortunes of Texas: Cowboy Country)

Suddenly a Father

Kissing Mr. Right

MICHELLE MAJOR

Montlake
Romance

This is a work of fiction. Names, characters, organizations, places, events, and incidents are either products of the author's imagination or are used fictitiously.

Text copyright © 2015 Michelle Major
All rights reserved.

No part of this book may be reproduced, or stored in a retrieval system, or transmitted in any form or by any means, electronic, mechanical, photocopying, recording, or otherwise, without express written permission of the publisher.

Published by Montlake Romance, Seattle

www.apub.com

Amazon, the Amazon logo, and Montlake Romance are trademarks of Amazon.com, Inc., or its affiliates.

ISBN-13: 9781503945524
ISBN-10: 1503945529

Cover design by Shasti O'Leary-Soudant

Printed in the United States of America

To Lana and Annie, who believed in me and this book from the beginning. I wouldn't be here without you. XO

CHAPTER ONE

Kendall Clark adjusted the rearview mirror as her Jeep idled at a red light before taking out her makeup bag and fixing the mess on her face. She tried and failed to muster some enthusiasm for reapplying eye shadow for the third time that day. All the things she'd given up for this job over the past three years flashed through her mind—a social life, boyfriends, most of her dignity.

As a lifestyles reporter for Denver, Colorado's News Channel 8, Kendall would do just about anything for on-air time. Her boss liked to remind her that she needed to pay her dues, which meant Kendall was given the stories no one else at the station wanted. A lot of her assignments involved animals. This morning she'd been shadowing one of the vets at the Denver zoo. Who knew a walrus with a cold could blow snot so far?

She wished that being sneezed on by a three hundred pound walrus had been the most embarrassing moment of her career, but she'd been peed on, bitten, chased, and most humiliatingly, had her leg humped by an overzealous poodle—all with the camera rolling. Through each incident, she'd smiled and tried to look professional.

She was popular with the viewers for the entertainment value she provided. But even as she entertained, Kendall's goal was always to inform people. Her specialty was human interest stories, and there wasn't much she'd refuse to do so that her pieces got the airtime they deserved.

Lately Kendall's boss wanted her to focus on stories that were more sensationalized than thought-provoking. All in the name of ratings, of course.

But journalism was more than ratings to Kendall. It was about the people she covered, giving a voice to their stories and making a difference. She wanted to do her job well and finally make something of herself but wondered, not for the first time, if the sacrifices were worth the potential payoff.

And besides, how much walrus snot could one person take?

The zookeeper had handed her a roll of paper towels to clean the slime off her cheek and most of her makeup had peeled away with it. Stroking the mascara wand across her bottom lashes, she glanced up to see a ten-foot-tall billboard with her face plastered across it looming above her Jeep Cherokee. The caption, written in block letters across the sign, hit her like a ton of bricks.

No. Flipping. Way.

The mascara wand stabbed into the corner of her eye, and she blinked furiously against the sting as the applicator fell from her fingers, landing on her charcoal-gray silk skirt.

At that moment, the red light changed to green. Her working eye focused on the traffic moving in front of her.

Her muscles tensed and her foot slammed the gas pedal to the floor. An ugly crunch echoed as she crashed into the bumper of the large truck in front of her. Then there was silence.

She sat motionless for several moments, her hands curled white-knuckled around the steering wheel.

This is not happening. None of this is happening.

Her heart pumped a frantic rhythm against her chest. Adrenaline hummed through her body, and a bead of perspiration rolled down the back of her neck, alerting her to the stifling warmth that already pervaded the interior of her SUV. Because the Jeep's engine had stalled when her foot popped off the clutch, the air conditioner no longer blew puffs of cool air from the vents in the dash.

A knock at the window jolted her back into reality.

She turned to see a man peering in through the glass. His features were blurred by the sun's reflection hitting the window, but she heard his muffled voice ask, "Are you ok?"

She swiped a finger along the bottom of her profusely watering eye. Oh, God, she'd been in a car accident. She'd *caused* a car accident. Saying a silent prayer that no one in the truck had been injured, she unfastened her seat belt and opened the door of the Jeep.

Horns blew and motors hummed along Colorado Boulevard. The loud churning of a diesel engine sounded as a bus sped by, blowing a hot gust of pollution into Kendall's face.

Hoping no one would recognize her, she stepped onto the asphalt in her high heels, and although her legs tingled, she was relatively steady on her feet. She closed her eyes and took another deep breath, ignoring the smell of engine exhaust.

The heat of the April sun felt good against her face. The familiar warmth helped to steady her shaky nerves. She concentrated on the tickle of warm spring air against her cheek.

Feeling calmer, she turned and found herself staring into the most beautiful pair of blue eyes she'd ever seen.

She knew the man's mouth was moving, but for the life of her, Kendall couldn't have repeated what he was saying. His eyes mesmerized her, sucking away most of her brain cells in the process. Eyes that were the same clear blue as the cloudless sky that coated the Denver landscape most spring mornings.

Since moving to Colorado, Kendall had been fascinated with the contrast between that vibrant color overhead and the massive peaks of the Rocky Mountains where sky met earth along the Front Range. It was like that with those eyes. The face that surrounded them was rugged and tanned, making the blue stand out even more.

At the moment they were focused on her with a look of deep concern. She realized he was speaking and she still hadn't responded. Two large hands waved in front of her face.

She glanced up at her own oversize eyes staring down at her from the billboard and shuddered. In the photo, her eyes rolled heavenward and she was holding an umbrella above her head.

Instead of raindrops, the billboard showed tiny figures of men pelting against the umbrella. The blurb that ran across the puffy cloud at the top of the sign read, "Tune in to find out why it's raining men for News 8's Kendall Clark."

She'd told her news director there was no way she'd participate in the silly ratings promotion. It was the first time she'd refused anything at work, and she should have guessed that her boss wouldn't listen. The harder Kendall pushed to be given stories of substance, the more gimmicky her assignments became.

To Kendall, that sentence meant the end of her dream of making a name for herself in the world of hard-hitting journalism. Yes, her stories to date were almost all ratings gimmicks. But she had bigger dreams, real aspirations to make use of the journalism degree she was still paying off.

Her head hurt and she struggled to concentrate on the man with the beautiful eyes. What was he saying?

"Are you ok?" he repeated, adding, "Should I call 911?"

Finally his words registered. She shook her head. "I'm fine. What about the people in the truck?" She yelled to be heard over the noise from passing cars.

"We're ok." He put his hand on her cheek and for a moment her knees went weak. "I'm not sure about you."

Oh, man, he was something. "With you here, I'm fine." She jumped at the sound of a horn honking right next to her then clapped a hand over her mouth. Did she really say that out loud? "I mean, if you're ok—if everyone is ok—I'm fine."

One side of his mouth kicked up, just the hint of a smile, and she had a feeling she was digging herself in deeper.

They were standing just inside the far right lane of the street. A long line of cars waited behind her Jeep, turn signals blinking furiously as they tried to merge into the two unblocked lanes of the street.

He gestured to their vehicles. "Let's check the damage."

She followed him to the front of her Jeep, moaning softly when she saw the mangled bumper. It looked like it had suffered in the losing end of a fight with a large trash compactor. There was a deep dent in the center, with crumpled metal on either side.

Shifting her eyes to the back of the truck, she was relieved to see little damage. Maybe a few splotches of red paint along the bumper, but that was the extent of it.

There was just enough space between the two cars to squeeze through. She followed Blue Eyes onto the sidewalk, where they were less likely to be hit.

He rested his hand on the corner of the truck's back bumper and crouched down. "You got hung up on the trailer hitch."

His forest-green T-shirt stretched as he bent forward to examine the damage. Kendall's mouth went dry at the sight of muscles bunching across the broad expanse of his back.

Whoa, girl. She put the mental breaks on her rusty libido, which had picked a most inopportune time to come out of hibernation. Maybe she'd been more rattled by the accident than she first thought. She didn't have this sort of physical reaction to men. Besides, her type wore tailored suits, not faded T-shirts, cargo pants, and dusty work boots.

The passenger door of the truck opened, offering a welcome distraction. A tiny woman with a big halo of curly red hair hopped onto the pavement. Cell phone cradled between her head and shoulder, she strode to the back of the truck and bent forward. "Not much damage," she said into the phone. "We shouldn't be more than a half hour late."

Kendall didn't realize it was possible for legs to look so good in cutoff jean shorts and heavy work boots. But the redhead's did. Pocketing the cell phone, she turned to Kendall and did a double take. "Holy hell, what happened to your face?"

Kendall's gaze whipped toward the man straightening from under the Jeep. He frowned slightly. "Are you sure you're all right? You seem a little out of it. Do you want to sit down?"

While she appreciated his concern, the redhead's words stuck. Something happened to her face? She'd have a difficult time on-air with a big goose egg on her forehead. She grabbed the Jeep's side mirror and crouched in front of it.

An enormous clump of mascara stuck gooey and black to the inside corner of her eye. More of the mascara caked to the skin underneath her lashes. It smeared along her cheek where she'd wiped away tears after poking herself. Next to the unmarred half of her face, the mascara-strewn portion looked awful. So much for her perfect image.

"Why didn't you say anything?"

Blue Eyes cocked an eyebrow. "I did. You stared at me."

Kendall blushed as she thought of her reaction to him. Another reason she didn't go for the hot, hunky type. Too distracting. She opened the car door and dug through her glove compartment for the small stash of wet wipes she kept there.

Grabbing several from the container, she scrubbed at her face. The wipes felt cool against skin now heated from intense embarrassment. While she had been ogling Mr. Blue Eyes, he'd probably been wondering if she'd just come from her job as the main attraction in some circus freak show.

She did her best to wipe away the mascara.

"I'm sorry about the accident," she told him. "I was late for work and was trying to save time by doing my makeup in the car." She gestured to her face. "Obviously a big mistake."

"Obviously," the redhead repeated. Kendall noticed that she wore no makeup. To be so lucky.

The man reached out and took one of the crumpled wipes from her clenched fingers. Gently, he dabbed at a spot just above her left eyebrow. "You missed a little," he said with a smile.

A row of perfectly white teeth gleamed from behind that tawny skin and a small dimple winked at the corner of his mouth. Her breath caught. *Get a grip*, she told herself.

He shoved the wipe into his pocket and glanced at the two cars. "It's no big deal. Your Jeep got the worse end of it."

"The truck's a beater," the woman added, "but solid as a tank." Her head cocked to one side as she studied Kendall. "Do I know you from somewhere?"

She thought about the billboard towering above them. *Don't look up*, she inwardly pleaded. "Maybe. I'm a reporter on Channel 8."

"Omigod, you're Kendall Clark." The redhead tipped her head back and let out a hoot of laughter, then smacked the driver of the truck in the ribs. "Ty, it's Kendall Clark."

Kendall didn't know how to take that outburst, but she thought she might be the butt end of an inside joke.

"I know who she is," the man told the redhead, his gaze never leaving Kendall. "You've had some interesting stories."

"That could be the understatement of the year."

"Like when the cat from the shelter bit you," the woman interjected. "That sucker latched onto your hand for dear life."

Kendall grimaced. "I still have a scar. But it was adopted the next day. I guess people like a spunky animal."

"Spunky is good," the man said. Kendall tried to ignore the warmth that spread through her at his tone.

"Thanks for being so understanding about all this." She held out her right hand as she glanced at the watch on her left wrist. "Oh, boy. I'm going to be lucky if I make the five thirty broadcast." The billboard grinned down at her. *If I don't quit first,* she added to herself. "Again, I'm sorry about the accident. Did you call the police?"

He took her hand in his. His palm felt rough against her skin, but his grasp was surprisingly gentle. "I'm Tyler Bishop. And, no, I haven't called yet."

The redhead groaned. "Just exchange numbers and be done with it, Ty. She needs to get to work, and we're supposed to be at my mom's by now."

Kendall saw a look pass between the two. They must be dating. She didn't know why she was surprised or why it bothered her. They made a cute couple—all natural and outdoorsy looking.

She offered a weak smile. "I really do need to get to the station. I'm sure my insurance will pay for the damage to your truck." Too bad her rates would go up. She could barely afford the car payment now. Between her student loans, the money she sent to her parents each month, and the mortgage on her condo, there wasn't much left.

"The truck isn't the problem. I use it for work and it gets banged up pretty regularly. But your Jeep's going to need some help with that bumper." Tyler stepped closer to the cars again and examined the mangled front end of the Jeep. "Why don't you try to start it?"

She walked between the two cars and opened her driver's-side door just enough to squeeze through. Her fingers closed around the keys still dangling from the ignition. To her relief, the engine turned over immediately and the Jeep hummed to life. She pressed down on the window lever. A warm gust of spring air blew into the interior of the car.

Tyler nodded to her from the front of the car. His head dipped from sight for a few moments, then reappeared. He gave her a thumbs-up sign. Dusting his hands together, he approached her window, the redhead hot on his heels.

"Sounds good. Nothing seems to be leaking. Just to be safe, I wouldn't drive far until you take it into a shop."

"I'll take it in first thing in the morning. What about your truck?"

He shrugged. "Don't worry about it."

"Really, Mr. Bishop, I'd like to pay for the damage."

"Call me Ty. It's not a big deal. I have a friend with a repair shop who will give me a good deal."

Kendall sighed. "Any chance . . . no, never mind. You don't owe me anything. I can't say I'm sorry enough."

Ty studied her for a moment. As if reading her thoughts, he said, "If you want, I'll give you the repair shop address. Bring the Jeep by around ten tomorrow?" The redhead laughed again. Ty shook his head. "Ignore her. Probably bumped her head on the dash."

She looked over his shoulder to see the redhead arch her brows. Was she worried Kendall was going to make a move on her man? After her last dating fiasco, Kendall wasn't looking for another relationship. Especially not with someone like Ty Bishop, no matter what her body said to the contrary. She should call her insurance company and let them take care of this.

But if she could save money, it was worth a try. "You're being so nice about this whole thing. I'd appreciate that."

He returned her smile. "It's easy to be nice to someone so . . ." He paused, shook his head. "My turn for never mind. Do you have a pen and paper?"

Reaching into the center console, she pulled out a small notepad and pen. Ty scribbled an address and phone number. A spark danced across her skin as his fingers brushed hers when he placed the notepad back in her hand. It was probably just the spring breeze.

She blinked rapidly to clear her head. When she spoke, her voice sounded squeaky in her ears. "Ok, well, I, uh, guess I should get going."

He looked like he wanted to say something but only nodded. With a quick tap on the Jeep's door he moved back, turning to survey the line of cars behind them. After a moment, he stepped into the center lane, his arm extended to stop the slow stream of traffic. He motioned her forward with the other hand.

Kendall gripped the steering wheel and turned the Jeep into the space he'd carved for her.

"I'll see you tomorrow morning," he called.

She gave a quick wave out the window but kept her eyes on the road ahead. No need for two accidents in one day.

◆ ◆ ◆

Ignoring the blaring horns from the cars stopped behind him, Ty watched Kendall speed away and then walked back to his truck and slid behind the wheel.

Jenny was waiting. "It's sooo easy to be nice to someone so *what?* What were you going to say? Lovely . . . uptight . . . shallow?" She stuck her finger in her mouth and gagged.

"You don't know that she's shallow."

"Maybe not, but she's too perfect. Always wearing fancy designer clothes and never a hair out of place."

"Did you see her face a minute ago?"

Jenny waved away his argument. "An exception to the rule. Stop thinking with your junk. Kendall Clark is expensive wine and four-course meals. You're beer and wings at a sports bar. It would never work. You think she's going to go for someone who's practically a laborer?"

"I own the company, Jenny."

"Semantics." She patted his arm. "Trust me, women like Kendall are more trouble than they're worth. If you need a date, let me set you up."

"I don't need a date." Ty turned on the radio and cranked up the volume, trying to block out Kendall's face in his mind. Despite the mess of black goop camouflaging most of the left side of her face, she was a stunner. With her big green eyes, high cheekbones, and slightly upturned nose, she was the only reason he tuned into the local news. He'd had a crush on her since the day he'd watched her kiss a camel on air last January. Something had flashed in her eyes at that moment, barely caught by the camera. A mix of vulnerability and determination that spoke to him.

Maybe he'd imagined the spark between them, but he believed there was more to Kendall than Jenny thought. It was the way she seemed to care about every one of her stories on the news, no matter how light or frivolous the topic. She might not look like the women he usually went out with, but outward appearances could be deceiving. His family was living proof.

As he pulled his truck to the curb in front of Jenny's mom's house, Ty thought about the next morning. He hadn't felt anything for a woman in a long time.

He was pretty damn sure Kendall Clark was about to change that.

CHAPTER TWO

Glancing at the dashboard clock, Kendall screeched to a stop in front of the KDPO station. It was three thirty, which made her a half hour late for the weekly news meeting, where the anchors, reporters, and producers met to discuss the upcoming broadcast schedule.

But instead of using the precious minutes on the ride over to call ahead so one of the production assistants could put together the footage from her zoo story, her mind had been occupied with thoughts of Ty Bishop and his sky-blue eyes.

Mary Samuels, the receptionist, looked up from her keyboard as Kendall burst into the lobby.

"Kendall, you're never late." The older woman pulled off her bifocals. "Is everything ok?"

Kendall took the stairs that led to the production offices two at a time. "I'm fine," she called down. "I'll tell you all about it tomorrow."

"As long as you're ok, dear." Mary's voice echoed from below.

Oh, she was peachy, if she discounted walrus boogers, a mild anxiety attack, eminent career disaster, and an unwanted attraction to a virtual stranger.

She raced down the second-floor hallway and veered into the conference room, slamming the door behind her. Her coworkers turned to stare as the questions started.

"What happened?"

"Where have you been?"

The evening anchor, Jeff Baumgartner, raised his eyebrows but made no comment about her disheveled appearance.

Ignoring the questions, she pointed at Tom Brogan, one of the station's interns. "Where are we on the zoo piece?"

"I've spliced together most of your report. Everything up until the walrus sneezed."

Kendall ignored the titters of laughter from around the room. "Tom, you saved me. I could kiss you."

His face brightened, but before he could reply, Kendall felt a tap on her shoulder.

"There's a penalty for missing the afternoon meeting," a voice as sharp as rusted metal said quietly in her ear.

Embarrassment and anger washed over Kendall as she thought of the reason for her late arrival. "I haven't *missed* the meeting, and this is the first time I've been late in three years." Kendall turned to Liz Blessen, KDPO's news director. "I'm fine, Liz. Your concern means so much."

"I get anxious when my reporters aren't here on time. Extra stress is bad for my high blood pressure." Liz straightened the hem of her St. John jacket. "Ward Davis is on his way in. Tell me why I shouldn't bump your story for his piece about the Highlands food festival."

"I'm not sure Ward's wife would appreciate her husband starring in your new dating show."

Something flashed in Liz's eyes that looked like guilt. "You saw the billboard?" she asked, her icy tone melting.

"I saw it and immediately rear-ended a truck. That's why I'm late." The news director cringed.

"You look great in the promo shots," Jeff said. "Like a real hard-hitting journalist fending off those tiny men." He chuckled at his own joke.

Kendall felt color rise to her cheeks. Jeff's reaction was one of the reasons she'd said no to *It's Raining Men* in the first place. He wouldn't be the only one to make fun of her for it.

"Was anyone hurt?" one of the other reporters asked.

"Luckily, it was a fender bender." Kendall turned to Liz and her voice became as heated as her face. "I said *no* to the dating show. *It's Raining Men*, Liz? You've got to be kidding me."

The news director pretended not to notice Kendall's temper and patted her arm. "We're glad you're safe. The walrus story stays, of course." She smiled, as if tossing Kendall that small bone would make the tension between them disappear. "Let's finish the meeting so everyone can get to work. Kendall, do you want to have a seat?"

"No." What she wanted was to stomp from the room or throw a fit and demand that Liz take her seriously. But demands and fits weren't part of Kendall's personality, and Liz knew it. Kendall loved the reporting part of her job but had never mastered cutthroat office politics or even the ability to advocate for herself.

"Fine." Liz stepped around Kendall to sit at the head of the conference table. "We're set for tonight and have already gone through the programming schedule for most of the week. Kendall, I've got your write-up on the flooring company owner who hires ex-cons."

Kendall squared her shoulders. She might not be good at advocating for herself, but even without notes, she could pitch a story she believed in. "It's more than hiring ex-cons," she told the group. "Here's a small business owner trying to make a difference in his community, to break that cycle of poverty and give unlikely employees a chance. He also invests in at-risk youth, offering scholarships—"

Jeff groaned. "Another tearjerker? What a surprise. You're a downer, Kendall. Viewers want to be entertained, not made to feel guilty for how much they *don't* do to make a difference."

"I'm giving people hope, Jeff. This man believes these kids and his employees deserve a shot at a different future."

"But it's in a similar vein to most of the features you do," one of the producers said, shuffling papers as she spoke.

That comment hit close to home, but no one at the station knew Kendall's motivation for the type of stories she reported. "Because there's too much hope in the nightly news cast?" Kendall shot back. "The point of human interest stories is to evoke emotion in viewers."

"Tell her about the baked bake sale," Jeff said with a laugh.

The young producer smiled. "A group of college freshmen have set up a bake sale outside one of the marijuana dispensaries on Colfax. They're raising money for a spring break trip to Cancun."

Jeff leaned forward in his chair. "They made five hundred bucks the first day. I wish pot had been legal when I was in school."

Kendall's jaw started to ache from clamping it shut. She glanced at Liz, unable to believe the news director would pull her story for this piece of fluff.

"The ex-con idea has merit," the news director said after a moment. "It's important to highlight people doing good work in the local community. I think it would be a great write-up for the station blog." She reached for the notes the producer was holding about the bake sale. "We'll go with the spring break piece for the broadcast, though. It's timely and viewers will either be entertained or outraged. But they'll be talking about it no matter what. We're *evoking emotion*, Kendall."

Kendall's mouth dropped open as Liz smiled at her.

"Great choice," Jeff said, standing and heading for the door. "Mind picking up a brownie for me while you're down there, Ken?"

Tom Brogan took a step toward Kendall. "Do you want to take a look at the zoo story?" he asked gently.

She nodded, forcing a professional smile on her face. She'd had worse assignments than a pot bake sale and wasn't going to push Liz. Yet. As awful as the dating promotion was, with the billboards for *It's Raining Men* already up, Kendall realized she finally had some small amount of power at the station. The trick was figuring out the best way to use it.

◆ ◆ ◆

Two hours later, Kendall dropped into the chair that faced her computer in the newsroom office, massaging her fingers against her jaw. She'd smiled her way through the *Live at Five!* broadcast, feeling like a complete fool each time she looked into the camera and imagined exposing her dating life on-air.

A knock sounded on the partially closed office door and Liz peeked her head around the corner. "Is it safe to enter or do you still want to kill me?"

"I haven't decided."

Liz smiled and stepped into the office. She perched one compact hip on the desk nearest the door and folded her arms across her chest. "*It's Raining Men* won't be that bad."

Kendall took a stack of papers off the printer next to her desk. "I've jumped through every hoop you've put in front of me for three years, but I want a legitimate career. You can't make me into a reality television joke. This was supposed to be a charity auction—win a date with a local celebrity. Not a televised dating show."

"It *is* a charity event."

She pointed a finger at the news director. "Because I don't date much? That's low, Liz. Even for you."

"I didn't mean it like that." She ran a hand through her crop of spiky blond hair. "I'm sorry, Kendall. Does that make it better? I'm sorry about the accident. I'm sorry we went ahead with the billboards. But we *are* raising money for charity. The two men chosen will have a thousand dollars donated to their favorite nonprofit. You'll go on a second on-camera date with the guy the viewers like the best. His charity gets another five hundred dollars."

"The men are paid to date me? Even better."

"You're looking at it wrong," Liz said, straightening. "It's two dates for a good cause. The publicity will be great for the station and for you. The promos started this morning and the response has been phenomenal."

Kendall's stomach rolled and churned like she'd just gotten off the steepest rollercoaster at Elitch Gardens, the amusement park near downtown. "There are promo spots as well as the billboards? I *did not* say yes."

"Do you know how much money we've already spent on marketing? Now that the spots are running you can't—"

"No." Kendall shook her head. "You won't bully me into this unless . . ."

Liz's mouth thinned and it looked like a vein in her forehead might explode. "Unless what?" she snapped.

"You give me the wildfire follow-up story."

Liz actually laughed. "You can't be serious. That story has already been assigned to one of the senior reporters."

Kendall shrugged. "I want it, and I want Bob to call his contacts at WRKU in New York." The station's president, Bob Cunningham, had worked in New York City before taking over the Denver station. Kendall knew he still had friends on the East Coast. "There's an opening at the weekend news desk. I'd be a good fit and will have a better chance with Bob's recommendation." She kept her voice steady, but inside she was a jumble of nerves.

Liz didn't reply for a few moments. When she finally spoke, her voice was quiet. "WRKU is the network's flagship station."

"I know."

"You think you're ready?" her boss asked with an arched eyebrow.

The eyebrow was Liz's trademark. She could communicate a dozen types of disdain with a few millimeters of movement. It had stopped Kendall from speaking up on more than one occasion. But not now. This was too important.

"Absolutely," she answered, almost surprised to find she meant it. "You know the publicity from *It's Raining Men* will pull us way ahead during sweeps. Bob must be salivating at the prospect. If he gets the ratings, I get his support."

"And the wildfire story," Liz added.

Kendall nodded. Three summers ago, shortly after Kendall had arrived in Colorado, a wildfire devastated the foothills southwest of Denver, making the area a local and national news story. Hundreds of people had spent weeks evacuated from their homes when the fires swept into heavily populated neighborhoods. Dozens of families living in the foothills of the Rocky Mountains lost their homes and most of their possessions.

Even miles away in Denver, a heavy coat of ash had hung over the south end of the city, turning the normally clear sky into a churning mass of smoke and debris.

Viewers had watched scenes of destruction with horrified fascination. Kendall had been given the opportunity to interview a few of the families since all of the station's manpower had been focused on the fires. She'd been touched by the stories she heard from people who lived in the area. The way the community had banded together to support families who lost their homes, as well as the firefighters and police officers working the scene, had made a big impact on her, especially since she'd never felt that kind of community connection growing up.

Restoration of the area was well underway, and she wanted to be the one to tell the stories of people whose lives had been affected by the disaster.

"I can't believe you're making demands," Liz murmured. "I didn't think you had it in you, Ken."

"I guess I wasn't the only one shocked today."

Liz gave a reluctant smile. "If I agree, you'll go forward with *It's Raining Men*? The dates, the interviews, social media? Plus enthusiasm—at least on camera?

Kendall pressed her fingers to her temples. She focused on the reaction of people back in her tiny hometown in Kansas if she was on the national news. She imagined the ladies who lunched at the country club, where her father worked, seeing her on TV just like Diane Sawyer. That would cause a few mouths to drop. "The men will be decent, right?"

"We'll make sure of it."

"If you promise the wildfire story and New York, I'll do it."

Liz held up her hand, her littlest finger wiggling. "Pinkie swear."

Kendall laughed. As juvenile as it seemed, Liz took her pinkie swears seriously. She crossed her little finger with Liz's. Their relationship had been up and down over the years, but Kendall still felt a strange loyalty to the woman who'd given her a break in this top-25 market.

From the time she was ten years old, Kendall had wanted to be a television news anchor. She watched the national newscasts the way other kids watched reruns of Scooby Doo. The women she saw on TV fascinated her, especially Diane Sawyer.

Diane had been the epitome of female journalists to Kendall. She was a trailblazer, original and tenacious but always with a sophisticated elegance Kendall had longed to emulate. Growing up in small town on the outskirts of Kansas City, Kendall felt a connection to the woman who'd made it to the top of broadcasting all the way from rural Kentucky.

What Kendall lacked in pedigree, she made up for in determination. When she was twelve, one of her teachers helped her become the first scholarship student at the elite Graves Academy in Kansas City.

She'd been tingling with excitement the morning her mother had driven their battered Dodge Duster toward the affluent community that housed Graves. She knew a fancy education could open the right doors for her. But just as her mother pulled away from the curb, Kendall felt something hard hit her square in the back.

"Pull the car around, sweetie," a voice behind her taunted. Everyone knew her dad worked at the country club parking cars. Soft laughter followed, but when Kendall turned, cheeks burning, she'd only seen a set of keys lying at her feet.

She'd never forgotten the shame she felt at that moment. Each morning after, Kendall had kissed her mother good-bye and exited the car three blocks away from the school. Her mom hadn't mentioned the change or the fact that Kendall never brought home fliers about school activities. She kept her parents far away from Graves.

It had been a struggle to fit in at the prestigious school. During the six years she attended Graves, she'd written papers and finished homework assignments for other students. She'd allowed them to copy from her tests during exams. In exchange for this, Kendall was given a tenuous position on the fringes of the popular cliques at the school, but it was constant work to keep her so-called friends satisfied.

She always felt like her presence polluted the rarified air that normally smelled of wealth and privilege. So she'd held her breath, snuffing out her childhood like a candle in a coal mine.

Ignoring her family became so second nature that the lines between who she was on the inside and who she pretended to be had blurred. Her parents had made plenty of sacrifices so she could succeed. Now she hoped her future success would make up for treating them so badly.

She could manage her way through anything if it got her closer to her goal of becoming a respected journalist. But there was still something that worried her about dating on camera. "What if they don't like me?"

Liz was at the door but turned at Kendall's question. "What are you talking about? One thing no one can deny is that viewers love you. This is a chance for them to know you better. They'll take you even further into their homes and hearts."

Kendall shook her head. "Not the viewers. I'm talking about the men." The words tumbled out of her in a rush of nervous breath. "What if none of the guys like me? What if the dates are busts and then they get played on-air and everyone sees that I have no chemistry with men?"

"Is this about Greg Davies?"

Kendall winced at her ex-boyfriend's name. "He called me a frigid ice princess."

"Refresh my memory," Liz interrupted. "Did he tell you this before or after you found out he was going at it with your real estate agent? He was an ass, Kendall."

"Agreed, but did he have a valid point?"

Liz threw her hands into the air. "Don't sell yourself short. Go on the dates. Meet a few nice guys. When was the last time you felt a rush of attraction for someone?"

A pair of deep blue eyes popped into Kendall's mind. She shook her head to clear the image. "I've agreed to it, but I'm not looking to meet someone right now. This is about my career, not my nonexistent love life. If there's one thing Greg reinforced, it was that romance belongs at the bottom of my priority list." She nodded, needing to convince herself as much as her boss. "It's a distraction I don't want or need."

"Smart girl." Liz nodded then headed out the door. Kendall could hear her humming the cheesy song the promotion had been named after as she strolled down the hall.

Kendall stared at her computer screen, but inside she was doing a big production happy dance. For the first time in her career, she'd fought for more than a story she believed in. She'd stood up for herself.

It felt unsettling . . . exhilarating . . . right.

As silly as *It's Raining Men* seemed, maybe the promotion would really be the start of something good. Pulling a notebook out of the bottom drawer of her desk, she flipped to the page labeled "Life List." The list was over ten years old now, but the goals on it hadn't changed much. Some of them were crossed off—valedictorian, college scholarship, working in a top-25 market.

But the one she'd written in bubble letters as a teenager was still there—New York City. Her ultimate goal, working as a reporter in the big city. It had felt almost too ambitious for a girl from Nowhere, USA, but now adrenaline buzzed through her as she took a pen and outlined the words once more.

The dream she'd worked toward all this time was finally within reach, and nothing was going to stop her from achieving it.

◆ ◆ ◆

Ty let out a long breath as the Jeep turned into the lot of the body shop. He'd convinced himself that Kendall Clark wouldn't show this morning and didn't like the flood of relief that pounded through him now. Did it really matter so much to him if he saw her again?

Apparently it did.

As she stepped out of the banged-up car, he approached with a friendly wave. The parking lot was littered with cars and trucks in various states of repair. Kendall, in her lavender sweater, neat trousers, and low heels, looked as out of place as Martha Stewart at a monster truck rally.

Tortoiseshell glasses screened her eyes from view. Her brown hair was pulled back into a neat ponytail at the nape of her neck. The morning air blew one loose strand against the side of her face.

Ty's fingers itched to reach out and tuck it behind her ear, to trail his finger along the graceful column of her exposed neck.

Instead, he handed her one of the steaming cups he held in his hands. "There's a little coffee shop a few blocks from here. I didn't know how you like it, so the coffee's black. They have cream and sugar in the shop. But Ray's coffee is about as palatable as tar."

There was a slight hesitation before she took the cup, as if no one had ever bought her a coffee before. "Black is fine. Thanks." She looked toward the large plate-glass window at the front of the brick building. "Is Ray the owner?"

Ty nodded. "He and I go way back. He's serviced my trucks since I started my business six years ago. He knows his way around an engine. Also does a lot of bodywork. He'll take good care of your Jeep."

"What type of business are you in, Mr. Bishop?"

"Ty. Call me Ty. I own a nursery, Rocky Mountain Landscapes. Actually, we just opened our second location on the south end of town."

"Congratulations."

"It's hard competing against the big-name chains, but we do all right. We also do a lot of residential landscaping and some commercial. We just finished the grounds of the governor's mansion." God help him, he was babbling.

"I've driven by there. The flower beds in the front yard are beautiful." She smiled, but it seemed forced. Maybe Jenny was right, and the spark he'd felt yesterday had been only one-sided.

"Thanks." He motioned toward the building. "Let's find Ray and see what he thinks about your car."

The whir of pneumatic wrenches and the clang of hammers against metal grew louder as they walked toward the entrance of the body shop.

He held the door for her and drew in a breath as she moved through it. The crisp scent of her perfume mingled with the clean smell of soap and made his head spin.

In contrast, the pungent odor of stale sweat, grease, and cigarette smoke permeated the lobby of Ray's Body Shop. Ty watched Kendall take in the stained upholstery of the worn couch. She eyed the swimsuit pinups from various years. The blare of heavy metal music coming from the back office practically shook the paint off the grimy walls.

He gave her his most encouraging smile. "Ray doesn't go all out on the décor, but don't let it fool you. He's really good with cars. He'll give us a great deal. I wouldn't have brought you here if I didn't trust him." *Shut up, shut up, shut up,* he told himself.

"Maybe you should find Ray," Kendall suggested. She nodded to the small bell that sat on the counter of the empty reception area. "I don't think he's going to hear that over the music."

"It's Metallica."

She gave him a funny look. "Yeah, I know. Could you find him?"

With a quick nod, Ty disappeared around the corner of the wall that led to the back of the building.

CHAPTER THREE

Kendall eyed the stained couch. There wasn't enough money at the Denver Mint to convince her to sit on those cushions.

It was probably a bad idea to show up here this morning, but she wasn't sure she could have stopped herself. A good night's sleep should have dulled her reaction to Ty Bishop, but that hadn't been the case. As soon as she saw him waiting for her, she'd had trouble catching her breath. This morning he wore a green plaid flannel shirt tucked into faded jeans. Since when had flannel become attractive to her?

Maybe that attraction explained why she'd barely been able to form a coherent sentence. She hoped it wasn't the memories that the body shop brought back from her childhood. The place looked and smelled exactly like the garage where her dad did part time work between his shifts at the country club. When he wasn't drying out in rehab, anyway. Her dad was a great guy when he was sober, doing his best to take care of Kendall and the medical bills from her mom's rheumatoid arthritis. But at least once a year he'd fall off the wagon and go on a months-long binge, getting suspended from work and putting their already dismal finances in real peril. The worst episode had lasted almost half a year and landed Kendall and her mother in a homeless shelter for Thanksgiving. Kendall had been ten years old. Eventually, he'd cleaned up his act, but the fear and uncertainty of those times had stayed with Kendall.

The thumping music stopped abruptly. A minute later, Ty Bishop returned, followed by a stocky, slightly balding man wearing a shirt with the name "Ray" printed above the breast pocket.

Ray held out his hand. "Pleasure to meet you, Ms. Clark. The wife and I tune in every night."

"I appreciate that. Please call me Kendall."

Ray gestured to the empty chair behind the reception desk. "Gloria, she's my wife, is usually here to greet people. But she had to take our seven-year-old to the doctor this morning. Ear infection." He grinned. "Sorry about the music. I wasn't expecting anyone, and I only get to play what I like when Gloria's not around. She keeps the radio tuned to country." He rolled his eyes. "Blake Shelton is ok, but a few of them ladies make my head pound."

Ray Sharp reminded Kendall of some of the locals from Grady, Kansas. Although she'd hightailed it out of her hometown, sometimes she missed the easy friendliness of the people there. She dropped her voice to a whisper. "Between you and me, I'd take Metallica over country any day."

The tension in Ray Sharp's shoulders eased. He waggled a finger in her direction. "I knew I'd like you. Let's take a look at your car. Ty tells me the front bumper's destroyed."

Ray led the way out of the building into the bright morning sunlight. He whistled softly as he took in the damage to her car.

Ty came to stand next to Kendall. "How bad is it, Ray?"

The other man straightened and ran a hand through his hair. "It doesn't look like more than body work. I'd like to put it on one of the lifts and check underneath to make sure." He turned to Kendall. "Could you leave the car with me for about an hour?"

"That would work," she said, checking her watch. "I have a noon meeting but left the morning open. Should I wait in the lobby?"

Ray grinned. "If you don't mind Metallica."

She returned his smile. "They're better than country, but . . ."

Ty stepped forward. "Actually, I don't have anything going on this morning. We could grab a muffin at the coffee shop I told you about."

She considered declining, knowing it would be safer to keep her distance from this man who made her feel things she hadn't expected. Then she looked into his blue eyes and forgot everything else. He looked so hopeful, watching her like it really mattered that she said yes. "My treat," she told him. Her mouth had gone dry. "It's the least I can do."

Ray spoke before Ty could answer. "I hope your wallet's full," he laughed. "Ty eats like a horse."

"Hey," Ty said in mock protest. "I resemble that remark. Besides, it makes Gloria happy when I take a second helping."

"Or third," Ray added. "Are the keys in the car?"

She nodded.

"Great. See you two in an hour." Ray climbed into the Jeep and drove it toward the back of the building.

Kendall turned to Ty. "Third?"

"What can I say? She makes a hell of a lasagna." He pointed down the street. "The coffee shop's this way. And don't worry that I'll drain your bank account. I'm not a huge fan of breakfast."

She fell in step beside him. "What's not to like about breakfast? Eggs, bacon, pancakes." She sighed. "What could be better?"

He gave her a dubious look. "You eat a lot of pancakes?"

"Well, no," she admitted. "Mainly fruit and yogurt these days. But a girl can dream."

"And you dream about pancakes?"

"Stacks of them. Dripping with real butter and maple syrup." She held a hand to her grumbling stomach. "Oops."

His wide smile caught her off guard, and her step faltered for a moment.

He continued to grin as he reached out an arm to steady her. "Fruit and yogurt doesn't hold up next to visions of pancakes, huh?"

"I guess not." Kendall felt the color rise to her cheeks. First she could barely put a sentence together and now she was practically having an orgasm over the mere thought of pancakes.

"I don't think The Daily Grind has pancakes. But we'll get you a big blueberry muffin." He leaned in closer. "With a side of butter?"

She laughed, because as strange as this banter felt, it was refreshing to joke around with him. "Thanks, but I take my muffins plain."

They rounded a corner and the coffee shop came into view.

She stepped through the front door and breathed in the rich scent of coffee.

Ty motioned to a small cluster of café tables positioned near the front of the shop. "Why don't you grab a table and I'll get the food? Do you want another coffee?"

"Water would be fine." She reached for her purse. "Let me give you some cash."

He waved her away. "Don't worry about it."

"I told you I wanted to pay."

Ty was already making his way to the counter. "You can buy the next time," he called over his shoulder.

She stared after him, his words ringing in her ears. Next time. When was the last time there had been a next time after one of her many first dates?

Not since Greg.

After Kendall had discovered her boyfriend was a ratfink cheater and ended their relationship, it had taken months before she was ready to date again. At that point, plenty of people had tried to fix her up, and she'd had first dates with a variety of eligible, upwardly mobile men.

She hadn't wanted a second date with any of them.

After a while, the routine had gotten old and she'd shifted her personal life to the back burner and focused on her career instead. She wanted more than the silly stories assigned to her, so it hadn't felt like a sacrifice to devote herself exclusively to her job. If she missed romance . . . well, she could always binge watch the Hallmark Channel on a Saturday night.

How long had it been since she'd been on a date? Six months? Eight? That had to be the reason for her physical reaction to Ty. Because she'd never in her life wanted to lift a guy's shirt to see if the body underneath was as good as it looked. She could imagine doing all kinds of wicked, wonderful things to that body.

But it was more than the body and the crazy chemistry she'd like to deny. He was laid-back and clearly comfortable in his own skin, something Kendall had never quite managed. It appealed to her on a level she didn't care to examine, especially since it made her agree to meet him at Ray's this morning. Even with her finances tight, she could have handled the repairs to her Jeep. But she hadn't been able to resist the lure of the spark between them, which made agreeing to this non-date even more foolish.

She pulled at her sweater as she selected a table near the front window, trying and failing to cool down her overheated imagination. She could ignore the spark. Absently, she played with a container of sugar substitute and watched Ty select their food. He looked almost elegant, despite his casual shirt and jeans.

Jeans that, she couldn't help but notice, covered one fine ass. This is not a date, she repeated over and over again. Don't check out his ass, fine or not.

Ty gestured to the pastry case next to the coffee shop's front counter. The young woman who waited on him smiled attentively then giggled at something he said. When he turned to walk toward the table, she noticed the girl cocking her head for a better view of his butt. At least Kendall wasn't the only one.

Ty set a tray with muffins and two glasses of orange juice on the table and slid into the chair across from her. "I watched the news last night. You sure pulled it together after the accident."

"Luckily, one of the production assistants took care of the footage for me. It was still tight, but everything worked out."

He studied her over the rim of his juice glass. "I hope the poor walrus feels better. The story ended kind of abruptly."

"It ended when the *poor* walrus blew a gallon of snot all over me. But it's fascinating how much the vets can do for animals so that little problems don't escalate like they would in the wild. In fact, at the Denver Zoo—" She cupped a hand over her mouth. "I'm sorry. You asked a simple question and I started rambling."

"It's interesting rambling. Besides, I like how your eyes light up when you talk about your work." His mouth quirked at one end. "It's sexy."

The piece of muffin she'd just swallowed lodged in the back of her throat. *Oh, yes. Sexy. That was her.* She coughed and sputtered until Ty stood and leaned over, thumping her hard between the shoulder blades.

"Sorry." He grinned when she was breathing normally again. "That wasn't the reaction I was going for."

"What reaction did you expect?"

"I don't know—another smile?"

She waved a hand in front of her face. "It's ok. You just caught me off guard."

"Obviously. I'll let you finish that bite before I ask my next question."

Kendall's fingers clenched around the glass of juice. Here it was, she thought, he was going to ask her out.

And, God help her, she wanted him to.

Even though she knew he was wrong for her and she was completely wrong for him. Kendall had goals and ambitions that didn't involve a guy like Ty, even if a few minutes in his company made her feel alive in a way she hadn't in years. She wanted love when the timing was right. When the guy she was with could fit into her world. She hated what that said about her, but her own insecurities wouldn't let her function any other way.

"Why does someone like you need to be a part of a dating show? I'd think the men of Denver would be lined up at your doorstep."

The question surprised her before she realized Ty would have no knowledge of her non-existent love life. At least the frustration she'd felt the previous night had eased enough so she could see the humor in the situation.

"The path to my door is clear at the moment," she answered honestly. "And the dates are for a good cause."

He raised a brow. "Is that so?"

She laughed softly and shook her head. "I didn't mean it like that. Viewers submit the names, profiles and photographs of the potential dates. If the man they've submitted is chosen, the station will make a donation to the charity of their choice." The irony of repeating the words that had annoyed her so much when Liz spoke them last night wasn't lost on Kendall.

"What do you get out of all this?"

"Would you believe me if I told you the chance to make a connection with a great guy?"

"Nope."

"You've only known me about thirty minutes. How can you be sure?"

He tapped one finger on the neat pile of trash on the edge of the table. "You've collected all of our combined garbage, folded the empty muffin wrappers and used napkins. Anyone who is so . . . what's the word I'm looking for?"

She grimaced. "Anal?"

"Particular," he provided. "Anyone who is so particular about stacking trash isn't going to let someone else choose her man." He leaned back and crossed his arms in front of his chest. "I bet you have a two-page, typed list of qualities for the perfect guy."

"I do not. The list is only one page, and it's not typed."

"What's the real reason? Think it's your philanthropic duty to date for charity?"

"Career ambition," she mumbled.

He leaned forward. "What was that?"

"There's an opening at the news desk on the *Wake Up Weekend!* show in New York. If I do *It's Raining Men*, my boss will get me an audition."

Ty whistled softly. "A national morning show. That's big time."

"It's an exciting opportunity." She tried not to sound as hopeful as she was. "Plus, they've given me my first real news story since I agreed to the promotion. I intend to make the most of it. It's an in-depth report on the regeneration of the burn area from the wildfires a few summers back. There are plans to redevelop the community that was hardest hit."

A look flashed across his face that Kendall didn't understand. He smiled, but it seemed strained compared to a few minutes ago. "The fact that you're doing this, though, means you're not seeing anyone seriously."

"Not at the moment."

His smile turned devilish. "So there's still time to get a jump on the competition. Have dinner with me on Friday?"

Her girlie parts did some elaborate dance moves until Kendall's brain shut them down. "I don't think . . ."

"C'mon," he coaxed. "We'll have a nice meal. I'll dust off my cheesiest lines. You can, with grace and charm, politely rebuff my advances. Think of it as practice for the dating show."

She laughed, tempted to accept his invitation. She could easily imagine a romantic dinner with Ty. If her racing pulse and the tingles shooting up and down her spine were any indication, it would take a lot more than charm to resist his advances.

Even entertaining the thought of a date with the gorgeous land-scaper was ridiculous. Not when she'd already reacted so strongly to him. Kendall's life was built on staying calm and keeping her game face through any situation. She was so close to the next step in the career she'd worked so hard for. There was no room in her well-ordered life for a relationship with anyone.

"I appreciate the offer, but it wouldn't be a good idea."

His eyes narrowed. "Why?"

So much for an easy brushoff.

"What about the redhead? I thought she was your girlfriend."

Ty laughed. "Jenny? No. She works for me, and we've been friends since we were kids. She's like my sister."

"Ok, well," Kendall stammered. "I have a lot going on right now. Between my regular job and this dating show deal, things are going to be kind of crazy for the next several weeks." She smiled apologetically. "It's just not a good time. I'm sorry."

He continued to pierce her with his deep blue gaze. That gaze seemed to see her. Not just her image—not who she'd been and who she was determined to become. It was like he shined a light on the dark corners of her soul to see the woman she'd hidden away under makeup and a fancy wardrobe she could barely afford. The woman she barely recognized anymore. That fact alone was enough to shore up her resolve. Ty Bishop might be easygoing, but he was dangerous in all the ways that counted the most.

"You don't plan to eat in the next month?" he asked gently.

Kendall drummed tense fingers against the table. Her palms had started to sweat. She needed to end this conversation before her body's desire for him short-circuited her brain. "Listen, Ty, the truth is, you're not really my type."

His smiled never wavered, but something sparked in his blue eyes, as if this exchange was the beginning of a chess game he would take great enjoyment in winning. "What if I wore an expensive suit, drove a fancy car, and worked in a hot-shot office building? Would I be your type then?"

"I can't believe you said that. What you wear or the car you drive has *nothing* to do with it."

He leaned forward and in a husky whisper said, "I don't believe that for a second. What's the matter, Princess? Afraid to get your hands dirty messin' with the common folk?"

Kendall sucked in a sharp breath. The accusation that she was a snob would be almost laughable if the insinuation wasn't so offensive. She'd navigated through the worst kind of snobbery in her life, and that wasn't who she wanted to be. There was nothing wrong with being clear about her priorities.

Her physical reaction to Ty convinced her that spending time with him would shake up her life in a way she wasn't prepared to deal with at the moment. She let her irritation and fear coalesce, drowning out her unwanted lust for him. She was a reporter, and it was time to dig a little deeper into this story.

She brought her face near enough to Ty's that she could feel his breath against her skin. "I'm sure your rippling muscles and baby blue eyes have gotten you far with women. Why me? Why does it matter that *I* agree to a date? Is it possible your ego can't handle someone saying no?"

She'd wanted to make him mad. Instead, one end of his mouth quirked slightly. "I've been asking myself all morning why it matters." He shook his head, almost rueful. "All I can tell you is that I feel a connection to you I can't explain."

Blood pounded in Kendall's head and her mouth went dry. Of all the answers she'd expected, the idea that his persistence was about her and not just the conquest hadn't crossed her mind. She'd never felt so off-balance or desirable. It was a precarious combination. She licked her lips and whispered, "There's no connection."

Their heads were so close she didn't notice him raise his hand until she felt the gentle pressure of his fingertip against her bottom lip.

Her eyes widened but she made no move, her breath catching in her chest. His eyes were focused on her mouth, which had gone completely dry. Little lightning bolts of sensation sparked along her skin as he traced a path from her lips, across her chin and down the column of her neck to where the collar of her silk sweater began.

He hooked his finger into the soft fabric, his knuckle lightly brushing the sensitive skin at the base of her throat. An involuntary shiver skittered across the back of her neck.

Slowly, Ty sat back and folded his arms across his chest. Desire darkened his eyes as his gaze slammed into hers. "No connection at all?" he repeated.

Kendall could barely hear him over her pounding head. She dropped her eyes to the front of his shirt, unwilling to meet the intensity of his stare. The sleeves of his shirt were folded just below the elbows. His forearms were tanned and muscled, with a smattering of golden hair flecked across them. His right hand rested in the crook of his left arm. The lean finger that had, moments earlier, wreaked havoc on her insides tapped benignly against the flannel.

She was losing her cool and it scared her. The way Ty Bishop made her feel was too much of a distraction from her dream, and she was smart enough to know it. Smart enough to take a deep, if shaky, breath to calm down before meeting his eyes. Smart enough to sit back against the hard wood of the chair, clasp her hands tightly in front of her and dig her thumbnail deep into the soft flesh of her palm. The sharp pain burst the sweet bubble of lust that enveloped her.

When she felt like she'd be able to speak without squeaking, she plastered on a fake smile and said, "Sorry to disappoint, but you just don't do it for me."

He focused his stare on her mouth, as if he had every intention of licking the lie from her lips. "Right."

Unable to stand his scrutiny for one more moment, Kendall stood. "We'd better get back."

She reached for the neat pile of trash, grateful for the distraction. Before she could pick it up, one of Ty's hands covered hers. "Let me get that."

She snatched back her hand as if she'd been scalded. Which, to Kendall's chagrin, made him laugh out loud.

Reluctantly, she followed him toward the coffee shop's entrance. A few steps from the door he turned and lifted a casual arm. "See ya later, Amy," he called.

The blond behind the counter leaned so far over the display case Kendall thought she might land on her head. Either that or those perky breasts were going to fall right out of the top of her shirt. "Bye, Ty." Her voice dripped with honey. "Come back soon."

He gave another noncommittal wave and pushed open the door, holding it until Kendall was through. "I guess not every woman is immune to my charms."

Kendall rolled her eyes and fished around in her purse for her sunglasses case. "No doubt the poor girl's senses are impaired by caffeine overload."

He shook his head. "You're a piece of work, Princess."

"Don't call me *Princess*." She unfolded her tortoiseshell frames, pushing them onto her face.

Ty fell in step beside her. They walked back to the body shop in a silence that felt almost companionable. Surprising, given the awkwardness of their recent exchange.

Kendall felt Ty watching her. The hair on her neck stood at attention under his scrutiny. She kept her gaze straight ahead. He didn't seem angry with her. In fact, she was unable to get a read on what he was thinking.

Maybe it was better this way. His touch had made her body yell a big, fat *yes*, and it had taken every amount of willpower she possessed not to give in to his advances. The sooner she was away from him the better.

As they walked around the chain-link fence that marked the body shop's perimeter, there was no sign of the Jeep. It wasn't parked in the lot or in one of the open work bays.

"I'll find Ray," Ty suggested. He placed his hand on the small of her back to steer her toward the body shop's office. Even that casual touch made her stomach flip. From the look he sent her, Ty damn well knew it.

She picked up her pace, and he dropped his hand. She ignored the soft chuckling behind her and made a beeline toward the office.

A blast of stale air assaulted her as she swung open the office door. Ray sat behind the counter in front of a computer monitor and the red-head, Jenny, stood behind him, studying the screen over his shoulder. Both looked up as she stepped into the lobby area. Ray's eyes remained on her, but Jenny's assessing gaze traveled between Kendall and Ty, who'd followed her into the building.

"Good news," Ray told her. "Only the bumper needs to be replaced. The dent in the side is shallow enough that I can take care of it with a buff and touch-up paint." He shuffled through a stack of papers on the counter then handed her one from near the top. "Here's the breakdown of parts and labor."

Kendall studied the estimate. The total amount was less than her deductible. At least something positive had come from this morning. "When can you get started?"

Ray glanced back at the computer screen. "I should be able to have it back to you Monday morning."

"You want me to leave it with you now?"

Ray looked surprised. "Wasn't that the plan?"

Kendall nodded. "I guess. I'm sorry, my mind's a little scattered." She dug in her purse for her cell phone. "I just need to call someone to pick me up." She wasn't used to feeling so emotionally unsteady.

She noticed both Ray and Jenny staring over her shoulder at the place where Ty stood. They expected him to offer to drive her somewhere, while he most likely regretted the time he'd already wasted with her. She punched in a number, but before she could hit the "Send" button, Jenny spoke.

"I can drop you off wherever you need to go."

"Thanks," Kendall replied, "but I don't want to inconvenience you. I'm meeting a couple of friends for lunch. One of them can come and get me."

"It's not a problem. I'm on the clock." Jenny gave her a conspiratorial wink. "My boss can be a real prick when he sets his mind to it. I wouldn't mind a personal errand on company time."

Kendall looked over her shoulder and almost laughed at Ty's expression. She gave him an innocent shrug and turned back to Jenny. "That would be great. I just need to grab a few things out of my car."

"It's around back," Ray told her. "I'll show you." He motioned toward the door that led to the work bays.

She followed him without looking back, wishing she could ignore her body's reaction to Ty as easily as she could ignore his presence.

CHAPTER FOUR

As the door shut behind Kendall, Ty stepped closer to Jenny. "My boss can be a real prick? What the hell was that about? Yesterday you called her shallow and suddenly you're offering her a ride?"

Jenny shrugged. "She looked so jumbled standing there. I felt bad." Her eyes narrowed and she shook a finger at him. "What did you do to her?"

Ty's mouth dropped open. "What did *I* do to *her*? How about what she did to me? You were right about her being trouble." The anger he'd felt at Kendall's rejection came rushing back.

He began to pace the small lobby. "I don't do it for her, my ass," he mumbled to himself, forgetting that Jenny stood a few feet away. "She practically jumped out of her skin when I touched her."

He stopped in his tracks when Jenny cackled.

"What's so funny?"

Her gray eyes widened in amusement. "You're pissed."

"Of course I'm pissed."

She shook her head. "I take back what I said about Kendall not being worth the trouble. It's entertaining to see you all hot and bothered. What is it about her that has you so fired up?"

Ty blew out a sigh and raked one hand through his hair. "I don't know. She's snooty, compulsive, probably a control freak."

"All attractive qualities in a woman," Jenny interrupted, popping her gum.

"Yeah, right. There's something about her that gets to me and I can't seem to let it go." He massaged his forehead with his thumb and forefinger. "But she turned me down flat. What do I do now?"

Jenny tapped one finger to her chin, as if she was contemplating an answer. "You could track down a boom box and stand outside the TV station blasting old Peter Gabriel songs. That would get her attention."

He smiled. "I'm thinking of something that won't get me slapped with a restraining order."

"But taking no for an answer doesn't seem like a viable option?"

"No." Although it probably should. He didn't know Kendall well enough to subject himself to more rejection, despite his attraction to her. But other than building his business, Ty hadn't taken a risk on anything in a long time. Now that he'd made Rocky Mountain Landscapes a success, he'd begun to feel restless, like he wanted more than the simple life he'd created for himself. He'd been burned once before when he'd fought for something he believed in, but maybe it was time to try putting himself out there again. He wanted Kendall, and he suspected she felt more for him than she was letting on.

Jenny continued to watch him, elbows against the laminate countertop, her chin resting in her hands. "What?" she asked. "Are you going to aerate her lawn?"

"Funny. Can you check on the Donnelly house after you drop her off? I've got something I need to do."

"Aren't you going to fill me in on the big plan?" Jenny asked, straightening from the counter.

Ty already had one hand on the front door. "Let's just say if you can't beat 'em, join 'em," he called over his shoulder.

"What does that mean?"

Kendall heard Jenny's yell as she came in from the garage. The door to the front of the office swung closed. She watched Ty stalk across the parking lot toward his truck. She tamped down the wave of disappointment that spilled over her as she watched his retreating form. That was the last she'd see of Ty Bishop.

She ignored the disappointment that shot through her. Of course he was gone. She'd blown him off. He'd hardly wait around to say good-bye.

The other woman noticed her and walked around the counter, grabbing her battered backpack from the top. "Where to?" she asked with a smile.

"I'm sorry if I caused a fight," Kendall said.

Jenny fished around in the bottom of the backpack and pulled out an industrial-size ring of keys. "Aw, honey, Ty and I go back too far to fight. Besides, that man is easy like Sunday morning. Not much gets to him."

An image of the muscle pulsing in Ty's strong jaw flashed into Kendall's mind, but she didn't argue with Jenny. The striking redhead had a long relationship with Ty Bishop. Kendall barely knew him.

She followed Jenny toward another beat-up pickup truck. "So tell me about the landscaping business," she said, trying not to sound too interested.

By the time Kendall hopped to the curb in front of the farm-to-table restaurant where she met her two best friends for lunch every Friday, she decided she liked Jenny Castelli's candor and confidence. "Thanks for the ride," she said through the open door on the pickup's passenger side. "And for helping with my car. I appreciate it."

Jenny smiled. "No problem. The Jeep will be good as new when Ray's done."

Kendall swung the door closed and waved as Jenny drove away. The ancient pickup backfired as it turned a corner at the end of the block, attracting several raised eyebrows from people walking along the street in the trendy Cherry Creek North neighborhood. She imagined Jenny thumbing her nose at the onlookers and grinned.

When she walked into The Cherry Kitchen, the young woman behind the host stand smiled. "They're at your usual table."

Kendall bypassed the people waiting for tables. The restaurant was popular and there was always a crowd for Friday lunch.

The Cherry Kitchen served locally sourced food and the décor combined industrial flare with farmhouse comfort. The walls were painted a muted gray with rich mahogany trim. Vintage American art hung in neat rows along the walls. Each of the stainless steel tables sported a mason jar with fresh flowers. The lighting was soft and ambient.

A number of eyes followed her as she made her way to the back of the restaurant. Kendall liked being recognized in the community, but not for the reasons most people would guess. A lot of people were fiercely loyal to their local news channel. It gave her a sense of belonging to be invited into someone's home via the television.

She set her purse and bag next to a chair at a four-person table positioned in a quiet corner of the busy restaurant. "Hello, ladies."

Two women turned to smile at her.

"Well, if it isn't Denver's answer to *The Bachelorette*," one of them drawled.

"Sam, you promised you wouldn't tease her," the other chided.

"I lied."

Kendall rolled her eyes at Samantha Carlton and Chloe Daniels, her two best friends, who couldn't be less alike.

A decade ago, Sam had been one of America's reigning supermodels, gracing magazine covers and fashion spreads with her honey blond hair, almond shaped blue eyes, and killer body. These days, she favored baggy sundresses and cowboy boots over designer duds and heels. She wore no makeup and her hair was typically fashioned into a sloppy knot on the back of her head. But no amount of dressing down could completely hide Sam's traffic-stopping good looks.

Next to her, Chloe was a throwback to another era. Short and curvy, she looked a little like a modern day Betty Boop with raven-hued curls framing a pixie face.

"Tell me the truth." Kendall groaned. "Is it going to be a total disaster?"

She'd called Chloe from the station yesterday to tell her that she and Sam should watch the broadcast introducing viewers to the concept for *It's Raining Men*. She wanted the opinion of friends she could trust to be honest with her.

Before either of the women could respond a waiter approached. They ordered and when the waiter disappeared, Chloe leaned forward and patted Kendall's hand.

"Internet dating is all the rage right now, so it will bring attention to you and the station."

Kendall sipped her water. "But is it the wrong kind of attention? Will I look pathetic dating on camera?"

Chloe shook her head, curls bouncing against the side of her face. "You're the star of the show. The star never looks pathetic."

"She's right," Sam agreed, her long fingers wrapped around a steaming mug of herbal tea. "It's the losers applying to date you who will look pathetic."

Kendall cringed at the description of the men she would be dating. "They might not be losers. They might be *nice* men who haven't had much luck meeting a *nice* woman."

Sam looked skeptical but Chloe said, "Like us."

"As in we're nice or we're losers?" Kendall asked doubtfully.

She'd met Sam and Chloe three months after moving to Denver. She'd had no social life and no friends. Most of the people she worked with were either several years older than her and settled in their lives or young and into the party scene. She didn't fit into either group.

On a whim, she'd signed up for a class at a local community center, *Discovering the Wild Woman Within*. It wasn't her first choice, but the only one that fit into her odd schedule. Halfway through the first class, she regretted her decision. It had quickly turned into a bitch session about her classmates' husbands and boyfriends.

She'd walked out during the break, planning not to return, and found Sam and Chloe, both women she'd recognized from class, sitting on opposite ends of the building's main staircase. Too embarrassed to quit with an audience, she'd stood near the entrance mulling her options. When the break was over, Sam had suggested that the three women skip the rest of class in favor of margaritas and lunch at a nearby Mexican restaurant.

After two pitchers of margaritas and a mound of nachos, the three had discovered something better than their inner wild women: friendship.

From that afternoon, Sam and Chloe had become Kendall's two best friends. They'd held each other's hands through bad boyfriends and worse breakups. Their abysmal luck with men was one of their tightest bonds. Sam nicknamed their love lives *No Sex in the City*.

"We're not losers," Kendall assured Chloe. "We could get dates if we wanted them. We're discriminating."

"Speaking of discriminating," Sam interrupted. "Do you have any veto power over the men?"

Kendall grimaced. "Not really. I filled out a detailed questionnaire about my preferences, but other than that, it's anyone's guess which men the producers will choose. Liz promised to sneak me a few of the audition tapes to watch so I'd get an idea of what the men might be like."

Sam smiled around a forkful of spinach leaves. "You are a brave girl, my friend."

Kendall stabbed at her salad. "Stupid is more like it. You know my luck with men. Plus, I've been so distracted worrying about these dates that I'm behind on my other work. I've got a meeting this afternoon for the wildfire follow-up series—my first real story—and I haven't even begun my research because I'm too freaked out about this." She sighed. "All I know is this New York job better come through."

"Who knows," Chloe said, reaching for a piece of bread from the basket that sat in the middle of the table. "Maybe you'll meet Mr. Right."

"That's exactly what Liz said," Kendall told her. "But I don't think it's going to happen."

As if on cue, a tall man appeared at the side of the table. He was wearing black-checkered pants, a white chef's shirt, and he sported close-cropped dark hair with just a hint of gray around the temples. When he clasped his hands together in front of his chest, a gold pinkie ring sparkled in the light. That was the only hint that the renowned chef at Denver's favorite local eatery was a Jersey boy at heart.

"And how are you ladies enjoying lunch?" he asked with a broad smile.

"It's perfect as usual, Anthony," Sam told him.

He eyed the half-eaten salads and tsked. "One day I will convince you three to try something that would take skill to prepare."

This was the usual conversation the trio had with Anthony Kulaski, the restaurant's gregarious head chef. First, he confirmed that the food was good before launching into a few minutes of unabashed flirting, mainly with Sam. Wrapped up in her own thoughts, Kendall paid little attention to the innuendos traded back and forth until she realized Anthony had spoken to her.

"I'm bringing the digital camera to my sister's tonight," he told her. "I don't trust the quality on my phone. You need to see exactly what you're getting." Kendall smiled and nodded, not wanting to admit she had no idea what he was talking about.

Anthony wiggled his bushy eyebrows. "Robbie is quite a catch, you know."

"Isn't your nephew married?" Chloe asked.

"The divorce papers were finalized last week," he replied, with a dismissive wave of his hand. "Good riddance as far as I'm concerned." He gave Kendall an encouraging smile. "Besides, third time's a charm, right?"

Her eyes widened. Robbie was Anthony's forty-something nephew. Anthony had been trying to set up Robbie with Sam, Chloe, or Kendall since they'd started their regular lunches at his restaurant. She'd met Robbie once. He was a short, pudgy man with a well-oiled pompadour and a thick mat of chest hair, accentuated by several heavy gold chains. She was pretty sure he ran a pawnshop.

"So Robbie is living with his mother again?" Sam asked innocently. Kendall glared at the teasing gleam in her friend's big eyes.

Anthony nodded. "Just until he finds a place of his own. You have a nice condo nearby, right?" he asked Kendall.

Her mouth opened but no words came out. Luckily, she was saved from answering when one of the waitstaff tapped Anthony on the shoulder.

He turned back to their table with an apologetic smile. "If you'll excuse me, ladies, there's something that needs my attention in the kitchen."

Kendall stared at her half-eaten salad for several moments after his departure. Sam and Chloe did not speak. Finally, she looked up to find both of her friends watching her and trying hard not to laugh.

She dropped her head into her hands. "Fantastic. The guy I'll be dating with all of Denver watching is a twice-divorced forty-year-old who lives with his mother."

"It could be worse," Chloe mused. "He could be unemployed."

Kendall covered her mouth with her hand, but a burst of hysterical laughter escaped her lips. A moment later all three of the women were doubled over with laughter, ignoring the strange looks they received from the other diners.

"This is going to be great." Sam grinned, wiping tears from the corner of one eye.

Kendall shook her head. "What have I gotten myself into?"

◆ ◆ ◆

When she returned to the station, Kendall pushed away all thoughts of *It's Raining Men* as she got ready for her first meeting on the Silver Creek fire project. She'd been up late last night preparing for her meeting with the soil scientist who would serve as her guide to the burn areas.

The more she learned about the restoration efforts, the more certain she was of her decision to demand this assignment. She wanted to tell the stories of the families rebuilding their lives after this tragedy. Her coworkers might not appreciate the emotional angle of many of her features, but Kendall needed to give a voice to the community that had been so affected by the Silver Creek fire.

Nerves fluttering with excitement, she pushed open the door to the conference room. She put her heart into each one of her stories, but she had a feeling Silver Creek was going to be a significant turning point in her life. The scientist sat at the large conference table facing Liz, his back to Kendall. She was glad Liz would be producing the series. The news director might not always act in Kendall's best interest, but her instincts for how to tell a story on-air were impeccable.

Liz looked up as Kendall entered and motioned her to the far end of the table.

"Sorry to keep you waiting," Kendall said as she placed her notes and research on the table next to the news director.

"Have a seat," Liz told her. "We were just getting started. Kendall, I want you to meet the scientist who'll be working with you on the project, Dr. Tyler Bishop."

Kendall's body jerked. Her rear end slipped off the chair as she locked eyes with Ty. She caught herself before she plopped onto the floor. Braced on her elbows, she managed to keep her face expressionless. Ty Bishop was her soil scientist?

No. Way.

A crisp blue button-down that matched the color of his eyes had replaced the worn flannel shirt. A muted yellow tie was neatly knotted at his throat. His jaw was clean-shaven and his blond hair looked shorter than she remembered. Had it been trimmed in the past couple hours?

Was this the same guy she'd shared coffee with a few hours earlier? Then she heard the soft chuckle she remembered from outside the repair shop. The one that said he knew exactly what she was thinking and thoroughly enjoyed how uncomfortable he made her.

Her files slipped off the table and she felt her face grow hot as she leaned forward to collect the scattered papers.

"Need a hand?" A smile played at one corner of his mouth.

"Kendall, are you all right?" Liz's voice sounded both concerned and disbelieving. "What happened?"

"I'm fine." Kendall turned to Liz. "What is *he* doing here?" And why does he look like he just stepped out of *Hot Scientist Monthly*, she added silently.

Liz's eyebrows furrowed. "Dr. Bishop? I told you, he's the soil scientist for the wildfire series. Is there a problem?"

Kendall leafed through her stack of papers. She slapped a single sheet onto the table. "Yes. According to the information I was given, Dr. Miles Roundtree from the National Forest Service is my scientist. I have his resume right here."

Liz glanced at Ty. Kendall narrowed her eyes at the easy smile he bestowed on her boss. "I apologize for any confusion," he said with total sincerity, shifting his gaze to Kendall. "Miles was looking forward to working with you. But with the recent budget cuts at the Forest Service, he's understaffed and was concerned he wouldn't have time to devote to this project. So he asked me to fill in."

"But you're a . . . a . . ."

Before she could finish the sentence, Ty slid a piece of paper across the table toward her. The sleeves of his button-down shirt were rolled up to the elbows, revealing the corded muscles along his forearm that had fascinated Kendall earlier this morning.

"Here's a copy of my resume," he told her, the long finger that had unnerved her at the coffee shop tapping against the paper.

The last bit of control Kendall felt like she had slipped through her fingers. She released her tight hold on Miles Roundtree's biography. She gingerly picked up the sheet that Ty offered.

She read the words printed in a classic typeface across the top of the page, *Tyler Bishop, PhD.*

As she scanned the rest of the page, a feeling uncomfortably close to guilt settled in the pit of her stomach. The label she'd placed on him had been woefully inadequate. He was the real deal. The resume highlighted his work with Rocky Mountain Landscapes but there was a lot more to Ty Bishop than he'd let on.

According to the information she held in her hand, his undergraduate studies had been in biology at the University of Colorado. He held a doctorate degree in soil conservation, and in a volunteer capacity had led a forest recovery team that was still working to return the forest to its pre-fire state.

Why would someone with such a scholarly background choose to spend most of his time planting bushes in a suburban backyard?

That thought was replaced by a more alarming realization. Dr. Tyler Bishop was the perfect person to act as the expert researcher for this project. He had the right credentials and because of his work in the commercial and residential sectors, could discuss technical matters in a way the general viewing audience would understand.

Kendall was stuck with him.

"How did this happen?" she whispered, shaking her head in disbelief.

"Kendall, you don't look so good," Liz said, worry creasing her brow. "Do you feel sick? Can I get you something?"

Kendall placed a fingertip to each temple. "I'm fine. A little surprised, that's all. I didn't expect to see Ty here."

The news director glanced back and forth between Ty and Kendall. "Do you two know each other?"

A deep pink rose in Kendall's cheeks. Her glossed lips opened and closed several times before she stammered, "Not really. Well, sort of." Her eyes shut and her chest rose as she took several deep breaths.

Suddenly Ty was riveted by the sight of Kendall's full mouth. Maybe it hadn't been such a good idea to pursue her if this was his body's reaction to something as innocuous as breathing. He remembered how soft her skin had felt under the pad of his finger. Soft as the petal of an early spring tulip.

The level of heat that passed between them in the coffee shop had dumbfounded him. Kendall denying that heat had pissed him off. Usually it took a lot to get under Ty's skin. But with her icy blow-off, Kendall Clark had made his blood boil.

When he'd left Ray's shop earlier, he'd called Miles Roundtree. Ty guessed correctly that Miles, as regional director of the National Forest Service, would be involved in any type of media coverage of the burn area. Ty had worked with Miles on and off for years. First, as a summer intern during college, and later, as a volunteer to help with the wildfire containment and clean-up.

Always overworked, Miles had been happy to relinquish the task of guiding a news reporter through the regeneration efforts to Ty.

Ty'd met women like Kendall in the past. Smart, sophisticated women who only dated guys they felt were worthy of their time and attention. Ty Bishop, landscaper, wasn't part of that mold. But Tyler Bishop, PhD, could hold his own, and he'd wanted to prove that to Kendall.

Liz placed a protective hand near Kendall's elbow and eyed him suspiciously. He gave her his most disarming grin, but when her expression didn't change, he started talking.

"We met yesterday," he explained. "There was an accident."

The woman turned to Kendall. "Dr. Bishop was involved in the car crash?"

"Apparently," Kendall replied cryptically.

Ty made a dismissive gesture with his hand. "It was a fender bender. No big deal. I'm sure Kendall didn't imagine we'd run into each other again so soon." *Especially after she'd cut him off at the knees.*

The news director nodded. "Then there's no problem with the two of you working together," she said, her tone determined.

"I'm looking forward to it," Ty told her, earning an approving nod.

Kendall said nothing. She sat rigidly still across from him, staring at his resume, her fingers clenched so tightly around the corners that he thought the paper might rip in half. At any moment, Ty expected to see smoke curling from the sides of her head.

A pang of guilt over her obvious discomfort stabbed at his conscience. He hadn't been lying about the connection he felt, and it wasn't just physical. Too late, he realized that intruding on the news story that meant so much to her wasn't the smartest way to curry favor with her. It had been a long time since Ty had made a decision based on an emotional reaction, and it had led him to nothing but trouble in the past. If he was smart, he'd excuse himself right now and find another wildfire expert to take his place.

But he couldn't make himself leave, not with the way Kendall's gaze had turned challenging and curious at the same time.

"Kendall," the news director prompted, "is this arrangement all right with you?"

"As long as he's serious. I won't let anyone mess up this story."

"His credentials look perfect to me," Liz answered, without a moment's hesitation.

Kendall's lush mouth curved into a brittle smile as she turned to Ty. "I hope you've got what it takes to make this work."

He smiled. He liked that her spunk had returned. "I've got it, all right."

The news director ignored the crackling tension between them. "Great. Now that everything is settled, let's get down to business."

CHAPTER FIVE

The next afternoon, Kendall sank into the cushions of her overstuffed couch with her hand cradling a pint of Rocky Road ice cream. It was the first time she'd had a chance to process the events of the prior day. From the meeting with Ty and Liz, she'd gone immediately into preparations for last night's newscast.

This morning she'd had a commitment to appear at a community Easter egg hunt at one of the downtown parks. It had been cold but sunny, with the kids bundled up in winter coats and hats as they searched for plastic eggs. Although she worked Monday through Friday in an official capacity, she often spent a portion of her weekend representing the station at local events. She didn't mind the imposition because her social calendar was normally empty.

She loaded a spoonful of ice cream into her mouth and pushed the power button on the remote. CNN clicked on, but she muted the perky anchor and concentrated on the headlines that ran along the bottom of the screen.

She jabbed her spoon back into the frozen container, digging absently for marshmallows. At this point she wasn't sure what was most disconcerting—four blind dates in as many weeks or working with Ty Bishop.

Once she'd recovered from her shock, the wildfire meeting had been productive and exciting. Under different circumstances, she would've applauded Ty's nerve at proving wrong the woman who had dismissed him as not worthy of her precious time. Because Kendall was the woman in question, she didn't feel so generous.

Only she knew that the reason for her rejection hadn't been entirely based on what he did for a living. Ok, maybe that was part of it, but not in the way Ty had assumed.

If she had told him the truth when turning him down, it would have sounded more like, "I've met you twice and both times you've made me hornier than a fifteen year old boy. I'm afraid that if I spend any more time with you I may do something embarrassing like rip off my clothes and jump you. That sort of behavior doesn't mesh with the image I've created for myself. So I'm going to go home frustrated and full of explicit fantasies starring the two of us, but at least I'll retain my dignity."

Oh, yeah, that would have gone over well.

At least then she wouldn't have had to deal with Ty horning his way into her professional life. Even if he *was* perfect for the role he would play in the wildfire project.

Just as she'd expected, Ty was able to translate his technical knowledge into terms that were both understandable and interesting to the average viewer.

Liz and Kendall were banking on the fact that locals would be interested to see the clean-up efforts to date. On Monday morning, Kendall, Ty, and one of the Channel 8 cameramen would drive down to the burn area and begin taping segments for the series.

The thought of spending an hour confined in a station van with Ty, then following him through the burn sites, had Kendall digging for another spoonful of Rocky Road. The spoon hit the bottom of the empty carton.

Damn. By the time this project wrapped, Ty Bishop was going to have her not only frazzled but also fat.

A knock at the door interrupted her thoughts. It had to be Liz with the flash drive of submissions for *It's Raining Men*. Sam and Chloe were coming over later to watch since Kendall was too much of a chicken to face the videos on her own.

She swiped the back of her hand across her mouth. Padding to the door, she ran her clean hand through her hair. Her fingers stuck on the elastic band she'd secured on the top of her head when she'd given herself a mini-facial earlier. She thought about pulling out the rubber band but didn't bother.

Although Kendall rarely went out without at least a dab of lip gloss, she knew Liz wouldn't care how she looked. Her need to maintain a perfect image stemmed from growing up a very poor fish in a sea of rich friends. Back then she'd tried to compensate for being the girl without the right clothes, the right shoes, or the right family by always looking put together.

"What have you got for me?" she asked, opening the door to Channel 8's news director.

But it wasn't Liz who waited on the other side.

Ty Bishop stood on her front porch with a large envelope and a stack of papers tucked under one arm. He brought his other hand around from behind his back to reveal a colorful bouquet of flowers.

He shoved the blooms toward her. "Would you take a peace offering?"

Stunned at the sight of him, Kendall's fingers unconsciously curled around the large cluster, a sweet floral fragrance drifting up to her. No one ever brought her flowers. Well, Greg had on one occasion. They'd been a sorry arrangement of generic flowers from the local supermarket—she knew because he'd left the half-price tag stuck to the cellophane.

Unlike that arrangement, the mass of stems she held in her hand was exquisite. She couldn't name many of the blossoms that made up the bouquet, but they were the exact combination she would have chosen if designing her perfect arrangement.

"They're gorgeous." She brought her face closer to enjoy the heady fragrance.

"They reminded me of you. I'm glad you like them."

A thought struck her. "Did you pick these flowers and arrange them yourself?"

One of Ty's broad shoulders lifted in a shrug. "I have some flowers in my yard. Part of the job," he told her, with a self-conscious smile. "They bloomed early with the hot weather last week and needed to be cut thanks to this morning's cold snap."

"You picked flowers for me," she repeated.

"It's not a big deal." His gaze lowered from hers and swept along her body, taking in her old college T-shirt and faded sweatpants. "I like the outfit."

She shook her head, wishing desperately for a baseball cap. "You said you wanted peace. Why would you make fun of me?"

He looked genuinely surprised. "I'm not making fun. Honest. I've gotten used to watching you on the news. You're always perfect with your suits and matching sweater things . . ."

"Sweater sets. They're called sweater sets."

"Right. It's nice to see you looking more like the rest of us. Makes you more real." His smile turned seductive. "I like real women."

She pulled on the hem of her shirt as her pulse leapt at his tone.

Before she could form a coherent answer, Ty raised his head to peer over her shoulder. "Are you going to invite me in so I can show you the rest of what I've brought?"

She looked down at the papers under his arm.

"Some of the recent reports on the rejuvenation effort," he told her. "Mainly statistical stuff but I thought you'd want to see it before we visit the burn area on Monday."

He shifted the documents as she continued to stare at him. "I stopped by the station to see if someone there could get them to you. Liz told me she had this envelope and a flash drive to drop off and gave me your address. You must be really dedicated to have work delivered on Saturday."

Her gaze switched to the flash drive. She tried not to let her eyes bug out of her head. Did he know what it held? She'd kill Liz for this.

Kendall crossed her arms across her chest and leveled a steely look at him. "I wasn't lying when I said I've got a lot going on right now."

If Ty remembered her reason for turning down his offer of a date, he ignored it. He gave her another one of those melting smiles that made her insides turn to mush. "So can I come in?"

After a few beats, she stepped to one side of the entry, "Oh, why not."

As he walked past her, Ty flicked a finger at her messy topknot. "Nice touch."

Mortified, Kendall's hand flew to her hair. She yanked at the elastic band and combed her fingers through the curls that tumbled against her forehead.

She followed Ty into her living room. He said he liked real women. Sweats and scrubby ponytails were about as real as it got in her world. *I don't care what he thinks about me*, she reminded herself. He was a guy she was stuck working with, not her boyfriend.

Glancing around the large area that served as both her living and dining room, his brows furrowed. "Did you move in recently?" he asked, indicating the open and extremely under-furnished space.

"No. I'm a minimalist," she explained, adopting the term Sam always used when describing Kendall's decorating style. It was difficult to have a certain style when she refused to furnish her space. Most of her extra money went to help out her parents. Besides, she was moving to New York soon. This place was merely an investment—not a home.

She followed Ty's gaze, seeing her condo through his eyes. She was so used to having almost nothing that she'd gotten used to it. A slipcover draped the couch in a soft beige fabric, and two occasional chairs in sage green and a cherrywood coffee table sat in front of a built-in entertainment center that held a television, stereo, a few pillar candles, and one framed photo of Kendall with her two best friends.

The photo had been a birthday gift from Chloe, who was horrified by Kendall's indifference toward decorating. Like everything else in her life, she'd put her desire to furnish her home on hold, reasoning that the style that fit her spacious Denver condo, with its vaulted ceilings and maple floors, wouldn't be the same if she was living in a small apartment in New York City.

Ty's brows rose at her description, but he didn't argue. He nodded at the muted television screen. "What are you watching?"

She gritted her teeth, knowing how the answer would sound. "CNN. I have it on almost all the time. Geeky, I know, since there are so many news outlets available. But I like watching other journalists and how they present themselves and the news."

He nodded and sat in one of the upholstered chairs that flanked the sofa. "You're dedicated," he said quietly. "I like that."

A surge of electricity radiated from his gaze that made goose bumps spring up on Kendall's arms. "You said you came here with a peace offering." She needed to change the subject before she melted into the couch. "But I probably deserved what you did to me."

He blinked a couple of times before answering, as if he'd also been trapped in the current that flowed between them. "I don't know what you mean," he said finally, his tone innocent. The effect was ruined when he winked at her.

"Be honest. You got yourself on the Silver Creek project because you were mad I wouldn't go out with you when I thought you were a gardener."

"Am I more your type with a couple of letters behind my name?"

"Yes. I mean, no." She shook her head. "I can't think straight when I'm around you."

"And that's bad because . . ."

"That's bad because I need to believe you're not a part of the story only to get back at me. This assignment is important, Ty, and not just because of what it means to my career. The Silver Creek community went through hell during the fire. Those people need to be recognized for how they've rebuilt their community."

His gaze turned serious. "I understand the importance of Silver Creek. There's no one better than me for this project."

"Maybe," she admitted, "but for your professional reputation only. As for the rest of you . . ." She waved her hand in front of him. "You're a distraction I can't afford right now. I've got three blind dates looming and need to do my best to retain my dignity so I can be taken seriously in New York. I don't have time for personal complications."

He lifted his palm in front of his mouth and pretended to yawn.

She tried another tack. "I didn't mean to offend you. It isn't what you do for a living that made me say no to a date. Like I asked in the coffee shop, why do you even care? I'm sure you have lots of women who'd like to date you. Why bother with me?"

He shook his head. "Princess, I've been asking myself that same question for the past two days."

"I am *not* a princess," she muttered.

He stood and walked the two steps that separated the chair from the sofa. When he sat next to her, his denim-clad knee brushed the thin cotton fabric of her sweatpants. A flash of heat shot through her and she looked down at her leg, half expecting the material to have been singed by the light contact.

When she looked up, Ty was watching her with an unreadable expression. His eyes were dilated, making them look almost more black than blue. This close she could see the fine network of lines that spread out from their corners. She wanted to trace those lines with her finger and run her hand along the hard contour of his jaw where sand-colored stubble covered his skin.

His gaze traveled across her face as if she were the main dish on his favorite restaurant's menu. "I don't know what it is, but I haven't been able to stop thinking about you since the crash." He touched his finger to the tip of her nose. "You are the most irritating woman I've ever met," he murmured as his eyes devoured her. "Stubborn, snooty, argumentative . . ."

She started to move away. "Is this your idea of sweet talk? I'm shocked you're still on the market."

Ty caught the material of her T-shirt between two fingers and pulled her back. "Let me finish. You are also exciting, passionate, hardworking, smart, and sexy. Jesus, sexy should be at the top of the list. You've got me tied in knots." He smiled. "You say the word *ratings* and it's like you're talking dirty."

"Ratings, ratings, ratings."

A wide grin spread across his face. "There you go again with your combative nature."

His features blurred as he brought his face closer to hers. He was going to kiss her. At this moment, she wanted his mouth on hers more than she wanted the regional Emmy, more than she wanted the job in New York, more than she wanted to breathe.

The realization terrified her.

"Don't," she whispered.

He stopped a hair's breadth from her mouth. He said nothing, made no move to back away, made no move closer. "Tell me you don't want this," he said, his voice thick.

"Shhh," she whispered. "I need to think."

"You think too much."

Kendall watched his mouth form the words. God, his mouth was beautiful. For the first time in as long as she could remember, she did exactly what she wanted to with no thought to the consequences. She traced the seam of his lips with her tongue. She heard his sharp intake of breath, felt the tightly reined desire pulsing through him. His lips were as soft as the petals of the flowers he'd given her, a sharp contrast to his hard-etched features and lean body. They tasted like salt and man and ChapStick. She licked her way from corner to corner while Ty stayed perfectly still.

When she finished her exploration, she ran her tongue across her own lips and covered his mouth with her own. Still he remained motionless.

"Why aren't you kissing me back?" she asked against his mouth.

"You said no. I'm waiting for you to tell me you've changed your mind."

She met his gaze and smiled. He was letting her choose, allowing her to set the boundaries.

"I've changed my mind," she said against his mouth.

In an instant she was on her back, Ty balanced above her.

He cradled her head between his hands, as if reminding her with the touch of his callused skin who he was. A man who worked with his hands, who spent most days outside with the sun beating down to etch those lines along the corners of his eyes, those lines that fascinated her.

Kendall knew that being kissed by this man, no matter how much it didn't fit into her long-range plan, was exactly what she wanted. She flashed a smile. "What are you waiting for, an invitation?"

When he finally lowered his mouth to hers, she realized her delusions of being the one in control had been just that. He commanded her lips with a delicious sensuality she had no desire to resist. The temperature in the room jumped several degrees as he slid his tongue to mingle with hers. She lost herself in the kiss, all of her doubts melting away under the intensity of his intoxicating warmth.

His hand slid from her face to trace the curve of her body. When he brushed the swell of her breast, she was sure she would spontaneously combust from the heat generated by his touch.

He broke the kiss and settled his lips against the sensitive column of her throat. She was too turned on to be embarrassed when a moan escaped her lips.

She felt him smile against her throat. "That's perfect," he murmured. The vibration of his lips touching her skin made her shudder.

She turned her head to one side to give him better access to her neck and noticed that the muted television set was still on. One of CNN's female anchors gave a rundown on the day's headlines. Reality slammed into Kendall like a bucket of ice water. She was sprawled on her sofa with a man she barely knew who made her body feel things she hadn't even known were possible.

It felt so good when he sucked on the soft flesh of her earlobe. So right for his hands to be cupping the curve of her hip, pressing her body against his until she could feel his erection straining against the fabric of his worn jeans.

Wrong, wrong, wrong.

The words echoed in her lust-fogged brain. But why was it so wrong? They were both adults. And there was an undeniable chemistry between them. They could enjoy each other without any strings attached. As long as they both understood that was what was happening.

"Ty?"

His tongue traced hot patterns on her neck. "Mmmm . . ." he said, moving to the base of her throat.

"What we're doing here, whatever this is," she mumbled, having difficulty forming a coherent thought.

"I think what I'm currently doing could best be described as necking," he told her. "What about it?"

"It doesn't mean anything."

"Ok," he said, sounding uninterested in the conversation as he moved on to a particularly sensitive spot behind her ear.

She unwrapped her hands from behind his neck and pushed against his shoulders until he lifted his head back enough to meet her gaze. "Ok?" she repeated.

He heaved a sigh and rested his forehead against hers. "I told you before, you think too much. We are two consenting adults, giving each other some major-league pleasure. It doesn't mean you have to wear my ring on a chain around your neck for everyone who watches the news to see. This is between us."

She'd made a plan for her life. "You won't have a problem if this is all I can give you? No public declarations or long-term commitment or anything."

He lifted his head. "Have you ever heard of the word *spontaneous*?"

"I don't do spontaneous very well."

"Shocker," he said with a smile. "How about casual? Fun?"

"Casual?" She ran her hand over the muscled wall of his chest, watching his eyes darken at her touch. "Casual is good."

"Some things you can't deny," he whispered. "This kind of chemistry is one of them."

He remained still as her hand continued to explore his body. Her fingers curled under the hem of his shirt, running up his soft skin and then scratching softly with her nails.

Ty sucked in a breath.

"We can manage the chemistry," she told him.

He smiled but didn't answer.

"Control ourselves." She shifted closer and he tightened his hold on her hips. She cupped his face between her hands, leaning forward to nip at one edge of his mouth.

"I like when you're in control," he told her, his words gruff. "You can trust me, Kendall. I'm not going to pressure you for anything you're not comfortable doing or giving."

She looked deep into his brilliant blue eyes and saw that he was telling the truth. "No pressure," she echoed.

He flashed her a suggestive smile and moved against her. "None that you don't ask for."

That he could make her laugh made her want him all the more. His hands slid into her hair and he took her mouth, suddenly rough and possessive as if he was done entertaining her worries. This is what she wanted, she realized. Needed. To let go, even for a few minutes. Their kiss deepened, and she lost herself in the force of it.

CHAPTER SIX

He hadn't expected to have his world rocked by a simple kiss. But he should have known nothing with Kendall would be simple. With her plastered against his body, her hands all over him, he wasn't too worried about complicated. He sucked her bottom lip into his mouth, growing impossibly hard when she moaned. He cupped her breast through her T-shirt, flicking his thumb over the nipple.

He wanted to see her, touch her, taste her. All of her.

Then the doorbell rang.

Kendall's eyes flew open. She looked as affected by the kiss as he felt.

He thought about covering her mouth again and kissing her until she forgot about whoever was at her door, but since he'd moments ago promised to keep any involvement between them casual, he eased away from her.

She scrambled up next to him, and they sat side by side, both trying to catch their breath and regain their balance.

The doorbell rang again.

"Are you expecting someone?"

Kendall blinked several times, and then her eyes widened in horror. "It's Sam and Chloe," she said, as if that should mean something to him. "My two best friends," she explained at his blank look. "Act normal. I don't want to explain you to them."

"You better fasten your bra," he suggested. "The way it looks now you might have some 'splainin' to do, Lucy."

She bent her head to look at the front of her shirt, where her bra clearly hung loose under the wrinkled fabric. She shot him an accusatory glare.

He held his palms up and shrugged. "Seemed like a good idea at the time."

She groaned and marched toward the front door, her fingers working at the clasp of her bra. Ty got a quick view of the creamy skin of her back before she righted her shirt. He straightened his own shirt and concentrated on thinking thoughts that would ease the monumental stiffness in his pants. He'd make an interesting impression on her friends flying more half-mast.

He heard the sound of female voices and turned to see Kendall return to the living room, flanked by two women. One was tall, blond, and gorgeous. The other was shorter, curvy, and cute in a girl-next-door sort of way.

The trio stopped and stared when Ty came into view.

"And what do we have here?" the knockout drawled, with a sly glance at Kendall. Something about the tall beauty struck Ty as familiar. "Is this an in-person audition?" she asked.

"Don't be ridiculous, Sam," Kendall said. "This is Ty. Dr. Tyler Bishop," she amended, slipping into her TV reporter tone.

Ty realized that Kendall adopted her on-air persona when she felt uncomfortable. Evidently, her friends knew this, too. The curvy woman joined the other one in a sideways glance.

"We're working together on the wildfire story I told you about."

The bombshell sidled toward him before Kendall could say any more. "Hey, there, hot stuff," she purred, giving him a slow onceover. "I can believe you're the fire expert."

The model's identity clicked into place. "I miss seeing you on the newsstand," Ty replied. "I was a fan."

She flashed him the seductive smile that had sold a million magazines. "We need to do something about your use of the past tense."

"We'll see." He turned from the former supermodel to where Kendall stood, a look of shock on her face. He didn't understand her friend's blatant flirtation any more than she seemed to.

He smiled and held out his hand to the curly-haired woman who stood at her side. "I'm Ty Bishop."

"Chloe Daniels," she said, and placed her small hand in his. "It's nice to meet you. I know Kendall feels strongly about keeping the community's attention on the burn areas."

"I do, too. But I'll get out of your way." He gestured to the bottle of wine Chloe held in her hand, along with a large bag of chips. "Looks like you're ready for some serious work."

"Brain food." Chloe grinned.

"Of course," he agreed. He looked at Kendall. "I'll see you Monday morning at the station?"

"Yes." Her tone was all business. "We'll take one of the news vans down to the burn site in case there's any initial footage Steve wants," she replied, referring to the cameraman who would accompany them. "Thanks for bringing everything by. I'll show you out."

He shook his head. "No need. I won't get lost." The urge to lean forward and kiss the frown off her lips was strong, but Ty walked past

Kendall without touching her. "Nice to meet you ladies," he called over his shoulder to her two friends. "Enjoy your night."

Kendall watched him turn down the hall toward her front door, wondering why it was so difficult to see him leave. When the door clicked shut, she whirled on Sam, but Chloe was already speaking.

"You shouldn't do that," Chloe admonished Sam quietly. "It isn't right."

"Isn't right?" Kendall bit out. "Sam, you put the moves on a man I work with. What were you thinking?"

Sam looked genuinely hurt at Kendall's outrage. "I was just trying to help. I don't want you to end up with another weasel like Greg."

"And how is coming on to one of my coworkers supposed to help me?"

Chloe opened her mouth to speak, but Sam held a hand in the air to silence her. "Wait a minute." Her eyes pierced Kendall with a dubious gaze. "Are you saying the gorgeous hunk of man who just left was only here in a professional capacity?"

Kendall laughed, although it sounded more like a nervous squeak. "I told you, we're working together on the wildfire story. He's a soil scientist."

"Bullshit," Sam responded evenly.

"No, really, he is. I can't figure out why he runs a landscaping company when he has such an impressive background." She tapped one finger against her bottom lip, which was still swollen from his kisses. "But it's true. I called the university to verify his degree." Her gaze shot back and forth between her two friends. "You can't honestly think I'd get involved with someone like Ty." She rolled her eyes. "He is *so* not my type."

Chloe gave her a reassuring smile. Sam grunted. "Not involved, my butt. You've got a big hickey in the middle of your neck."

Horrified, Kendall's hand shot to her neck. "So much for being able to trust him." She turned on her heel and stalked out of the room toward the mirror that hung in her foyer.

A few moments later she returned to the living room, hands on hips, a hard stare leveled at Sam. "There's no hickey on my neck."

Her friend shrugged. "No, but based on your reaction, I'd say there was a lot more going on with Hunky McDirt than you're telling us."

"He doesn't fit into my master plan."

Chloe groaned as Sam snorted. "Not the plan again."

"The plan is important to me." Kendall took the bottle of merlot Chloe held and led the way into the small galley kitchen. Growing up, prioritizing a life plan had been a way to feel in control and compartmentalize her insecurities. The list had been straightforward and it kept her motivated when balancing all the balls of her life got to be too much.

She opened a drawer and handed Chloe the wine opener, then pulled out three wine glasses. Chloe uncorked the bottle and poured.

Kendall took a long drink before she spoke. "New York City is the dream, marriage and kids come after that. I can't risk being sidetracked."

"You're talking about your mom," Chloe said softly.

Kendall nodded. "She could have done so much more. She had her own dream but sacrificed everything for our family. My dad had to work through a lot of demons before he could be the man she deserved. She paid a steep price for loving him, and I always felt like she was a shell of the woman she could have been. They're in a good place now, but was it worth all the sacrifices she made to get there?"

"Have you asked her?"

"She'd tell me I was worth everything, but that only makes me feel more guilty. If she hadn't gotten pregnant—"

"If the life she chose makes her happy," Sam said, "it isn't a sacrifice. It's a decision."

Kendall blinked away tears. "But it always seemed like the *wrong* one."

Sam squeezed her hand. "Not for her."

"Focusing on my career is the right decision," Kendall said, swallowing back the emotion that clogged her throat. "I can't lose focus now, and Ty would only be a distraction." She studied her friend over the rim of her wine glass. "But if you suspected something was going on between the two of us, why were you flirting with him?"

Sam and Chloe exchanged a look.

"What?" Kendall asked, exasperated to be the only one not in on the secret. "What is it I don't know?"

Sam sat cross-legged on one of the barstools tucked underneath the counter. Even in her battered cargo shorts and utilitarian Birkenstocks, her legs were long and graceful. Kendall couldn't imagine any man saying no to the prospect of having those legs sprawled across his bed.

"There's no easy way to say this," Sam told her, shifting in her seat, "so I'll cut to the chase. While you were dating Greg, he made a pass at me."

Kendall's hand jerked. Burgundy-colored liquid splashed out of her glass and ran down her arm. Chloe pulled paper towels off the roll and handed several to her. Kendall wiped at the spill, her eyes never leaving Sam's.

A broad sweep of emotions left her numb for a moment before a rush of questions, denials, and accusations leapt to the forefront of her mind. "Explain," she said succinctly, not trusting herself to say anything more.

"Nothing happened," Sam said quickly, with none of her typical flippancy. "Swear to God, Ken, I would never do that to you."

Kendall nodded. She could see the remorse in her friend's amber brown eyes.

Sam brushed a hand through her tumble of thick blond hair. "I'm sorry. I should have told you. At first, I thought I was imagining it. When we'd all go out, he'd give me a look or brush up against me. Nothing overt, mind you. Then he started helping me with the bookkeeping software."

Kendall's mouth tightened into a thin line. She had been the one to suggest that Greg use his accounting skills to help Sam set up the books for her nonprofit summer camp.

"I don't know what it was," Sam said, shaking her head. "He still didn't make any direct advances. But I know when a guy is giving me 'come on' signs and Greg Davies was lit up like a neon marker."

Kendall didn't think for a minute that Sam might have misread Greg's intentions. With her looks and background, Kendall knew Sam had been a target for men's advances since she was a preteen. She could spot a sexual advance a mile away.

"Did you confront him?"

"I needed to be certain I wasn't overreacting and that I had a witness in case the tables were turned on me," Sam continued. "I asked Chloe to come over and hide in one of the bedrooms before Greg arrived one night."

"I wasn't as blunt as 'take me to bed or lose me forever,'" she said, borrowing a popular movie line, "but there was no mistaking my intent. I'll spare you the nitty-gritty. Let's just say he showed a fair bit of interest in the prospect."

Kendall glanced at Chloe.

"I heard the whole thing." Chloe nodded. "He was all over her like white rice."

"White *on* rice," Kendall and Sam corrected in unison.

"Why didn't you tell me what had happened?" Kendall asked Sam. "If I'd known he was such a slime ball, I could have dumped him before he went after my realtor."

Sam sighed. "The guy should have been an actor," she told Kendall. "When he realized he'd been set up, he started crying like a baby. Went on about how much he loved you and didn't want to lose you. Blubbering about me being some sort of teenage crush for him and he'd never acted like this before." She gave a bitter snort. "He must have been laughing his cheating butt off all the way home. Chloe and I bought his sob story hook, line, and sinker."

"He just *seemed* like a good guy," Chloe added. "You know how men react to Sam. We thought he was telling the truth."

"You still should have told me," Kendall said quietly.

"I'm sorry," Sam said.

"Me, too," Chloe echoed.

"So that's the reason for the Mae West routine tonight?" asked Kendall.

Sam looked sheepish. "Not my brightest idea. But the sparks flying between the two of you could have set fire to wet logs. I wanted to get a read on the guy before things got serious."

"Trust me, nothing is going to get serious between Ty and me," Kendall said, with more determination than she felt. She couldn't help asking, "What did you think of him?"

"Not too much to go on since he rushed out after my little spectacle," Sam answered, taking a sip of wine. "He's certainly easy on the eyes. You said he was a landscaper?"

"He has a doctorate and, according to Google, extensive experience in soil conservation, biology, and resource inventory and assessment." When Sam gave her a blank look she added, "To answer your question, yes. He owns a landscaping company. That's what he does for a living."

"I don't know much about the science stuff," Sam said with a salacious grin, "but I'd pay good money to watch that man dig a hole in the ground with no shirt on."

"Mmmm hmmm," Chloe echoed.

Kendall made a face. "That's part of the reason I couldn't be serious about him."

"Why?" Sam asked. "You only go for the scrawny geeks like Greg?"

"Greg was a cute geek," Kendall protested. "And despite some of the problems we had . . ."

"Like the fact that he was a rat-bastard cheater," Sam interrupted.

"I prefer ratfink. Despite that," Kendall continued, "he's what I'm looking for in a guy: successful, polished, professional. We fit."

"But you didn't fit," Chloe argued. "You only thought you did. A man who could hurt you the way Greg did is not someone you want in your life, no matter how much he looks the part."

Kendall said nothing. Chloe's quiet insight cut directly to the heart of the matter.

Kendall didn't want to think about Greg's cheating or Ty Bishop. Especially Ty and the way his body fit perfectly over hers. The way her heart had softened when he'd held her then pounded as passion consumed them both. She grabbed the bag of chips from the counter.

"Let's go check out my other prospects," she said lightly.

Chloe touched her arm. "I mean it, Ken. You deserve someone who will respect and cherish you for who you are."

Too bad Kendall wasn't sure who she was.

She saw the pain in Chloe's pale gray eyes and knew her friend also spoke from firsthand experience with a bad man. She put her arms around Chloe's small shoulders and squeezed. "We all deserve that," she murmured against Chloe's dark curls.

Kendall felt Sam's arms tighten around her back and the three friends stood in the kitchen in an awkward hug. Sam's voice was as gentle as Chloe's had been when she said, "I still think you should give the hottie a chance."

Laughing, Kendall rolled her eyes. "Fine. Anyone for dating profiles?"

"I can't wait." Sam grinned and walked into Kendall's living room.

The application was straightforward. It asked for the man's name, address, age, height, weight, occupation, and why he should be chosen to date Kendall. It also requested that a photograph of the applicant be included, along with a short video introduction. Kendall had expected maybe a dozen men to apply, but by the time Chloe finished pulling the one-page forms out of the envelope, there was a stack of more than sixty applications sitting on the coffee table.

Kendall took a fortifying drink of wine. "I can't believe it," she breathed.

"The ads only started running two days ago," Chloe said. "You have a ton of possibilities here."

"Want to take a couple for yourself?" Chloe hadn't been on one date since they'd become friends. Kendall knew Chloe's first marriage had ended badly but believed her sweet friend deserved a second chance at finding love.

Chloe shook her head. "My cat provides all the companionship I need."

Before Kendall could respond, Sam snatched several sheets from the top of the stack. "Don't think of foisting any of these potential swains on me either. But they like you, Ken. They really like you. I've got a lawyer, a doctor, and a mortgage broker here." She flipped through a few more of the applications. "Ha. This one says he'd be a good fit because his favorite color is blue and you wear blue suits on the news a lot."

"I do?"

Chloe rifled through another stack of papers. "This guy is six four and a banker." She pushed a photo across the table toward Kendall. "He looks like your type—buttoned up but still cute."

Gingerly, Kendall picked up the picture. The man smiling back at her in an elegant suit looked exactly like the sort of guy she would normally be attracted to: handsome, professional, and sophisticated.

She couldn't muster one speck of interest.

She told herself it was because of the bizarre situation. Men applying to date her on camera should be what accounted for her indifference toward any of the potential candidates. She would have sworn on a mile-high stack of Bibles that it was not her increasing attraction to a certain gorgeous landscaper with golden skin and work-roughened hands that made her wish she could back out of the dating show. But she knew it was a lie.

Sam and Chloe stayed for another few hours, creating details about the applicants that became more salacious as they neared the bottom of the pile. The raunchy banter put the situation into perspective. At least to a point.

"Yuck. I can't believe you think someone would name his dingle Tex," she complained to Sam after a particularly graphic analysis of one candidate. "How am I going to keep a straight face if I end up going to dinner with that guy?"

"I can't believe you can say the word *dingle* with a straight face," Sam shot back. "What is this, third grade? Besides, if the producers set you up with a guy who poses next to his pick-up truck, sporting leather chaps, his beer gut, and a smile, you're going to need to laugh your way through the date just to keep your sanity."

Kendall glanced at the glossy photo and grimaced. "They wouldn't, would they?"

Chloe patted her hand. "There are a number of nice men who are interested in being part of the show. You filled out a similar questionnaire and the people at the station know you. I'm sure it will be fine."

"Just to be on the safe side . . ." Sam said, folding the picture of the overweight cowboy and placing it, along with the corresponding application, in the empty chip bag.

"Thanks," Kendall said.

Sam winked. "My pleasure."

Chloe stood, picking up the crumpled bag and empty wine bottle. "I should get going. I have a clown and a face painter scheduled in the store tomorrow so there's bound to be a crowd."

"Do you need help?" Kendall offered. Every so often, she got to pitch in at the toy store Chloe owned.

"Thanks, but I'll have reinforcements," Chloe said over her shoulder as she walked toward the kitchen to throw out the night's trash.

When she disappeared, Sam leaned forward. "Ken, about Greg. Don't blame Chloe for anything. She wanted to tell you, but I made her promise."

Kendall squeezed Sam's long fingers. "You need to tell me if you get a bad feeling about someone I'm seeing. I trust you." She tightened her grip until Sam winced slightly. "But lay off with the big time come-ons. A guy hardly has a fighting chance when you bring out the heavy artillery."

Sam met Kendall's gaze squarely. "Trust me, honey, I could have walked into the room naked and barely caused a raised eyebrow. He only had eyes for you."

A flush of warmth spread through Kendall. She didn't want Sam to see how much it meant to hear that, so she stood quickly. Immediately, the room started spinning and she plopped back down on the couch. "Ugh."

Sam gathered the wine glasses and headed toward the kitchen, calling to Chloe, "Someone's hit the sauce a little heavy tonight."

Kendall lay flat against the cushions, staring at the ceiling, until the walls stopped dancing around her. She lifted her head when Sam and Chloe returned to the living room. "Was I the only one drinking tonight?"

"The second bottle was pretty much all you," Sam answered.

"There was a second bottle?"

"It's ok," Chloe tried to reassure her. "You're not driving. Can we get you anything before we go?"

Kendall shook her head and lights danced in front of her eyes. She lay back against the sofa before she made herself sick. "I'm fine. Would you make sure the front door locks behind you? I don't think I can make it there on my own."

First Sam then Chloe bent down to kiss her cheek. "Try a hamburger in the morning," Chloe suggested as she brushed the hair off of Kendall's forehead. "The grease helps a hangover."

"That's disgusting," Sam complained.

Kendall gave her a bleary smile. "Whatever works."

Chloe dimmed the living room lights and the two women left. Kendall tried closing her eyes, but the room spun again. Staring at the ceiling, she crossed her hands over her chest and propped her feet against the armrest at one end of the couch.

She tried to clear her mind, but thoughts and memories trickled across. She was so grateful for Sam and Chloe, two friends who really knew who she was and liked her anyway. She had the unnerving suspicion that the same might be said about Ty. He seemed to have a remarkably accurate insight when it came to her.

She always hoped if she tried hard enough, she could one day forget about the girl who lived beneath the surface.

That girl had wanted nothing more than to fit in at the private school her parents couldn't afford. After her humiliating first day, all she'd wanted was to be invisible to the other students. Kendall had been grateful for the plaid jumper that helped her look like all the other girls.

As it turned out, too much like one of them. On her second week at Graves, when she'd cautiously set her lunch tray down at one of the cafeteria tables near some of the kids who were in her class, the bubbly blond ringleader of the group asked loudly, "Is that my old uniform you're wearing? There was hole at the bottom of the skirt so I got a new one this year."

Kendall had answered honestly, "I don't know." She hadn't known where her mother got the uniform, hadn't questioned its appearance at their house two weeks earlier. More than likely, it was the girl's uniform, bought secondhand and mended by her mother's stiff fingers.

The feeling of utter mortification she'd felt all those years ago was still so strong the muscles of her stomach quivered in response. She rubbed her fingers against the flat of her abdomen, wishing she'd been able to soothe the embarrassed little girl she had been so easily.

That little girl had wanted to run from the bright lights of the school's lunchroom back to her white-trash neighborhood with its double-wide trailer homes. All the kids she knew from home wore hand-me-down clothes and broken-in shoes with scuffed toes as well, but she didn't fit in there either.

She'd swallowed her embarrassment and began saving money to buy a new uniform. She studied the girls in her class as intently as she did her homework, watching how they dressed, wore their hair, what they scribbled on their textbook covers. Without being too obvious, she imitated everything they did until she blended in so seamlessly they almost forgot she wasn't one of them.

In a way, she was still using that method. Only these days, she studied her favorite anchorwomen. It was the reason she took time every morning, even on her days off, to apply makeup and style her hair. Even when she and Greg had spent the night together, she'd snuck out of bed before he woke to brush her teeth and dab gloss across her lips.

A lot of good that had done since he'd cheated on her. She studied a hairline crack running the length of her ceiling as she thought about that pain. He'd blamed her, said she'd been too cold, too wrapped up in her career to support him. Her friends had convinced her Greg's infidelity was his problem, but his accusations still hurt.

Ty's words came back to her, "It makes you more real." The only place Kendall felt real was in her job. But in Ty's arms, she'd wanted more. She'd wanted to let down her guard and allow him to see every piece of her, the bits she'd never shared with anyone else.

The questions and self-doubt swimming around in her head made it pound even harder. She focused on the future. Getting promoted to a real news position in New York would be the culmination of everything she'd worked for since that first year at Graves. It would finally prove that she was worthy of the life she'd craved for so long.

Her cell phone buzzed as a text came through.

Everything ok with your friends?

Ty. The fact that he was checking on her made her heart flip. She should ignore him, pretend the kiss never happened and focus only on his help with her story. But while she was used to being alone, some nights it felt . . . lonely. And the wine wasn't helping.

Her thumbs were texting him back before her common sense could stop them.

They said you gave me a hickey.

When the screen stayed blank, she texted again.

You didn't.

Her cell phone buzzed.

I wanted to taste you.

She smiled despite herself. Another text came through.

Do you want that too?

Now it was more than her brain that felt fuzzy. Her whole body flushed as she thought of his mouth on her skin. Flirting with Ty was not part of her plan. She tossed the phone to the side then picked it up again and typed in three letters. Stupid, but she couldn't resist hitting "Send."

Yes.

CHAPTER SEVEN

Kendall arrived at the station Monday morning to a couple dozen elementary school students gathered in the lobby.

She briefly spoke to the teacher in charge of the group then approached the reception desk. "Is Julia a no-show again?" Channel 8 offered weekly tours to local schools, and it was the responsibility of the newest staff member to lead the tours. But the current junior reporter had a convenient habit of calling in sick most Monday mornings.

Mary nodded. "I had a voice mail waiting when I arrived. The tour was scheduled to start twenty minutes ago, but I can't get anyone upstairs to answer my pages." The older woman's eyes narrowed. "I know they're hiding from me, and I'm about to march up those stairs—"

"I'll take them," Kendall said with a laugh. "I came in early to work on my new assignment, but I can spare a few minutes."

"You're a lifesaver. Again." Mary reached up to pat Kendall's hand. "And in a good mood for the start of another work week. Must have been a good weekend?"

"Fantastic." Kendall glanced at the kids milling about the reception area. She could tell by their faded T-shirts and well-worn sneakers that they weren't from an affluent part of the city. These were the students she most enjoyed introducing to the newsroom, knowing how much that would have meant to her when she was that age. "There's someone meeting me here in a half hour," she said to the receptionist. "If he arrives before I'm through, please ask him to wait."

"Or I could tag along on the tour," a deep voice said from directly behind her.

Heat spread down the length of Kendall's body at the sound of that rumbling tone. She spun around so fast she bumped against the receptionist desk. Ty Bishop stood silhouetted in the bright light spilling in from the large windows that encircled the lobby.

Wearing dark blue jeans, hiking boots, a burgundy button-down shirt, and a gray fleece vest zipped half way up, he looked like the poster boy for clean mountain living. He smiled and Kendall's knees turned to rubber. It had been a much more enjoyable sensation when she'd been drinking.

She thought about her own outfit. She wore a snug fitting crew neck sweater, tennis shoes, and blue jeans. She'd changed several times, wanting to find the jeans that showed off her figure to the best advantage without being too obvious. Obvious like the blush she could feel creeping up her cheeks as he watched her, a smile curving one side of his mouth.

"I'm sorry," Mary said quickly. "I didn't have a chance to tell you. Your appointment is already here."

Kendall struggled to keep the whirling emotions out of her voice. "That's fine. Dr. Bishop can come with us."

She introduced herself to the students, chaperones, and teachers and briefly explained how the station operated and what they'd see. Kendall had enjoyed leading the tours when she'd been new to her job and she didn't mind filling in, especially when it gave her time to curb her reaction to Ty.

As she led the group toward the newsroom on the main floor, Ty followed close on her heels. "What was so fantastic about your weekend?" he asked, his voice pitched so only she could hear.

"Nothing special. It's my standard Monday morning response."

"I had a great weekend, too," he said. "Want to know why?"

"Nope."

"There's this woman," he continued as if she hadn't spoken. "She smells like vanilla but tastes like chocolate. I think I may be addicted."

She stumbled, her shin banging against the edge of the raised platform in the news studio. "Damn."

"Ok there?" Ty took her elbow.

She shrugged off his touch and straightened. As the students filled into the rows of seats in the studio, she turned to face him. "I was eating ice cream when you came over. That's where the chocolate taste came from."

"What flavor?"

"Rocky Road. That doesn't matter."

He raised an eyebrow and flashed her a grin that turned her insides liquid. "I don't know. I would have pegged you for more of a strawberry girl. Rocky Road adds something to the equation."

"Stop distracting me. And don't talk about how I taste. I'm working here." She waved him away. "Go sit down."

He gave her a small salute. "Yes, ma'am."

She explained to the kids how the news broadcast was formatted then gave them a demonstration of the teleprompters and meteorology equipment, which was always the most popular part of the tour. She guided the tour upstairs for a walkthrough of the station offices before ending back in the lobby. After those first minutes, Ty hung back with the parent chaperones, which allowed her to gain a modicum of self-control.

The tour ended in the lobby, where she answered questions from the students. After a few random queries about their favorite TV shows and a reminder from the teacher to keep the questions focused on the tour, a small boy in front raised his hand. "Did you know there are over 200 dinosaur species that haven't even been discovered yet?"

"That's interesting," Kendall answered.

"Have you ever been on an airplane?" he continued, ignoring the teacher who was shaking her head.

"It's ok," Kendall told the woman then smiled at the boy. "I have. Have you?"

"Nope." He frowned. "They took away Mom's car last month so now we take the bus. But when I grow up I want to be a paleontologist and fly all over the world. I'm going to discover at least fifty new kinds of dinosaurs."

The girl standing next to the boy jabbed him in the ribs. "Shut up, Danny. You're not going nowhere."

The boy swatted at his classmate's arm but continued to look at Kendall, his gaze both determined and self-conscious, as if he hadn't meant to share his dream out loud.

"I have no doubt you'll be a great paleontologist, and even if you decide to study the dinosaurs we already know, I'll do a story on you." Kendall bent so that she was at eye level with the kid. "As long as you work hard at what you love, that's the important part. You remember that, ok?"

"Ok," the boy answered, nodding solemnly.

The teacher stepped forward and thanked Kendall, then instructed the class to give her a round of applause. As they filed out of the lobby, one of the mothers told her how much she was looking forward to watching the dates on *It's Raining Men*. Kendall smiled and made a joke about hoping she'd attract the right kind of men, but stopped when Ty winked at her over the woman's shoulder.

"Thanks again, Ken," Mary said as the lobby door closed behind the final students. "You have a real gift with the kids."

"I don't know about that," Kendall said, "but I like talking to them." There was always one, like the boy Danny, who tugged at her own memories of childhood. Wanting more than life seemed willing to offer.

She turned to see Ty staring at her with a mix of thoughtfulness and puzzlement that unsettled her more than his flirtation in the studio. "What?"

He smiled. "The more I know you, the more I like you."

She could tell he was sincere, and that threw her off balance more than anything. Maybe she could brush off a spark, but the tenderness in his gaze was harder to ignore.

"We should go," she said, and moved past him, trying hard to hold onto her self-control. She led the way to the back of the building, where Steve was loading gear into one of news vans.

"Do you need help with anything?" she asked.

The burly cameraman slammed the rear door shut. "We're all set. Hop in."

"Great." She slid open the side door and turned to Ty. "You can sit in the front so you can give directions once we get into the burn area." Without waiting for a reply, she scrambled into the back of the van.

Ty had a brief moment to enjoy the sight of Kendall's backside as she bent forward to step into the vehicle. A moment later the door closed, leaving him staring at his own reflection in the darkened glass window. He shook his head and climbed into the passenger seat.

He didn't know what he'd expected from this morning, but watching Kendall charm a roomful of elementary-age kids hadn't been it. He'd seen a vulnerability in her response to the aspiring paleontologist that made him want to know more about what made her who she was.

That proved easier said than done when she remained silent in the back seat for most of the ride. Yet the sweet, clean smell of her perfume drifted into the front seat, curling around Ty's senses in a way that left him distracted and dazed.

It took all his concentration to follow the conversation the cameraman started as they left behind rush-hour traffic on the interstate and cruised up the two-lane mountain highway that led to the national forest and the burn area.

"You grow up in Denver?" Steve asked, easing the van around a turn.

"North of the city," Ty answered, "in Boulder."

"No kidding? I'm from Arvada," Steve said, naming one of the small towns that made up the Denver suburbs. He slanted Ty a curious expression. "Did you say your last name was Bishop?"

"Yeah."

"When I was in college, there was a kid named Bishop who played wide receiver for CU."

"My brother Charlie," Ty said. "I played in high school but didn't have the discipline for college ball."

Steve slapped a meaty hand against the steering wheel. "That was your brother." Ty saw him glance in the rearview mirror. "You should have seen this guy, Kendall. Hands like Velcro—the ball absolutely stuck to them."

"Really," was her only response.

"Did he go pro?" Steve asked. "He had what it takes."

"Blew out his knee his junior year."

The cameraman whistled softly. "Tough break."

Ty shrugged. "He's a doctor now, an orthopedic surgeon."

"Put those hands to better use than catching pigskin." Steve laughed. "Good for him. Always nice to have a doctor in the family, huh?"

"I guess," Ty said and rolled down the van's window to let in the crisp morning air. The truth was, he and his brother barely spoke. Both Charlie and his sister, Clare, had been as angry as their parents when Ty turned his back on the prestigious scientific career he'd been groomed for. Charlie resented the fact that he and Clare toed the family line but still had to live with the ramifications of their mother's disappointment in Ty.

He leaned his head toward the open window and took a deep breath, trying to clear his head of dark thoughts and the smell of Kendall's subtle perfume. As the van climbed higher into the foothills, the conversation with Steve turned to sports in general. Ty kept up his end while continuing to watch the breathtaking scenery that unfolded around them.

The morning was bright, the sunlight that streamed through the pine trees that bordered the road danced in wavering patterns against the pavement. The forest was thick in this area. Although they were less than an hour from the city, the dense canopy of pine and aspen trees made it feel like they were deep in the Rocky Mountain wilderness.

Ty envied the people who lived in the scattered homes that dotted the clearings they passed. To wake up every morning to the smell of air not polluted with smog and car exhaust would be amazing. But he liked the convenience of the city, liked having friends close despite his occasional need for quiet and the solace of the mountains.

The van rounded another bend toward the area known as Silver Creek and the first evidence of fire damage was evident. Ahead, Ty could see the blackened outlines of trees on a hillside once ravaged by the wildfire. As they drove deeper into the burn area, no one spoke. The only sound he heard was the van's engine and the whistling of air rushing in through the open window.

Silence seemed appropriate. Unlike the hillsides they'd just passed, these slopes were covered with blackened trunks, charred skeletons of their former selves. No underbrush surrounded the trees, only the scrubby grasses and plants that had grown in since the wildfire.

Despite the devastation, many of the trees stood tall, their naked branches reaching proudly toward the sky, still trying to soak up the sun's warm rays. It was as if they didn't know their lives had been consumed by blazing flames two summers ago.

Ty still remembered the smell of smoke that had settled over the area right after the fires were contained. He'd been among the first to volunteer to help with the regeneration of the land, and the devastation and emotions had been intense.

"You can pull off here." He indicated a small dirt path on the right side of the road.

Steve swung the van onto the wide dirt shoulder next to the highway and cut the engine. One hundred yards from the edge of the pavement was a gate with a "No Trespassing" sign.

"We can see the worst of the damage from the top of that rise," Ty said, pointing to a nearby hilltop. "We'll need to hike. There's a stream that passes through here a little ways in so the van won't be able to cross."

Steve shifted in his seat to look at Kendall. "You two go ahead without me. I want to get some footage from the drive in while the morning light is still good."

She looked like she wanted to protest but said, "Sure thing. We'll scope out the shots and you get them when you catch up."

"Sounds like a plan." The cameraman turned to Ty. "Is the path clear enough to find on my own?"

Ty nodded and grabbed his backpack, which contained the supplies he'd need to gather initial soil samples. "It leads straight up the side of the mountain. We'll wait for you on the other side."

Ty heard the back door slide open and got out of the passenger side, swinging it shut behind him. Steve reversed the van until it was perpendicular with the highway and then slowly pulled forward onto the pavement, heading back the way they'd just come.

Ty glanced at Kendall, who was studying the surrounding landscape. Birds chirped noisily in the distance, the sound carrying farther without the forest to muffle it. An occasional car sped along the highway, its engine loud in the stillness of the morning. The only other sound was the soft whistle of the wind as it blew through the burnt pine needles that clung to branches on some of the trees.

"Nice morning for a walk." He chuckled softly at the suspicious look she gave him. He lifted his arms, palms out. "Don't worry, we're all business today."

She nodded. "It's better that way."

He walked forward and unhooked the latch on the gate, holding it open for her to pass through. "Whatever you say, Princess."

She muttered something as she marched by him. Ty figured it was better he didn't hear her. He swung the gate closed and followed her up the path, content to let his gaze wander between the natural scenery and the sway of Kendall's hips as she maneuvered around rocks and ditches along the path. It should be a crime for jeans to shape a woman so perfectly. Twice he got so distracted he almost walked off the path.

She stopped at the edge of a small stream that cut through the underbrush. Shielding her eyes from the sun, she looked around and then turned to him. "Is there a bridge or a log we can use to cross?"

He glanced at the brilliantly white gym shoes she wore and grinned. "I take it those aren't waterproof."

She shook her head.

"I can't believe you don't own hiking boots."

"I do. I'm just not wearing them today. Don't ask." She inched toward the water's edge until her toes almost touched the rippling current and bent forward to examine the stream. "It doesn't look that deep," she said, straightening. "My feet won't get too wet."

Before she could test her theory, Ty strode forward. Placing one arm across her back and the other behind her knees, he scooped her into his arms. Her light scent curled into his nostrils, mixing with the smell of the mountain air. He felt the warmth of her body beneath her jacket and the delicious pressure of her rounded hip pressing into his lower abdomen.

A wisp of her hair tickled his chin as she turned toward him, their faces only inches apart. He watched her mouth open in protest and wanted nothing more than to kiss whatever objection she came up with off her lips. But she said nothing. Instead she bit down into the soft fullness.

His knees almost buckled.

He gritted his teeth and walked through the shallow stream, thankful when the freezing water splashed against his legs. Holding her, even for practical reasons, made him so hot he wouldn't have been surprised to see steam rise from his body.

What the hell was the matter with him? He didn't get this worked up about anything, let alone women.

When they were on the path again, he dropped her to her feet. She opened her mouth to speak, but he cut her off with a wave of his hand. "Don't lecture me on professional behavior. You'd have a hell of a time trekking up this mountain with wet feet."

"I wasn't going to lecture. I was going to say thank you." She flashed him a smile and continued up the trail.

Ty stood on the bank of the stream for several moments, willing his body and mind to relax. Kendall stopped walking where the trail curved, her full attention on the charred evergreen near the path.

"It's so depressing," she whispered as she stepped forward to run her fingertips along the trunk. "I haven't been up here since right after the fires. It seemed surreal then. Now the forest looks sad."

He glanced at the sky through a canopy of scorched branches. "It's the natural order of things."

"How can you say that?" she asked. "The fire destroyed thousands of acres of forest and started from someone's carelessness."

"What do you see here?"

She looked at him as if he'd just asked her to take off her clothes and dance a jig. Not a bad idea, actually.

"What do I see?" she repeated. "A forest full of burned, dead trees that should be alive."

"Look closer."

She turned her head from side to side. "I don't know what you're getting at," she told him. "Why don't you spell it out for me?"

He moved forward until he stood directly in front of her. Then he bent and picked up a bright yellow wildflower and a handful of the dirt that it grew from.

"This forest has given us a precious gift," he told her, reaching forward to place the bloom in her palm. He opened his fingers to let the dirt trickle out. "We get to witness the miracle of nature renewing itself."

"Yes, I know," she replied, her tone indulgent. "The fire helps by giving the soil nutrients. I took biology in college." She shrugged her shoulder in a helpless gesture. "It still seems tragic to me to lose so many trees."

"It is tragic," he agreed. "But it's beautiful, too." He placed his hands on each of her shoulders and spun her around so that her back was pressed against his chest.

"Let me show you," he said, lifting his arm until it grazed the side of her cheek. "This hillside was consumed by the fire. Two years ago there was nothing here but blistered earth and blackened trees. It might as well have been the surface of the sun for all that could survive the heat. Now the ground is covered with grasses, flowers, sage, and other scrub bushes."

He breathed in the scent of her clean hair. "Can't you see how vital and alive this place is? It may not look like much driving by at fifty miles an hour, but this forest is full of life. It's a miracle, and we get to watch it."

Kendall turned in his arms. "You're right."

He looked down at her beautiful, upturned face and knew she wanted him to kiss her. He wanted that, too. Wanted to press her tight against him and lower her gently to the soft ground.

Instead, he took a deep breath. "This section of forest is like a lot of things in life," he murmured, his lips almost touching hers. "At first glance, not that remarkable. The question is, are you willing to look beyond the surface and see the value of what's underneath?"

Kendall stared up at Ty, wishing and waiting for his mouth to brush against hers. She heard his words but didn't register their meaning until he took a step back. Cool mountain air rushed into the gap between their bodies, washing over her like a bucket of ice water.

"The ball's in your court, Princess," he said, tracing one finger along the seam of her lips. "Let me know what you decide." He gave her a crooked smile and headed up the path toward the top of the mountain.

Kendall stared at his retreating back. It was a fantastic view, his broad shoulders strong and his gait easy as he kicked loose rocks from the trail. It was hard to believe she'd been kissing him as if her life depended on it only a few nights ago.

He'd offered her casual and that's what she wanted. But she was learning there was more to Ty Bishop than she'd first expected and that made it difficult to keep her feelings out of the equation.

She kicked her foot against the trunk of a fallen tree. Wincing, she cursed the sooty smudge on the toe of her new shoe instead of her own weakness. Emotions were not part of the plan.

As she followed him up the trail, Kendall admitted that she was angrier with herself than him. She knew better than to let him become a distraction. It was the same reason she'd given to him last week when she'd turned down his offer for a date.

When she got closer, she saw Ty gathering soil samples from different parts of the hillside. He spoke about the rejuvenation efforts for this section of the forest, and she was soon caught up in his words. He had a gift for blending technical facts with personal observations to weave a compelling narrative. He would make an excellent teacher. She wondered again why he wasn't putting his prestigious degree to better use than planting trees in suburban lawns.

It was best he hadn't kissed her today. If she didn't have the willpower to resist him, at least he had enough for both of them.

Now she could focus on the story, which was what she wanted. She tried not to notice the way his hair curled in the morning breeze, how his long legs ate up the length of trail, the reverence in his tone as he spoke about the mountains. She tried to keep her mind focused on the business at hand.

It wasn't easy.

CHAPTER EIGHT

Steve caught up with them soon after they reached the top. Kendall turned on the microphone he'd packed along with the other remote location equipment. With Steve shooting from behind her shoulder, she asked Ty to explain the rejuvenation work to the viewing public. The three of them spent another hour on the mountain and then hiked back down to the van. Ty remained cordial but aloof. It was what she wanted, so why did it disappoint her so much?

When Steve parked the van behind the Channel 8 building, she and Ty climbed out simultaneously. They stood in awkward silence until the cameraman joined them.

"I'll put the footage from this morning together and e-mail it to you," Steve told Kendall. "Are we still on for tomorrow?"

She nodded. "I have appointments scheduled with two families who lost their homes in the fire." She felt Ty's questioning gaze and turned to him. "Do you know about the potential land development deal for the valley? We're going to talk with some of locals and get their views on it."

Ty stiffened and she noticed his hands clench at his sides. "A land deal?" His voice was hard.

"Do you think that's a problem?"

"Not necessarily," he said but glanced at his watch instead of looking at her. "I need to get going." Turning to Steve, he extended his hand. "Nice to meet you. I'll let my brother know you remembered him. That kind of stuff makes his day."

The cameraman shook Ty's hand. "Thanks for the tour. I'm not a nature buff, but you make it almost interesting."

One side of Ty's mouth inched up slightly. "That's what I'm here for." He shifted his gaze to Kendall. "I haven't heard anything about the land deal from my contacts in the area, but I'll do some digging. Let me know what else you need from me."

She tried to gauge if he was hiding something, but his eyes gave away nothing. "I'll walk you to your truck," she said. "Steve, I'll see you inside."

"Sure thing," the cameraman replied, and he began unloading equipment from the van.

Ty led the way around the side of the building to the front lot. He stopped next to a truck that was newer and nicer than the one she'd crashed into last week.

She wanted to say something that would bridge the distance between them but didn't know how to make it better without giving him the wrong impression. Which could also be considered the right one, depending on whether she listened to her brain or her body.

"Thank you for your time today," she said, hoping he would use his natural charm to ease the strain.

"Sure."

So much for that natural charm.

"I'll give you a call next week," she said. "I'd like to get some footage of the volunteer teams working. And maybe something on what's being done in other areas of the forest to prevent future fires from getting out of control. Would you be available for a couple more trips into the foothills?" She smiled tentatively. "I'll wear my hiking boots next time so you don't have to strain your back."

"No big deal," he replied, not returning her smile. His tone was so cool it made her wince. He reached into the pocket of his fleece vest and pulled out a set of car keys. "I'll talk to you next week."

She watched him unlock the door of the truck and climb in. "Ty?"

He angled his head around the side of the truck's cab to look at her.

Staring into those penetrating blue eyes, she had no idea what to say. Her emotions were so jumbled she couldn't keep them straight in her head, let alone make sense of them in the middle of a parking lot. "Thanks again," she said with another try at a smile.

He didn't reply, only lifted one hand in a casual wave. He closed the door and started the engine. Kendall moved to the side as the truck reversed out of the parking lot. Ty didn't look at her as he drove away.

She stood in the parking lot for several minutes after he disappeared from view. Finally, she shook her head and walked toward the building.

She had a long day ahead of her and a lot of work to do.

♦ ♦ ♦

The following evening, Kendall shifted nervously in her seat at the downtown Denver restaurant where she was meeting her first date. At seven o'clock on a Wednesday night, the place was half filled. The other customers divided their attention between their own dining companions and the table where she sat near the back of the room. She glanced at Steve, who stood behind her, a camera perched on one beefy shoulder.

"Having second thoughts?" he asked, shifting so the camera lens focused on her.

She nodded. "Third and fourth thoughts, too." Not to mention the fact that she couldn't get Ty and the way their morning had ended out of her mind. "Are you taping me?"

He shook his head. "Not yet."

"I'm freaking out," she confided. "Is it too late to bolt?"

He patted the top of her head like she was a puppy. "You'll be fine. If you get any sort of weird vibes from the guy, give me a sign and I'll knock a drink in his lap or something."

"You're the best." Kendall smiled.

Liz hurried over to the table. "He's here," she said excitedly. "You remember which one this is, right? Scott Jenkins, thirty-four, hot shot investment banker."

Kendall rolled her eyes. "I've studied his profile and you've been lecturing me on his stats for the past half hour."

"Are you ready?"

Kendall ran her fingers through her hair. "Ready as I'll ever be."

Liz tapped her finger twice on the table. "That's my girl." She gestured at Steve. "Come with me. I want to get some shots of his entrance and Kendall's expression when they first meet."

Kendall jerked to attention. "My expression? How am I supposed to react? Is there something wrong with the guy that I need to know about?" Liz left with Steve following, ignoring her frantic questions.

She folded her hands on the table and tried not to panic. As it turned out, there was no need for worry. The man walking toward her looked just like his picture, down to the tailored suit and matching red tie.

She stood as he approached the table. "Scott? Hi, I'm Kendall. It's nice to meet you."

He took her hand and brought it to his lips, smearing a sloppy wet kiss across her knuckles. "It's a pleasure to meet you, Kendall."

Aware of Steve filming her behind Scott's back, Kendall kept a bright smile on her face. She pulled her hand from her date's grasp and gestured to the table. "Have a seat," she said, wiping her hand on her napkin. It was an effort not to shudder.

As he sat down, it struck her that the last time she'd sat at a table across from a man was during her breakfast with Ty. Right now she needed to stop wishing Ty was with her on this date and start focusing on the man in front of her.

The man whose eyes were currently roaming all over her body. "You're even better looking in person than on television."

Kendall couldn't quite hide her surprise at his blunt remark. "Um, thank you."

He leaned forward and stared into her eyes. "I mean it," he told her earnestly. "They say the camera adds ten pounds and you look about perfect on TV so I thought you'd be scrawny in real life." He winked. "But you've got curves where it counts."

Kendall's shocked gaze darted to Steve and the camera. He gave her a questioning glance. Almost imperceptibly, she shook her head. "Tell me a little bit about yourself, Scott," she said, trying to redirect the conversation. "I understand you're an investment banker."

He gave her a knowing smile. "That's always a hit with the ladies. Let's just say, I've got a good-size bulge where a man needs it."

"Excuse me?" she sputtered, hoping she'd misheard him. If she hadn't, she'd be going on one blind date instead of two. This one would be left on the cutting room floor. Even when Ty had been flirting with her, he'd been a gentleman about it. That was something she was appreciating more by the second. Once again, she tried *and failed* to stop thinking about Ty.

"In my wallet." He laughed. "Thanks to my job, I'm never short on cash." He pointed one finger at her in mock accusation. "You, little lady, need to get your mind out of the gutter. We'll save that sort of thinking for the end of the evening."

An end that couldn't come soon enough. She stared in abject horror at the lounge lizard in banker's clothing sitting across from her. She'd reviewed the bios of each of the guys she'd be dating for *It's Raining Men*. Like the other men, Steve had looked perfect on paper, but that didn't matter when he was such a jerk.

Her mind drifted to Ty once more. She'd tried to ignore the spark she'd felt because he was a complication she couldn't handle. But she was quickly coming to understand how rare that kind of a connection could be. Did she really want to let him go?

Right now she had to figure out how she was going to make it through this date without strangling Scott Jenkins. She gestured to the waiter hovering near the table. "Could we get a wine list, please?"

◆ ◆ ◆

Kendall pulled to a stop in front of the cozy brick house nestled in a recently gentrified neighborhood not far from downtown. She rested both hands against the steering wheel and propped her head against them. The digital clock on the dashboard shone brightly against the Jeep's darkened interior. It was almost ten o'clock.

Had it really only been two and a half hours since her disastrous date with Scott Jenkins began? She couldn't stand to think any more about that lecherous cheese ball. A cool gust of night air washed over her as she opened the car door and got out. One lone streetlight glowed dimly overhead, illuminating large trees that were just beginning to bud. The night was clear, the street silent but for the hum of cars in the distance.

She walked up the short concrete path that led to the house's over-sized porch. A wooden swing hung from the rafters on one end, while several empty flowerpots huddled in the corner on the other side.

Was this a mistake? *Of course it is,* her rational inner voice advised. She ignored the voice and rang the doorbell before she lost her nerve. Being on the date had made her feel lonely, even in the middle of a crowded restaurant with a camera filming. Her empty condo held no appeal tonight, and of all the places she could go, this was where she wanted to be. The porch light flicked on, bathing her in an iridescent glow.

The door swung open, and Ty peered out at her behind the mesh screen, his usual unreadable expression darkening his striking blue eyes.

"Hi." She smiled. "I was totally *not* in your neighborhood and decided to stop by."

A slow grin spread across his face. He pushed open the screen. "Come on in."

"Sorry it's so late," she said as she scooted past him into the entry.

The screen door banged behind her, and she jerked around. Ty stood in the doorway, his gaze still enigmatic. "The kitchen is straight ahead. Would you like something to drink?"

"Sure. Thank you." She walked forward, studying his home as she went. Shelves overflowed with books in the living room and a small table held a TV and stereo equipment. The furniture was overstuffed and comfortable. Framed prints of black and white landscape scenes hung in a row above the leather sofa.

"How long have you lived here?"

"A few years. I'm kind of remodeling it in stages."

"The house fits you."

"Thanks. I think."

She heard the smile in his voice. "Yeah, it's a compliment. Don't let it go to your head."

He laughed.

The kitchen she stepped into was warm and inviting. Dark cherry cabinets contrasted with the soft yellow walls. It was a room that made her want to sit down and stay a while.

"Did you redo this room yourself?" Kendall asked, sliding her hand over the smooth granite countertops.

Ty walked to the stainless steel refrigerator. "For the most part. I meet a lot of contractors in my line of work so I had some help with the plumbing and electrical. Jenny picked out the yellow," he said, gesturing to the walls. "She swore it wasn't too girlie and it's grown on me. What can I get you to drink?"

"A glass of white would be nice."

He rooted around in the refrigerator and pulled out a bottle. Silently, he removed a wine glass from one of the upper cabinets and poured. He set it before her and turned back to the refrigerator. Kendall watched the muscles of his legs flex under gray gym shorts as he squatted down to grab a beer bottle from one of the lower shelves.

"To what do I owe the pleasure?" he asked. He propped one hip against the counter and took a long drink of beer.

Kendall rolled the stem of the wine glass between her fingers. "I had a date tonight."

Something flashed in Ty's eyes. "Shouldn't you be having this conversation with one of your girlfriends?"

"Probably."

"So how was it?"

"Awful. It was for the dating show and a complete disaster. The guy threw out every bad line in the book. It's a wonder he didn't ask my sign. I didn't take one bite of the food. It was all I could do not to gag every time he opened his mouth."

"That bad?"

She nodded. "Do you know the worst part?"

"What?"

She took a long sip of wine and met his brooding gaze. "The entire date, all I thought about was you. Even before I met the guy tonight. I was waiting at one of my favorite restaurants and I sat there wanting you to be walking toward me." She laughed. "I have two more dates for the show, and I want you on each one."

"I like the sound of that." He took another swallow of beer. "Why do I think there's a *but* in my future?"

"There are a number of *buts*," she agreed. "I've told you most of them. *But* you're not my type, *but* I don't have time for a relationship, *but* my career takes too much time and attention. If things go as planned I'm going to be moving to New York in a matter of months." She shook her head. "I should not be here, but when I got in my car after tonight's fiasco, I wanted to be with *you*. I like the way I feel when you're around. You make me feel so . . . real. Anyway, I dug out your resume to find your address and here I am."

She looked away from the intensity in his expression, embarrassed that she'd revealed so much. "How pathetic is that?" she asked weakly.

Ty ate up the distance between them in three long steps. He cradled her face between hands that were cool and slightly damp from the beer bottle. He tilted her head until she was forced to meet his gaze. "It doesn't sound pathetic at all," he murmured. "It sounds like the nicest thing I've ever heard."

He brought his mouth down to meet hers. The kiss was slow and gentle and tasted faintly of beer. This is what she'd imagined all night. The thought of Ty's lips against hers had kept her sane through the dreadful dinner.

But reality was so much better than any fantasy she'd created in her mind.

Her head spun, her knees went weak, and her stomach growled like an irate lion. "Oops," she said against his lips.

She felt his mouth curve into a smile. "I seem to have that effect on your stomach," he said, drawing back his head.

She flashed a grin. "What can I say, you make me hungry." It had been a long time since she'd flirted so openly, and she felt the heat rise to her cheeks again.

Ty's eyes darkened before he tucked her hair behind her ears and dropped a quick kiss on the tip of her nose. "First, let's get you fed," he told her, his tone gentle. "Then we'll do something about your hunger."

"Ok," she squeaked in response.

He smiled. "How do you feel about s'mores?"

"Those things you make over a campfire?"

He nodded.

"I've never had one."

He gave her an incredulous look. "You're kidding, right?"

She shrugged. "I've never been camping. It's not really my style."

Ty began opening cabinets, pulling out ingredients. "But you live in Colorado. It's an unofficial state law that you must like to camp to move here."

"What can I say? Maybe I'm the only person who ever moved here who's not into the outdoors. I don't like dirt and bugs." She thought about how he spent his days and cringed. "No offense."

"None taken." He turned to her, holding a box of graham crackers, a bag of marshmallows, and a large chocolate bar. "We're going to broaden your horizons, darlin'." He grinned. "When I'm through with you, you'll be begging me to backpack with you through the Rocky Mountain wilderness."

She thought about reminding him that when they were through, she'd be getting on a plane bound for New York City, but decided against it. There was plenty of time for reality to rear its inevitable head. Tonight she wanted to forget about the rest of her life. "Why do you have all that stuff?" she asked. "Are you some kind of Boy Scout troop leader?"

"Hardly." He laughed. "Jenny's son, Cooper, spends the night every so often. Making s'mores is part of our ritual." He balanced the boxes and bag in one hand and opened the French doors that led off the kitchen toward the back of the house.

"What's the deal with you and Jenny?" she asked, as she followed him onto a large deck attached to the house.

"Why, Ms. Clark, are you the jealous type?"

"Of course not," she answered too quickly. "You two seem close. I was simply wondering if there's a history there. She's very pretty."

The only light in the backyard came from the kitchen window so Kendall couldn't see much past the wooden rail of the deck. Ty set the packages on a wrought iron table and disappeared into a darkened corner of the deck. As her eyes adjusted to the night, Kendall could make out his silhouette bending over a large stone fireplace built into one side of the patio.

"Jenny's pretty," he agreed. "But she's like a little sister to me. Her mom worked as my family's housekeeper so we've been friends since we were little. Her dad was a gardener so she knows a lot about planting. I worked summers for Mr. Castelli in high school. Jenny was the first person I hired when I started my business. She's been with me ever since."

Her eyes widened. "Your family had a housekeeper?"

His shoulders stiffened. "Let's not go there. Please."

The please got her. "For now," she agreed. "What about Cooper's father?"

"Jenny was barely eighteen when Cooper was born. The jerk wasn't interested in being a dad. That's part of the reason she came to work for me. I could be flexible with her hours and it didn't bother me if she brought the baby into the office. It's worked out for both of us." He stood and turned. "I need to get some kindling from the garage. Do you want a jacket? Even with the fire, it'll be cool out here."

"That would be great."

He walked past her into the house. Alone on the deck, Kendall sank into one of the chairs that surrounded the oval table. She folded her arms across her chest to ward off the chill in the evening air.

She didn't know what to think about his family having a housekeeper. The kids she'd gone to school with had had housekeepers and gardeners, but they had come from families with money—old money and new money alike, but lots of money all the same. Ty didn't strike her as having had a privileged youth, but what she'd discovered online about his background focused on his work with the landscaping company and mentioned nothing about his personal life.

Ty didn't seem like the type to have grown up with paid help in the house. But as curious as she was to know the story behind that, she didn't want to encourage him to ask questions about her childhood. She knew from the time she'd spent with him hiking the burn area that he was smart. She assumed he'd put himself through graduate school with landscaping jobs and the money had been too lucrative to stop.

More compelling was the fact that he'd hired a young, single woman with a baby as his company's first employee, displaying a streak of protectiveness and loyalty that warmed both her heart and other parts of her anatomy. A heated body she could handle, her heart was another matter.

"Here you go."

Kendall jumped slightly at the sound of Ty's voice so close to her ear. He wrapped a thick fleece jacket around her shoulders and dropped a cotton blanket and a pair of wool socks into her lap.

"Those shoes look uncomfortable," he explained, pointing at her feet. "Plus, the socks will keep your feet warmer."

Kendall looked down at the three-inch heels she'd been wearing since her date with Scott. Now that she thought about it, her toes did feel cramped. "Thank you."

He walked past her to the fireplace. "I'll have this thing blazing in a minute and we can roast up those marshmallows. I can't believe you've never made s'mores."

"I've had a sheltered life." She slipped her arms into the oversized sleeves of the fleece. The weight of the soft fabric added a layer of warmth over her silk suit. The faint smell of laundry detergent mixed with the woodsy scent of male cologne drifted up to her. Ty smelled the same way when he was close to her. Little butterflies zipped around her stomach as she snuggled deeper into the bulk of the jacket.

Ty turned to look at her. Flames were just beginning to glow behind his back. "Has your life been sheltered?"

"It's a figure of speech," she said casually.

He gave her a wry smile. "I realize that. But I don't know much about you."

She kicked off her pumps and bent forward to slip on the socks. "There's not much to tell," she answered, not meeting his gaze. "I was raised in a small town outside of Kansas City. My parents still live there. I went to St. Louis University and took a job in Ohio right out of school. I came to Denver three years ago. You know the rest." She stood and picked up the bag of marshmallows, opening the plastic and popping one into her mouth.

"Brothers and sisters?" he asked, moving two chairs from the table to face the fireplace.

She shook her head. "I wish. I wasn't exactly the daughter my parents bargained for. It would be nice if they had a kid who was more like them."

"What are they like?"

Kendall inwardly grimaced at how much her comment had revealed. She never discussed her family. She waved dismissively. "You know, they have a small-town mentality. They got married the summer after high school graduation. My mom had a scholarship to the local community college, but then she got pregnant. I don't think they quite knew what to do with me. I spent most of my childhood wanting to leave behind the life they'd chosen."

"I know what you mean." Ty reached for two long sticks that lay next to the fireplace. "I doubt Cooper will mind if you use his," he said, handing one to Kendall. "So they aren't supportive?"

Kendall took the stick and poked the flat end of the marshmallow carefully with the blackened tip. "Oh, no. They were encouraging, as much as they could be while dealing with their own lives. They still are. But they didn't understand some of my choices."

"You're lucky to have their support," Ty said. He smiled at the marshmallow dangling off the tip of her stick. "You may want to push that down a little. Otherwise, you're going to lose it in the fire."

She watched him jam a marshmallow several inches down onto his stick and copied the action. "What about you? Do you have brothers and sisters?"

"One of each," he replied and held his stick toward the flames.

"That's right," she said, "you and Steve were discussing your brother's college football career. You grew up in Boulder. Do your parents still live there?"

He nodded.

She studied his hooded expression and waited for him to say more. When he didn't, she asked, "Are you close with your family?"

He gave a bark of laughter. "This feels like an interview. I see them regularly, if that counts. It's time to move your stick."

Kendall refocused her attention on the fire. The end of her stick was engulfed in hot flames, the marshmallow on its tip glowed as bright as the Olympic torch. "It's on fire." She yanked the burning end away from the fire. A tongue-like blue and gold flame shimmered from the top.

Ty cupped his hand around hers on the end of the stick she held and leaned it toward his face. He blew on the marshmallow until the fiery glow subsided. The charred confection left in its wake was as black as the burned-out tree trunks near the heart of the wildfire area.

"You really don't know how to do this." He laughed, plucking the stick from her fingers and replacing it with his own. He put her marshmallow back in the heart of the fire, scraping it against one of the logs until it dislodged from the stick and was consumed by the flames.

Kendall studied his marshmallow. It was evenly toasted to a lovely golden brown on all sides. "I didn't know roasting marshmallows was such an art."

Ty reached for the box of graham crackers. "You'll get the hang of it after a couple more." He arranged a piece of the chocolate on a graham cracker square, then surrounded the marshmallow with two sections of cracker and eased the gooey paste off the stick. "Some people like it burned to a crisp, but I think it's better when the marshmallow melts but doesn't char." He held the makeshift sandwich toward Kendall. "Here you go."

She shook her head. "That's yours. I can try another one."

"We'll share."

Unable to resist the sugary smell, she placed her fingers over Ty's on each end of the s'more and bit down. "Oh, wow," she groaned around a mouthful of food. "This is so good."

Ty slid his fingers out from under hers. "Finish it. I'll toast another one."

"Do you want a bite?"

He shook his head. "It's all yours."

She sank back in her chair and savored each bite. "I should have been a Girl Scout," she moaned. "This is like heaven."

Ty skewered two more marshmallows on the stick and held them toward the fire. "What are you doing for Easter?"

"Hmmm?"

"Easter is this coming Sunday. Do you have plans?"

Kendall finished the s'more and licked her fingers. "Nothing special."

He slid her a sideways glance. "The best way to explain my family is for you to meet them. Why don't you come to dinner at my parents' house?"

She opened and closed her mouth several times before replying. "I don't think your mother would want a stranger over for a family holiday."

"Sure she would," he argued. "My mom loves entertaining. She doesn't actually cook, but the more people to fawn over her flower arrangements and tablescapes the better."

A whole slew of objections darted across Kendall's mind. She hadn't wanted to get close to this man, but suddenly she was going to meet his parents? Then she thought about spending one more holiday alone in her empty condo. "That would be nice," she answered.

The brilliance of the smile he bestowed on her would have knocked her on her butt if she hadn't been sitting down already.

They continued to toast marshmallows until Kendall was stuffed into a blissful food coma.

He asked her more questions about her youth, to which she gave vague answers that satisfied his curiosity without revealing too much. They were the same ambiguous stories she'd been telling for years, but tonight they made her feel dishonest and guilty. Her parents had their problems, but they'd worked hard to overcome them, and they were good people. Kendall wished she felt comfortable enough with herself to reveal the truth about her trailer-park childhood.

The fire died down to a pile of hot embers. She glanced at her watch and stood. "It's late. I should get going."

Without warning, Ty grabbed her hand and tugged hard. She stumbled backwards and landed in his lap. His arms wrapped tightly around her. "Not hungry anymore?" he murmured against her hair.

"Are you kidding? I think I ate my weight in chocolate."

He nuzzled his face against her neck, pressing his lips to her earlobe. Gently, he bit into the soft flesh. Kendall tingled right down to her toes. "Maybe a little hungry," she said on a breath.

His soft laugh tickled the hair at the side of her face. "Good."

She turned until her face was level with his. "What about you?"

His mouth curved into a wolfish grin. "Starving."

CHAPTER NINE

He leaned forward and claimed her mouth with his. This kiss was not the soft seduction it had been earlier in the kitchen. It was hot and hard and demanding. She wound her arms around his back, her nails sinking into the smooth fabric of his sweatshirt, and hung on for dear life. Ty's fingers combed through her curls as his tongue mingled with hers. The sweet taste of the chocolate and marshmallow contrasted with the intensity of his passion.

"So good," he rasped against her skin, nipping at the pulse that thumped wildly on her neck. "You taste so damn good."

"It's the marshmallow," she answered, her voice hoarse. She dropped her head back as his breath blew in hot swells against her skin.

"It's you," he corrected. Dragging his mouth back to hers, he moved his hands to the fleece's zipper. He tugged it down and pushed the jacket off her shoulders. A cool night breeze cut into the thin fabric of her silk blazer. He undid the buttons at the front of the blazer as his lips fluttered along her collarbone. She wore nothing but a thin lace camisole and bra under her jacket. As the evening's chill swept along her bare shoulders, an involuntarily shiver coursed through her.

She shifted position, trying to get closer to the heat that radiated off Ty's body. He lifted her hips, positioning her so she straddled his lap, the folds of her knee-length skirt stretching across his thighs.

His hand fumbled for a moment on the seat next to her and then he drew the cotton blanket around her shoulders. His arms wrapped around her and pressed her tight to the muscled wall of his chest. The kiss he gave her was long and intense, his tongue gliding in and out in a rhythm that Kendall mimicked with her hips. She felt the length of his erection against her stomach grow harder beneath his cotton shorts.

"Jesus," he groaned against her mouth, "you make me crazy." He cupped her face in his hands and drew back. She gazed at him without really focusing, her vision clouded by lust.

After several moments, his steady blue gaze penetrated the fog that enveloped her. "I want you, Kendall," he said solemnly. "I want to see you, I want to taste you. Every inch of you. I told you no pressure, only as much involvement as makes you comfortable. That still stands and we'll stop right now if that's what you want. Just say the word."

She stared at him. Her heart hammered in her chest at the vulnerability she saw in his expression. The smart thing would be to walk away right now, before what was between them went any farther. She reached forward with both hands and tugged at the sides of his sweatshirt. "What I want," she said with a smile, "is for you to get rid of this."

Lightning fast, Ty ripped the heavy material over his head, tossing the sweatshirt into the darkness with the flick of one wrist. Just as quickly, the breath whooshed out of Kendall's lungs as her eyes feasted on the hard contours of his powerful body.

It was the body of a man who spent his days working his muscles to a fine precision. Hesitantly, she touched one finger to the hair-roughened skin. A muscle jumped and she heard Ty's sharp intake of air. The bronze expanse of his solid chest tapered into a flat abdomen, taut with muscles. His shoulders were broad, his arms strong.

He skimmed the skin at the neckline of her camisole with the tips of his fingers. He traced a path upward and hooked a finger from each hand under the straps that lay against her shoulders. Her gaze darted up to his when she realized his intent. With exquisite slowness, he dragged the straps of her camisole and bra down around her arms, revealing her breasts to the cool night air.

"Beautiful," he whispered, his eyes fixed on her face.

Her nipples puckered, more from the reverence in his voice than the crisp breeze that floated against her heated skin. Her lids drifted closed as his work-roughened palms grazed the sensitive tips. He circled his hand around the tender points, spinning her farther into a heated fervor.

Moisture pooled between her thighs as his head bent to capture one of her nipples in his mouth.

He rubbed his hands down the side of her body to her thighs. Pushing away the satiny fabric of her skirt, he pressed his palms along the curve of her inner thighs. He traced his thumb against the damp lace of her underpants.

Oh, my god. Whether she said it out loud or to herself, Kendall didn't know. Her mind was beyond reason, beyond rational thought. She was too turned on to care about the moans of pleasure that escaped her lips. Her body arched against his hand, silently urging him to touch her more deeply. He hummed his pleasure at her demand against the swell of her breast.

Gently, he moved aside the barrier of fabric. One finger slipped into her slick wetness, and she rocked with desire. Her breath came in short, ragged gasps as he delved deeper with his finger and pressed his thumb against her, stroking the tender spot in hypnotic circles. He captured her mouth for a soul-shattering kiss until she cried out her pleasure, the air whooshing out of her lungs and into his mouth.

The intimacy of the moment rocked her as hard as the sensations skittering through her body. Dragging her lips away from his, she buried her face in the warm skin of his throat. She shuddered uncontrollably as her body reeled from the force of her orgasm. His chest was heaving almost as hard as hers but the rest of his body remained rigidly still beneath her.

Her limbs, on the other hand, felt as soft as warm candle wax. She was afraid she might melt right onto the wood deck. After several minutes and with great effort, she lifted her head from Ty's shoulder. "Why did you stop?"

He gave her a crooked smile. "I may not be a rocket scientist, but I was pretty sure you—"

"No," she interrupted, heat coloring her cheeks. "I mean, yes. I did. It was very nice."

"Very nice?"

Her face felt like it was on fire. "Better than nice. Fantastic. Unbelievable. Mind-blowing."

"Mind-blowing." He grinned. "That's more like it." He wrapped the blanket tight around her shoulders and shifted her onto the bench next to him.

Set apart from the warmth of his body, the brisk night air chilled her damp skin. Holding the blanket closed with one hand, she readjusted the straps of her bra and camisole onto her shoulders.

Ty stood and collected his sweatshirt and her blazer. When he handed her the jacket, Kendall took it without meeting his gaze. "But you didn't, uh, you know . . ." she stammered, gesturing with her free hand. "So why did you stop?" Her ex-boyfriend's accusations about being cold and aloof rushed into her mind. She forced her lips to form the question, "Did I do something wrong?"

Ty let out a gruff laugh. "Are you kidding? I haven't been that close to losing control since high school. And I don't think it was the marshmallows. Look at me, Kendall," he said, tucking her hair behind her ears.

She shifted her gaze to meet his, swallowing hard at the latent desire burning in his eyes. "Being with you," he said, "holding you in my arms is fantastic, unbelievable, and *completely mind-blowing*. You are the sexiest, most responsive woman I have ever met."

Take that, slimy ex-boyfriend.

"Really?"

"Really. But when we make love for the first time, it won't happen with me, pardon the expression, going off half-cocked on a lawn chair in the middle of my deck. You deserve better than that."

How much better could it get?

He'd made her body feel things she hadn't known were possible. But the way he was looking at her now, all sweet and tender, made her heart zing. And that was a complication she didn't need. "Have sex," she mumbled.

"What?"

"You should have said when we have sex." She pulled the blanket from around her shoulders and quickly shrugged into her blazer. "The phrase 'making love' implies, well, an emotional connection between the two people involved. Our relationship, if you could call it that, is not about emotions."

Ty stood and his tone turned as cool as the night breeze. "What is it about?"

She took off his wool socks and slipped her feet into her heels. Her feet felt cold and cramped against the smooth material. "I don't know exactly. But now that you mention it, we should probably keep this professional."

"I didn't mention that, and I don't think it's what you want."

"Maybe not." She bundled up the socks and set them on the chair before glancing at him again. "But I can't get distracted. This story is too important."

He continued to study her, as if he could see how much more she wanted from him. A buzzing started low in her belly at the look in his eye. "Stop doing that."

"What am I doing?"

"Looking at me."

He smiled. "We're having a conversation."

"I can barely form a sentence when you're looking at me like that. It's not fair."

His gaze dropped and her nipples hardened.

"Don't look there either."

He laughed, a slow sexy sound, then made a show of covering his eyes with his hands. "You may need to lead me into the house."

She groaned. "Never mind." Pulling his hands away from his face, she tried not to notice the way the muscles of his arms tensed under her fingers. "But no more looks like you're imagining me naked."

"How do you know what I'm imagining?"

Her response lodged in her throat as her own imagination ran wild.

"Are you thinking of me naked?" Ty asked.

She swallowed. "Of course not. I need to go. Now." She picked up the socks and blanket.

As she turned for the door, Ty rounded on her without warning, dragging her against him and sliding his mouth over hers. Of their own volition, her arms wound around his neck.

They stayed that way for several minutes, teasing with their tongues, taking turns commanding the kiss. With a shake of his head, Ty dragged his mouth away from hers. "I guess that's the trick," he rasped, dropping his forehead to press against hers.

"What trick?" she asked, still dazed from the embrace.

"When your hackles rise, I'm going to have to kiss you into submission."

She lifted her head and threw him a glare.

"Or be kissed into submission," he amended.

"That's more like it. About this crazy chemistry between us . . ."

He touched a fingertip to the center of her lips. "We'll handle it, Kendall. We're both adults. You've told me you're leaving, and I don't do complicated. Let's enjoy the ride and not worry about the destination."

She wrinkled her nose. "Letting things ride isn't really my strong suit."

"This is a break from the norm, remember?

"I knew that would come back to bite me." She groaned, thumping the heel of her hand against her forehead.

Ty wiggled his eyebrows. "That's not the only thing that may come back to bite you. But right now, you need to get home. Beauty sleep and all that."

"Gee, thanks."

"It's the upside of working off camera. We laborers can just throw on a baseball cap and be done with it."

She rolled her eyes. "I'm not even going to go there. Speaking of on camera, we got some great interviews yesterday with the Silver Creek residents. There are several inspiring stories of families rebuilding their lives that the viewers will love, but the land development plan I told you about is shaping up to be a real hot button."

Ty's shoulders tightened as he led her to the front door. Pulling it open, he turned to face her. "What's the consensus with the locals?" he asked, his casual tone at odds with the muscle ticking in his jaw.

"As far as I can tell, it's a mixed bag. Some people feel like it's not right to turn over any of the forest for development, but a few of the homeowners I spoke with thought it would be worth a small sacrifice if it meant money for their families and future wildfire prevention efforts. There was one woman in particular, Helen Bradley, who has close to fifty acres backing up to the restoration site. The land has been in her family for years, and she's really struggling with her decision. If she sells to GoldStar, most of her neighbors will follow suit."

Ty mumbled something Kendall couldn't understand.

"What did you say?"

"Those residents will never see a dime of the money that's being dangled in front of them. GoldStar is as crooked as they come. Trust me, the company will find a way around any financial obligations they make to the locals." He flipped on the porch light. "I'll walk you to your car."

"Whoa, there," she said, trying to read his hooded features in the dim light. "That's a bold accusation, and you sound very sure of yourself when you make it."

"I am." He wrapped his arm around her shoulders as they walked down the front steps. "Let's not talk about this tonight. I'm still savoring the fact that you showed up on my doorstep. I don't want anything to ruin that."

Kendall relished the feeling of being pressed so cozily against him, but the reporter in her couldn't resist digging for more information. "I can't let this go after a bombshell like that. I've done my homework on GoldStar, Ty. They're a big player in land contracts around Colorado, but there's nothing shady in any of their deals."

"Have you researched the company's owners?"

"According to public records, GoldStar is run through a holding company, ERB Investments. The proposal for selling the land is a recent development. Silver Creek isn't an investigative report, unless you're willing to give me some facts to back your insinuations."

"Not tonight." He opened the driver's side door, and gave her a gentle push.

She inserted the key into the ignition and rolled down the window. "Fine. If you're too chicken to tell me what you know, I'll go to the source."

"What's that supposed to mean?" he asked, eyes narrowed.

"I've been dealing with GoldStar's media contact. My next step is to see what the CEO of ERB Investments has to say."

"Don't bother," he said through clenched teeth.

"You don't think some big shot owner will talk to a local reporter? I'll have you know—"

"You'll meet him on Sunday."

"What do you mean?"

His voice was hard and flat. "The crook who owns ERB Investments and GoldStar is my father." He turned on his heel and stalked toward the house. "I'll pick you up at three," he called over his shoulder.

Kendall stared, mouth agape, into the darkness where he'd stood moments before. Fumbling for the door handle, she wrenched it open and shot out of the SUV.

"Ty, wait," she yelled, rounding the Jeep's bumper just as the front door of his house slammed shut. She thought about following him and pounding on the door until he let her in. But she was too shocked to know what to say.

She climbed back into the SUV and closed the door. His father owned ERB Investments? It didn't make sense. The holding company was one of the largest in the state, with at least thirty companies in its portfolio. GoldStar had built dozens of subdivisions throughout Denver and its outlying suburbs.

Kendall tapped her fingers against the steering wheel. Ty called his father a crook but had done his best to act disinterested in the land development piece of the Silver Creek story. It didn't make sense.

He was a member of one of the wealthiest families in Colorado. And now the story they were working on had taken on a deeper meaning, both in terms of her career and what his accusations might mean for the Silver Creek community. Ty might not want complications in his life, but she was about to change all that.

◆ ◆ ◆

Ty heard the front door of the small office open. His attention remained focused on the computer.

"Hey, what's going on? You look like hell."

He dragged his eyes away from the data on the screen. Jenny's willowy frame filled his door. Her short denim cutoffs barely skimmed the top of her thighs and a tight yellow T-shirt made her red hair look even more vibrant.

"You go to the job site like that and some fool's bound to drive up on the McPherson's yard when they pass."

She shimmied her hips. "Just doing my civic duty. What about you? You look like you didn't sleep last night."

"A couple of hours. I'm doing some research on GoldStar's proposed land development deal up in Silver Creek."

Jenny's eyebrows lifted. "Are you going up against your dad? I thought those days were over."

"They are." He saved the document he'd been working on and swiveled his chair away from the computer. "Silver Creek is a beautiful area. I don't want to see GoldStar ruin it. I'm running some data for the Forest Service, that's all."

"Uh-huh."

"I mean it," Ty growled. "And don't look at me that way."

"Someone swallowed a grump-ass pill today." Jenny planted her hands on either hip. "Don't project six years of anger and resentment onto me, buddy. Besides, I'm thrilled to see you getting involved with the Silver Creek development, even if you're doing it to score on the hot news lady. It's high time you used the degree that put all those fancy letters behind your name. How long are you planning to hide your head in the dirt?"

"Who's hiding? I'm running a business here. One, I might add, that has kept you gainfully employed for these past six years."

"I'm eternally grateful," she said. Her tone softened. "You made a mistake, Ty, and you've paid in spades. It's time to move on."

"I have moved on. Rocky Mountain Landscapes is my job. I'm good at it, I enjoy it, and I have yet to let down one of my clients. Life is great." He locked gazes with his old friend for several long moments. "Let it go, Jenny."

"Fine." She gave an annoyed sigh. "Speaking of not letting down clients, did you finish the specs for Lakeside Park?"

"Shit," Ty whispered. "When is the meeting?"

She glanced at her watch. "Two hours. What happened? I thought you were going to work on the plans last night."

Ty shifted uncomfortably in his seat. He reached for the canvas case where he had stuffed the unfinished plans. "Yeah, well, something, uh, came up. I didn't get to the drawings."

Jenny bounded across the room. "You're blushing." She plopped into one of the upholstered chairs in front of his desk. "It has to be Kendall Clark. Tell me everything."

He pulled a roll of plotting sheets from the case and set them on the desk. "You're nuttier than a fruit cake. Men do not blush."

Jenny tapped one finger to the center of her mouth. "The last time I saw you blush I was twelve and caught you and Carol Dison in the back of your dad's Mercedes. As I remember, you were giving the full moon a run for its money."

"You were such a brat." Ty laughed. "I spent most of my Christmas vacation earning money to have that car detailed after you told on me."

"I was an impressionable child," she protested. "You freaked me out. Carol was making some scary noises."

"She was a screamer."

"Is Kendall Clark a screamer?"

Ty thought about the sweet, husky sounds Kendall had made against his mouth when he'd touched her last night. His body grew heavy at the memory. Shit. "I am not going to discuss Kendall with you."

Jenny smiled knowingly. "It must have been good. You're as red as a tomato. I've decided I like her. She seems kind of prissy on TV, but she was nice when I drove her from Ray's the other day. I bet she warms up in the right setting, huh?"

"Jenny." His tone held a warning note.

"All right," she said, not quite hiding the smile that played at the corner of her mouth. "More importantly, you like her."

Ty nodded. "I'm taking her to Easter dinner at my parents' house."

Jenny's eyes widened. "Holy crap, she's meeting the royal family? Forget about the bunny. Your mother is going to lay a chocolate egg on the marble floor."

Jenny had been referring to the Bishops as the royal family for as long as Ty could remember, so he didn't take offense. His mother, especially, acted as stuffy as nobility most of the time.

"When was the last time you brought a woman home to meet your parents?"

He shrugged. "I don't know. Grad school, I guess."

"Are you serious about this one?"

Good question. Based on the way he couldn't stop thinking about her and the fact that his chest clenched every time she was near, the answer was yes.

"Not at all," he said. "She's working on a story that involves GoldStar. It was only a matter of time before she figured out my connection to the company. I thought I'd cut to the chase and introduce her to Dad."

"He'll charm her."

"I know." Ty's father could take candy from a baby. "I told her he was a crook."

Jenny whistled softly. "That's a juicy bombshell to drop in a reporter's lap, even if she is your girlfriend."

"She's not my girlfriend."

"Whatever you say. Did she press for details?"

"She didn't have a chance. I stormed off right after I said it."

"How dramatic."

"And mature," he added. A ceramic mug sat on the top of his desk filled with pens and pencils. He pulled a yellow pencil out. "Enough about Kendall and GoldStar. I need to get these plans done before the meeting."

Jenny cleared her throat. "I've got drawings ready for Lakeside," she mumbled, examining the fingernails of her right hand.

Ty unrolled the unfinished sketches. He looked at Jenny, but her eyes were focused on her hand. It was unusual to see her looking uncomfortable. "What are you talking about?"

"They're not that good," she said quickly. "I like to practice so I do plans for each of the big jobs. I compare my ideas to yours. It's silly but helpful for me to learn that part of the business." She brought her hand to her mouth, nibbling at the side of one fingernail.

Ty stared at her, dumbfounded. "You've done mock-up specs for all of our jobs and never showed me? Why?"

"Why should I? You've got the flair for design, the big-time degrees, and the clients love your ideas," she said matter-of-factly. "Everything I know about this business I learned working for you. Hell, I didn't even finish college."

"Who cares? This is landscaping, Castelli. We're not splitting the atom." When she didn't respond, he shook his head. He was used to Jenny selling herself short because she'd dropped out of high school when she got pregnant, but it still annoyed him. "Are you going to sit there chewing your nails to the quick or are you going to get the plans? Time is wasting."

She dropped her hand from her mouth and stared at her fingers. "Hell, I'd been growing these babies out for two weeks without so much as a nibble." She glared at Ty. "See what the stress of this job does to me?"

"The plans," he repeated, removing the blank spec sheets to the side of his desk.

She stood, scowling. "They need a lot of work. Don't say I didn't warn you." Turning on her heel, she marched out of Ty's office. Moments later she returned with a roll of paper clutched gingerly between her hands. "Lakeside is pretty straightforward. I bet you could whip something together from scratch in time for the meeting."

He held up one hand, curling a finger toward his chest. "Give 'em up, baby."

"Don't call me baby, you jackass. I'll sue you for sexual harassment."

"Quit stalling."

With obvious reluctance, she dropped the papers on the space he'd cleared. "They're not—"

"Sit down," he ordered, "and shut your mouth for one lousy minute."

She plopped into the chair. "Your people management skills suck." Unconsciously, her hand strayed to her mouth.

At least biting her nails would keep her quiet. Ty unrolled the sheets of white paper. He studied the drawings Jenny had created. At one point, he glanced up at the woman sitting across from him. He'd known her almost his whole life but felt like he was seeing her for the first time. "Where did you learn how to draw?"

"I got some books out of the library. Cooper and I made it into a game at night. He picked the things I was supposed to sketch. I was really bad at first." She flashed an uncharacteristically sheepish smile. "I'm still not that great."

Ty rested his elbows on the edge of the desk and steepled his hands. "Jenny, this is fantastic. You've incorporated the important design elements but done it with a sense of fun that is perfect for a community recreation area and playground. The park board is going to go nuts over this."

Slowly, she brought her hand away from her mouth. "You mean it? You wouldn't blow smoke up my butt just because we're friends, would you?"

"I mean it." He shook his head in wonder. "I'm shocked. Not that you have this kind of talent," he added quickly. "That you've never shared any of your designs with me."

Jenny shrugged. "I thought you'd blow me off."

"You should know me better than that."

"Let me introduce you to a little concept called 'fear of failure,'" she said dryly. "Oh, wait, I forgot. You wrote the book on that one."

Ouch. He made sure she didn't see how close to home that comment struck. "We're not discussing me right now."

A huge smile broke across her features. "That's right. We're talking about my brilliant design talent. You'll use my plans?"

"Without a doubt."

"Promise you'll call me as soon as the meeting's over. I can't wait to hear what they think."

"You don't have to wait. I want you in the meeting with me. It's your work we're pitching."

She went perfectly still. "You mean it?"

"Of course." He tapped his fingers against his chin and studied the plans again. "I can give you a few tips on—" He broke off when he realized Jenny had bolted out of her seat and was heading for the door. "Hey, where are you going?"

She paused in the doorway to his office. "I've got to run home and change. I can't meet the clients looking like Daisy Duke."

His gaze skimmed over her skin tight T-shirt and skimpy cutoffs. He was used to the way Jenny dressed on the job site, but it probably wouldn't fly in a meeting with key members of the park board. "Good point. Call me on your cell and we'll go over the meeting setup so you're prepared."

She gave him a quick thumbs-up and disappeared down the hall. Ty took one last look at the design before rolling up the sketches. It still baffled him that Jenny had that much natural talent and hadn't shared it with him before now.

Summer was around the corner, and the landscaping business was moving quickly into high gear. But he ignored the pile of phone messages and bid requests Jenny had placed in his in-box.

He knew it was a mistake to get involved with his father's latest development, just like it was probably stupid to let things go any further with Kendall. He'd tried to move past his problems with his parents, but the Silver Creek story was going to bring everything to the surface once again. Plus Kendall had made it clear that her future was in New York, not Colorado, so it would be easier for both of them to cut ties now. But he was already in too deep to walk away.

He turned back to his computer and tapped a key. The Silver Creek development data blinked onto the screen.

CHAPTER TEN

Kendall checked her reflection in the bathroom mirror for the umpteenth time that morning. She pushed a curl off her forehead and jumped when the doorbell sounded from downstairs.

I can do this, she thought, smoothing her hands over the delicate linen of her pale yellow sundress.

Of course she could.

She'd been managing her way through dinners with families like the Bishops since grade school. She picked up her small purse from the bathroom counter and headed for the stairs.

A warm breeze danced across her bare arms as she pulled open the front door of her condo. The butterflies that had taken up residence in her stomach began a quick two-step at the sight of Ty standing on her stoop. He wore a finely woven slate blue sweater that was tucked into tailored khaki pants. The sweater accentuated the brilliant color of his eyes and molded over the contours of his upper body.

It was odd to see him without his typical uniform of jeans, flannel, and a T-shirt. Kendall caught a glimpse of the man who had grown up in a world of wealth and privilege. It was evident in the easy confidence of his posture. His clothes, although understated, hung gracefully in the way of expensive apparel.

"You look lovely," Ty said.

She smiled. "Thanks. You clean up pretty well yourself."

He stuffed his hands into the pockets of his slacks. "I figured this look would be more your style."

She thought about the night on his porch and felt color rise to her cheeks. She reached for the bottle of white wine on her entry table, hoping he didn't notice her blush, and stepped onto the front porch. "I can't believe I'm admitting this, but I sort of miss the ubiquitous flannel."

He grinned down at her. "What can I say? Chicks dig flannel."

With an eye roll, she turned to close the door, but he pulled her against him. His arms wrapped around her and she was enveloped in the scent of soap and man. "Thanks for coming with me today," he said, pressing a kiss against her temple.

She leaned into him, enjoying the feel of his body against hers. She tilted her head so she could just see his face out of the corner of her eye. "I was sort of surprised to get your message yesterday confirming. I thought you might cancel."

He leaned his head against hers and sighed. "By the end of today, you might wish I had." He took her hand and led her down the front walk.

"What does that mean?"

"Did you investigate my father?" He ignored her question.

She glanced over at him. He looked straight ahead, the profile of his strong features giving away nothing. "You know I've researched both GoldStar and ERB Investments."

"Let me rephrase the question." He opened the passenger door of the truck and turned to her. "Since I told you that GoldStar is my father's company, have you delved into his personal history?"

She stepped up into the truck's cab, feeling as if she were walking into a potential minefield. "Of course."

He nodded, his mouth drawn tight in a grim line.

"Ty, I still don't understand—"

He held up one finger. "Hold that thought."

Kendall shook her head as he closed the door and walked around the front of the truck. Rays of sunlight flashed against the shiny silver hood.

Ty climbed in and started the engine, shifting into gear and easing away from the curb. "Pretty impressive, huh?" he asked, his eyes never leaving the road.

"Your driving?"

One end of his mouth curved up. "My dad."

"Oh." She thought about what she'd learned of Eric Bishop. "It's a remarkable success story. A self-made man who started with nothing and built an empire in the span of thirty years."

Ty made a right-hand turn onto the ramp to the interstate. "It was a little more than nothing."

"You're referring to your grandfather's farm."

"Yep. Forty acres of prime real estate just inside the Boulder city limits."

"He called the subdivision Aspen Grove. That was the first piece of land GoldStar developed. He was twenty-five when he inherited the land, right?"

Ty nodded but said nothing. His wide shoulders went rigid. His tension clogged the air of the truck's interior. She felt her own muscles tighten and willed herself to relax.

"Ty, what is the problem? You tell me your father is a crook but offer no facts to back it up. I've looked at both the holding company and GoldStar from every angle I can think of and found nothing illegal or even unethical."

He glanced sideways, his expression hard as granite. "Keep looking," he told her with fierce calm.

"Damn it," Kendall hissed. "Why won't you tell me what you know?"

"He's my father."

"So what?" Her voice echoed in the confined space. She closed her eyes and took a deliberate breath. Shouting would get her nowhere. "Tell me," she said with a calm she didn't feel.

Ty was silent for a long time.

Finally, he opened his mouth as if to speak. Kendall watched him, her own breath held in anticipation.

His lips drew together tightly and he shook his head. "I'm sorry, Kendall. I can't explain my reasons to you right now."

She tilted her head back against the headrest and stared at the truck's ceiling. After several minutes she asked, "Why did you invite me to come with you today?"

"I thought it would be fun."

She arched one brow.

He ran one hand through his hair, giving the thick blond waves a tousled look that was at odds with the neat lines of his fitted sweater. "Ok, maybe fun isn't the right word. But I do want to introduce you to my family. My father likes to hide behind the holding company, but he can't resist the spotlight, so you'd have met him eventually. This will give you access quicker than you'd get through the station."

The warm feeling that spread across her middle because Ty wanted to introduce her to his family almost sidetracked her. Then she thought of what he had and hadn't told her about his father. "It would help if I knew—"

He reached over and grabbed her hand. "Not today. But I'll think about it, all right?"

She liked the feel of his rough hand enveloping hers. "You're the one who brought it up in the first place," she grumbled.

"I know." He lifted her hand to his mouth, rubbing his lips softly against the back of her knuckles. "But could you just forget about it for a while?"

"Only for a little while," she agreed, her shoulders easing as a shiver ran down her arm.

"Thanks." Turning her hand over, he rubbed his cheek along the delicate flesh of her inner wrist.

They exited off the highway after a half hour. The road turned and climbed. Large trees lined each side of the street, their branches speckled lime green with spring's first leaves. The neighborhood seemed familiar, although Kendall had never been here before. From the manicured lawns to the four-car garages, the prosperity of the residents was as clear as if tax brackets had been stamped on each mailbox. Kendall sighed and closed her eyes, concentrating on the sweetness of Ty's touch.

A moment later, the truck pulled to a stop.

"We're here," he said, giving her knuckles another kiss.

She turned to look out the window and sat up so fast her seatbelt snapped against her chest. She spun back toward Ty. "This is your parents' house?"

He leaned his head closer to hers to peer out the window. "Last time I checked, this is it."

She swallowed hard. "You grew up here?"

"My dad had the house built when I was around nine. Do you like it?"

"I've stayed in hotels smaller than this place."

He chuckled. "It's doesn't seem that big on the inside."

She gave him a doubtful look.

He kissed her bare shoulder. "Let's go," he said, pulling the keys from the ignition and opening his car door. "My mother is probably watching out the front window. She'll wonder what we're doing in here."

Kendall glanced once more toward the house. As if on cue, a curtain in one of the first floor windows fluttered. She took a fortifying breath. She'd been friends with children of wealthy families during her years at Graves, but the Bishops gave the word *affluent* new meaning.

The house was two stories, with massive limestone columns on either side of the expansive front porch. Kendall lost count of how many windows ran along the front of the house. Really, calling it a house was an understatement. The Bishops lived in a mansion if she'd ever seen one.

She pulled down the sun visor and checked her reflection in the small mirror. Ty opened her door just as she finished applying a fresh coat of gloss to her lips.

"Ready?" he asked, offering his hand.

"Ready." She wiped her damp palms against the upholstered seat and placed her fingers in his.

As they walked up the cobblestone path that led to the house, she tried to tug her hand away. She didn't want to give his parents the wrong impression about their relationship.

He released her fingers but looped an arm around her shoulder, pulling her close. "Don't worry," he said. "They're going to love you. You're just their type."

Her stomach heaved.

She knew exactly what type Ty was talking about: Kendall Clark, lovable staple of Denver's evening news. Right now she felt more like the insecure twelve-year-old with secondhand clothes and dime-store shoes. She'd worked long and hard to distance herself from what these people would call her "poor, white trash family." But at times like this the truth of her life came hurtling back at her, almost knocking her down with its intensity.

She was a fraud.

Ty felt Kendall's back grow more rigid with each step they took toward the house. Her feet dragged so much he thought she might stop in her tracks. He turned to see what the problem was, struck by the level of reluctance in her gaze.

"Hey." He rubbed what he hoped was a soothing hand along her back. "My problems with my dad are between him and me. Don't worry about it."

"It's not that," she said, her voice brittle. "It's me. I don't think—"

Whatever she was going to say was cut off when his mother opened the front door. "Tyler John," she called as she stepped onto the portico. "Where have you been? I expected you a half hour ago."

Ty sighed and waved. He steered Kendall up the path, worried she would bolt and run if he let her go. His mother walked to the edge of the porch as they approached. She stood on tiptoe, straightening his hair with her fingers.

"You need a haircut," she said with a frown.

Slowly, Ty pulled her hand away from his head. He bent forward and kissed her cheek. "Happy Easter, Mother." He straightened as his mother's gaze shifted. "Remember, I told you a friend was coming with me for dinner. This is Kendall—"

His mother swatted him on the arm. "Oh, my goodness," she breathed, her eyes alight with recognition. "You didn't tell me you were bringing a local celebrity. I thought it would be one of the floozies you usually date."

"Christ, Mom."

She swatted him harder. "Language, young man." Turning to Kendall, she said, "It's a pleasure to meet you, dear. I watch the evening news on Channel 8 most nights."

"That's so nice to hear, Mrs. Bishop," Kendall said in her television anchor voice. "Thank you for including me in your family's Easter celebration."

"Please call me Libby," his mother said. "Come and meet everyone." She took Kendall's hand in hers and led her into the house.

Ty followed the two women through the front door and tried to see his mother through Kendall's eyes. Libby Bishop was a petite woman, almost a full head shorter than Kendall. She reminded Ty of Candace Bergen without the sense of humor. Her blond hair was perfectly styled in the same neat shoulder-length cut she'd worn since Ty and his siblings were in high school. Even in her mid-sixties, her skin was creamy with only faint lines around the corners of her eyes when she smiled. She didn't smile often.

Today she wore a calf-length skirt in a muted floral print and a fitted silk blouse. Ty hadn't noticed when he'd hugged her moments ago, but he'd wager his mother was wearing a strand of pearls around her neck. Libby grocery shopped wearing pearls.

Two sets of heels clicked in front of him on the polished marble of the two-story foyer. Kendall had compared his parents' home to a hotel. Ty thought of it as a mausoleum. It was beautiful, cold, and almost completely devoid of life.

Or at least love. That's how it had felt to Ty growing up.

Voices echoed from the back of the house. He followed his mother and Kendall through the oversized doorway that led to the large family room. Charlie sat on the large leather couch positioned toward the back of the room while Clare stood near the fireplace, a glass of wine dangling between her fingers.

As he entered behind the two women, both his siblings turned to pierce him with similarly disapproving gazes.

Shit.

He shouldn't have brought her here today, to be subjected to his parents' scrutiny.

Not that they'd have anything to complain about. It was Ty who made trouble, who was the problem as far as his family was concerned. His stomach turned to lead. His misguided plan to introduce Kendall to his family was about to blow up in his face.

He concentrated on the back of her head as it tilted to take in the room's elegant but tastefully understated décor and the picture window that faced the elaborate gardens in the back of the house.

"Tyler is here," his mother announced, restating the obvious.

"About time you showed up, little brother," Charlie called out, not bothering to get up from the sofa.

His mother sent a warning look to Charlie. "And he brought a friend. This is Kendall Clark." She gave Kendall a warm smile. "The one with the large mouth is Charlie." She nodded toward the fireplace. "That's our daughter, Clare. Sweetie, you should switch to water until dinner. Too much wine will go to your head."

His sister walked toward the window, draining her glass in the process. "Whatever you say, Mother."

This was going to be worse than he'd thought.

Kendall's eyes widened fractionally. Libby's loud *tsk* filled the silence before she turned to Kendall. "Would you like a drink?"

Kendall kept her features as placid as his mother's. Damn, she was good. "No, thank you. I'm fine." She lifted the bottle of wine she carried. "I brought this for you."

His mother's fingers curled around the bottle's long neck. She studied the label for a moment and smiled her approval. "Thank you. What a lovely gesture. Tyler, your father is still in his office. I'll bring him in to meet Kendall."

"Hey, Clare-bear," Ty said as his sister ambled forward. He pulled her into a quick hug before she could resist. "Save some for the rest of us."

"There's plenty to go around." Clare extricated herself from his embrace and turned to Kendall. Her assessing gaze scanned her from head to toe. Ty held his breath, but his sister only said, "You're taller in person than you seem on TV."

Kendall smiled cautiously. "That's a beautiful necklace."

Clare fingered the colorful beads that sparkled against the fabric of her black tunic dress. "Thanks. I designed it."

"Really?" Kendall asked, stepping closer to his sister to examine the necklace. "Do you sell your pieces? Those colors would look great on camera."

As Clare smiled with genuine warmth, Ty wanted to hug Kendall. Not many people could cut through his sister's tough shell so quickly. "I do. As a matter of fact—"

"Clare has a master's degree in marketing," his mother interrupted from the doorway. "She works for our family business. The jewelry is a hobby."

Clare's face clouded. "No, Mother, it's not. And she asked . . ."

Libby's tone was sweet as honey when she answered, "Kendall is a guest in our home, Clare. She was being polite." She disappeared into the hallway.

Kendall's gaze shifted to Clare. "It's really lovely."

Ty reached out to touch his sister's arm. "I'm sorry."

She rounded on him, her voice rough with emotion. "Get real. I'm just the appetizer. They'll serve you up as the main course and in front of your fancy girlfriend, too. You've always been a glutton for punishment, Ty. He ruined you and now you're back to play nice. You should have stayed away when you had the chance."

Kendall stepped forward. "Ruined him?"

"It's nothing," Ty said. "Would you like a tour—"

"Wait." Clare poked him hard in the chest. "You haven't told her? You brought her to dinner and she doesn't know about you and Dad?"

He wasn't sure whether to smile or shake his head when Kendall stepped between the two of them like she was protecting him from his crazy sister. But Clare was right, he was the crazy one for allowing his parents access to Kendall.

His sister's hand dropped as Kendall spoke. "Ty wanted me to meet your father because his company is mentioned in a story we're working on about rebuilding the Silver Creek community."

"Don't start this shit again," Charlie said from the couch, his knuckles white as he squeezed the highball glass.

"I'm not starting anything," Ty muttered. "I promise."

"But you're working on a story that involves one of GoldStar's development deals?" Clare's voice was incredulous.

"No."

Kendall frowned.

"I mean yes." He scrubbed a hand along his jaw. "But my only part in the story is as an expert on the restoration efforts."

"An expert landscaper?" Clare asked with a snort.

"There's more to Ty than that," Kendall said, crossing her arms over her chest.

There she went defending him again, even if she didn't understand the reasons why Clare was going after him so hard.

With a disapproving look at Ty, Clare whispered, "You don't know the half of it," then stalked toward the wet bar built into the family room's far wall.

His mother walked back in the room, her fingers tucked into the crook of his father's arm. His parents only touched each other when there were guests in the house.

Ty wished he could follow his sister to the bar. Instead he stood with Kendall as his mother introduced her to his dad.

"It's a pleasure to meet you, Kendall," his father said, pumping her hand like he was a candidate running for office.

Kendall smiled. "You have a beautiful home, Mr. Bishop."

"Call me Eric. This place holds a lot of memories."

Ty heard Clare snicker. Memories of slamming doors and strained silences, he thought. The only room in the house he'd liked as a kid had been the kitchen with Jenny and her mother. There had always been the smell of something freshly baked and laughter and music playing. It was a sharp contrast to the rest of the unnaturally sterile house.

Kendall gestured to the row of windows. "The grounds are beautiful, as well. Did Ty design the landscaping?"

Charlie coughed wildly. Libby stiffened.

Kendall flashed a questioning glance toward Ty.

"My parents have used the same gardener for years," he explained. "Not me."

She turned to his mother. "Have you driven down to Denver recently? The work Ty did on the Governor's mansion is amazing."

The grim line of his mother's mouth could barely be described as a smile. "I'm afraid I haven't been to Denver recently. Eric, would you escort Kendall in to dinner?"

"I'd love to." His father set his glass on the mantel. "You must work with Bob Cunningham, Kendall." He placed a hand at her elbow and guided her from the room. "He and I golfed in a tournament last week."

She threw another look at Ty over her shoulder. He smiled reassuringly.

His mother patted his arm and said, "She seems like a lovely young women, Tyler. It's about time." Then she turned and followed her husband.

"Jesus." Ty sighed as he crossed the room to the bar. "She's in rare form."

Clare handed him a beer out of the refrigerator tucked under the granite counter. "I think it's menopause. I'm glad you're here so she has a new target. My back is bloody enough."

Charlie lifted his glass in Ty's direction. "Brave man, bringing home a girl to meet Mom and Dad."

"I'm an idiot," Ty mumbled.

"But you've got some bowling-ball-sized cojones." His brother nodded toward the dining room. "Are you going to leave her alone with them?"

Ty took a long swig of beer. "Better not. Let's go, you two. The more the merrier."

It was a shame that he only felt close to his brother and sister when they were trading digs about their parents. He knew they were still angry with him for defying their father, even after six years. He'd paid dearly for his independence from the family, and he wished Charlie and Clare could recognize that. All they saw was that he'd escaped Eric Bishop's oppressive control. They couldn't forgive him for it.

The dining room looked the same as it had since he was a boy. The walls were papered with an elegant stripe pattern of green and gold that shone in the light filtering from the picture window. The antique mahogany table was set with his mother's Spode china and Waterford crystal. Fresh flowers sat on the buffet, flanked by ivory candles perched in long silver candleholders.

Eric Bishop sat at the head of the table, with Libby and Kendall on either side of him. Ty took the seat next to Kendall. As he sat, his mother looked at him and raised her eyebrows. Without thinking, he held out his hands for inspection. "What? They're clean."

Libby rolled her eyes. "Why didn't you mention that Kendall was from Kansas City?" his mother asked.

He glanced at Kendall, who gave him a nervous smile. Kendall had responded to his questions about her family with vague, noncommittal answers. He hadn't pressed for details. His mistake. "My aunt lives in Kansas City," he said to Kendall, ignoring his mother's question.

"Yes, your mom told me."

Although her tone was composed, Ty could see Kendall's fingers working against the linen napkin in her lap. He reached over and placed his hand on top of hers. Her chest rose as she took a deep breath. When she met his gaze, the stark vulnerability in her eyes sliced across his middle. He didn't know what had her so rattled. He didn't particularly give a damn. At that moment, all he wanted was to get her out of his parents' house.

His mother's regal tone interrupted his thoughts. "Kendall attended the same academy as your cousins."

"That's nice," he answered, his gaze still focused on Kendall.

"Are you sure you didn't know them?" Libby asked Kendall. "The Truman family. They lived in the Carriage Hill neighborhood, just around the corner from the school. Two boys, one girl."

Ty watched the vulnerability vanish from Kendall's expression as her on-air mask slipped into place. She turned to his mother with a smile. "I'm familiar with the name. But I think the youngest boy was still a few years older than me."

His mother nodded her agreement. "That would be true. What did you say your father did, dear?"

Ty's hand still held Kendall's. He felt her fingers tense, though her smile remained in place. "He's involved in the automobile industry."

His mother opened her mouth to reply, but Clare interrupted, "Are you going to grill her all night, Mother, or can we eat?"

Libby's lips thinned. "I'm not grilling anyone, Clare. I'm getting to know Tyler's new friend."

Eric patted his wife's hand. "She's got a point, sweetheart. We'd better start on this feast before it gets cold."

Libby slipped her hand from under Eric's and fingered the pearls around her neck. "Of course," she agreed, her voice stiff. "Why don't you begin?"

"I'll do that." Ty's father ignored the fact that Libby was royally pissed at having her interrogation of Kendall cut short. "Ty, would you pour the wine?"

He filled the crystal goblets but ignored his own glass. The last thing he needed was to catch a buzz when facing his parents. Dinner with his family was usually difficult, but today was particularly strange, and he couldn't figure out what had Kendall so wound up.

She seemed to relax as the dinner progressed. Eric led the conversation to a variety of safe subjects from the weather to local sports teams. Kendall gamely answered questions about her work, the people she'd met, and stories she'd covered in the course of her career.

Toward the end of the meal, Ty's mother leaned across the table and asked, "Tell us, Kendall, how did you and Tyler meet?"

Kendall smiled sheepishly. "The truth is, I rear-ended one of his landscaping trucks with my Jeep. It was a minor accident. Thankfully, no one was hurt."

"That's awesome." Charlie howled with laughter and too much booze. "Did he threaten to fake whiplash if you didn't go out with him?"

"Real funny, Charlie," Ty said. "Only a guy as desperate as you would pull a stunt like that."

"We got to know each other better when Ty started working on a story with me," Kendall continued.

Shit. Ty pushed back from the table. "Uh, Ken, it's getting late. We should get going."

Clare and Charlie concentrated on their plates.

"What kind of story?" Libby asked. "Tyler, you didn't tell me you were going to be on the news."

"I'm not." At Kendall's puzzled look, Ty amended, "It's not a big deal, just a small piece on landscaping during drought conditions."

Kendall's features scrunched in confusion.

His mother sighed. "When are you going to quit mucking around in the dirt and do something worthwhile with your degree?"

Kendall leaned forward. "Actually, Libby, Ty is helping me—"

Ty yanked Kendall's chair out from the table, ignoring her yelp of protest. He grabbed her hand and pulled her to stand beside him. "I tried doing something worthwhile six years ago, Mother. You remember the results."

"Let it go, son," Eric said in his father-knows-best tone. "It's water under the bridge at this point."

Ty barked out a laugh. "Easy for you to say, Dad. I doubt you'd be so likely to forgive and forget if the tables were turned."

"Tyler, we just want what's best for you," Libby protested.

"No, you don't. You want what's best for the family and GoldStar. We all know you'll do anything to get it. Thanks for dinner, Mother. As usual, it's been quite an experience."

Before she had a chance to argue, Ty dragged Kendall from the dining room and through his parents' house.

She pulled to a stop halfway down the hall. "I didn't get a chance to thank your parents."

"Send them a note."

"Ty, what is going on with you?"

He started moving again, taking her with him. "I've got to get out of this house, that's what's going on. I've had about as much family bonding as I can take."

He threw open the front door and stepped onto the porch. Taking a breath of the clean mountain air, he turned to Kendall. "I'm sorry about today. I shouldn't have brought you here without telling you how things are with my parents."

"Will you explain it to me?"

"Are you asking as a reporter or my friend?" He looked past her to the perfectly manicured lawn of his childhood home. Damn, he'd gotten himself into a fine mess today.

"As your friend, Ty. I'd like to understand what happened in there." She looked like she wanted to press him for more details but squeezed his hand instead. "Are you ok?"

"I will be when we're away from here. Give me some time to settle down, then I'll tell you about my family."

"I think that's a good idea."

"And you can tell me about yours," he added.

Her mouth thinned, but she nodded.

CHAPTER ELEVEN

He was thankful she didn't start asking questions again because he wasn't sure he'd know how to answer. To explain how with one word, one pointed look, his parents could send him over the edge. How the taste of disapproval lingered in his mouth long after he left their house.

They drove in silence for the ride back to Denver. When they reached the city limits, he glanced over at her. Kendall sat staring out the passenger-side window with her head resting against the seat back. The light from the setting sun glowed against her porcelain skin. He wished this were simpler.

"Do you have a patio? I need some fresh air after that."

She rolled her head along the headrest until she faced him. "A couple of folding chairs on the deck out back."

"My house then. Is that ok with you?"

"Yes."

He shifted lanes and took the exit ramp for his part of town. "What are you thinking about?"

She smiled wistfully. "Family."

"Mine or yours?"

"Both."

"I know I owe you an explanation for today." Ty turned down the alley that ran behind the houses on his block. He pushed a button on his visor and a garage door cranked open next to a tall wooden privacy fence. The truck slid into one side of a two-stall garage.

"Let's have a drink first. You look like you could use one. Then we can talk."

She opened the door and hopped out before Ty could read her expression. But her tone sounded grave.

He had a sinking feeling that his relationship with Kendall was ending before it had even gotten started.

He got out of the truck and climbed the two steps to the door that led to his backyard, absently hitting the wall switch to close the garage door. The soft light of dusk flooded the doorway as Kendall stepped behind him into the yard.

She gasped and he whirled to face her. "What's wrong?"

She continued to stare past him into his backyard. He followed her gaze and couldn't hide his smile. "The yard, right? It's kind of unexpected when you first see it."

She shifted her gaze to him, her lips shaped in a small O. Damn, her mouth was sweet. She looked back and forth between him and the yard and then said quietly, "I've never seen anything like it. How long did it take?"

He dug his hands into the pockets of his pants and rocked back on his heels, considering her question. "Hard to say. I worked on it pretty regularly for a couple of years. Business was slow and I had a lot of time on my hands. I thought it'd be a good idea to have a kind of demonstration garden to show potential customers what I could do."

"I imagine your clients were impressed."

"It worked pretty well."

He'd bought the house right after the fiasco with his father. He'd been young, angry, and full of righteous indignation, determined to prove to his family that he could make it on his own. He'd poured all of his energy and frustration into building Rocky Mountain Landscapes into a viable business and making his own backyard his creative showpiece. In the process, it had become a private sanctuary.

"Do you mind if I look around?" Kendall asked, stepping forward on the stone path. She turned to face him, waiting for his reply.

Ty wondered if she could sense how personal the space was to him. Once the business had taken off and he had referable clients, he stopped showing these gardens to customers. In the past three years, only his close friends had been invited to this small refuge from the outside world. "Sure. I'll get the drinks. What would you like?"

She smiled. "White wine, please. I also need to make a quick phone call."

"Go ahead. I'll be right back."

She watched Ty stride down the path that led to the back of the house, his wide shoulders straight under the expensive fabric of his sweater.

She had a new appreciation for the work Ty did, for the beauty he created in the world. She imagined coming home to this type of sanctuary every night. A heavy warmth settled in her stomach that felt remarkably like contentment.

Whoa, there. She was talking about trees and grass. Nothing irreplaceable. They had grass in New York City. It was called Central Park.

She reached into her purse for her cell phone. She punched in the numbers and, after three rings, her mother answered.

"It's me."

"What an unexpected treat to hear from you, baby. Is everything all right?"

"Everything's fine. I just called to say Happy Easter."

"To you, too, sweetie. Your dad and I just finished supper. He made most of it."

"Are you feeling ok?"

"I haven't had a flare-up in a few weeks, but I was tired today. Don't you worry. Your daddy's been taking real good care of me."

"That's nice, Mom," Kendall interrupted. "Listen, I don't have a lot of time right now but I wanted to thank you—"

"Thank me? Thank me for what? Your birthday isn't for another couple of months."

She thought about the overt tension at dinner with the Bishops. They were the family she'd thought she wanted, perfect from the outside. But things weren't always as they appeared on the surface. She never considered herself lucky, but despite their struggles, her parents loved each other and her. That was something money couldn't buy.

"I wanted to thank you and Daddy for the way you always supported me growing up. When he had his drinking problems and was away at rehab, you always did your best. Even through your pain. He did, too, when he got sober. I wasn't easy to live with once I started at Graves, and I know we weren't as close as you would have liked. You were always there for me. Even when I acted like a total brat, you and Dad made so many sacrifices to make my dreams come true." Emotion clotted in the back of her throat. "Anyway, I should have said it before this, but I want you to know how much I love and appreciate everything the two of you did for me."

Swiping at her eyes, Kendall listened to silence at the other end of the line. Something that sounded like a hiccup filled the space. "Mom, are you there?"

"Yes, sweetie, I'm here." Her mother's voice was soft and thick with tears. "Well, it's a good thing we didn't go anywhere for Easter. You've got me crying like a baby. My makeup's running down to my knees."

She heard the muffled honking of her mother blowing her nose away from the phone. "Sorry about that."

"Don't you be sorry, Kendall Lee," her mother said forcefully. "Don't you be sorry. Your daddy and I couldn't be more proud of what you made of yourself. It wasn't easy for you, rubbin' elbows with all those fancy families. I wish we could have done more to help you, but you did right well on your own. I guess you showed all those ritzy-titzies what it takes to be a success."

"You did so much for me, Mom, so much."

"That's what mothers are for, baby doll."

Libby Bishop's disapproving scowl flashed across Kendall's mind. "Mom, I may be switching jobs this summer. I know I haven't been back home for a while. I could try to take a week to visit before I move."

"That would be wonderful." She could hear her mother's smile across the phone line.

"It's a plan. I've got to go now. I'll call again in a few days. I love you."

"I love you too, baby. You take care and don't work too hard."

"Bye, Mom."

She hit the button to end the call and slipped the cell phone back into her purse. If she got the job in New York City, the network would want her to start right away. Too bad. Come hell or high water, she was going to spend a week in the hometown she hadn't seen for more than three years.

She walked slowly down the path that led to the small outdoor waterfall. She could picture Ty, his face glistening with sweat, hauling each stone and setting it carefully into place as he built the wall around the small pond. Kendall's idea of a good workout was a three-mile jog around her neighborhood or a spin class at the gym. Her back ached just thinking about the effort it would have taken to lay the rock, move the dirt, and plant all the trees, bushes, and flowers in Ty's yard.

It was more than the physical strength the job required. The design of the yard was a work of art itself. It was early spring, but tulips and daffodils were already sprouting through the earth in cheerful group-ings. She guessed that as the season progressed, the bulbs would be replaced by wildflowers and other summer blooms.

Behind the garden, the fireplace rose from the side of the porch at the back of the house. The memory of her night there with Ty had warmth pooling in her belly.

She took a deep breath to steady her nerves. The air smelled clean but different than it had when they'd been hiking through the burn area. There was none of the spiciness she associated with the moun-tains. A sweet freshness permeated the air around her. When she'd first stepped through the garage door, she'd felt like Dorothy emerging from her black and white world into the brilliant color of Oz.

A branch snapped to her left, and she saw a bushy-tailed squirrel scurry up the limb of a tree. She watched it climb until it jumped out of sight. A flash of color on the other side of the tree trunk caught her eye. She walked forward around a bend in the path and smiled. Two short Adirondack chairs, painted cherry red, sat in a small clearing of grass. Several iron torches flanked the walkway next to the opening.

"I thought we could sit out here." Ty's voice came from the path behind her.

He'd changed from his dressy clothes to a faded gray college T-shirt and jeans so worn a sliver of his thigh peeked through a frayed tear above his knee. His approach had been silent thanks to the soft-soled sandals he wore.

At the sight of him, the warmth in her stomach grew hotter and traveled lower in her body.

Easy there, her inner voice warned. She swallowed to relieve the sudden dryness in her throat. "Ok," she said, mortified when the word came out a croak.

Ty didn't seem to notice. He walked forward, a glass of white wine in one hand and some brownish liquid—probably Scotch—in the other. "Since you're such a fan of flannel, I thought you could use this," he said, lifting one arm slightly. Kendall noticed a green and blue plaid shirt hanging across his forearm.

She reached for the shirt, careful not to touch him directly. She felt so charged even the lightest contact with him could set her on fire.

Although she'd slipped into her cardigan sweater on the way home, the early evening air was chilly enough to warrant multiple layers. Ty stared at her as she rolled up the sleeves that dangled over her hands. "What?" she asked.

"I knew you'd look good in those colors. Your eyes are as vivid green as the grass after a good, soaking rain."

She scrunched up her nose. "I try to stay inside when it rains. Was that a compliment?"

"Yes, indeed, Princess, that was a compliment. But I should warn you, the shirt you're wearing is my favorite. Don't get too attached."

Lifting the wine glass from his hand, she rolled her eyes. "No worries there, buddy." She wasn't about to admit how much she liked the soft, cozy feel of the well-worn fabric. Liked having something that belonged to him—that smelled of him—wrapped around her.

Nope, she'd keep that revelation to herself.

She took a seat on one of the wooden chairs and watched as Ty lit the candles inside the glass holders that hung next to the path. When the luminarias were lit, he folded himself into the seat next to her, stretching his long legs in front of him.

For several minutes, they sat in silence, water splashing into the small pond the only sound Kendall could hear. The waterfall's gurgle blocked out any of the city's noise, so she felt enfolded in a private paradise. If someone would have told her a month ago that she'd consider sitting on a wooden chair in a backyard paradise, Kendall would have laughed. But now she couldn't imagine wanting to be anywhere else.

Uh, oh. Bad sign.

Despite the cool evening air, beads of sweat broke out against the back of her neck. Her heart beat faster. One of the tricks she used to stay focused on the future was not to get overly attached to the present. This feeling of contentment might be fine for the moment, but it was not good for her long-term peace of mind. She had to get out of here, back to the well-ordered and empty existence that made it easy to think about leaving.

"Don't go." Ty's voice sliced gently into the silence.

She turned to stare at him. She hadn't spoken aloud, she was sure. Was she that transparent? "What are you talking about?" she said with a forced laugh. "I'm not going anywhere."

He straightened in his seat, taking a slow sip from his glass. "You look like you're about to bolt, and I don't blame you. You've had long enough to think about the fiasco at my parents' house. I'm sure you want to be as far away from me as possible right now."

That was true. Just not for the reasons Ty suspected.

She laughed softly. "Actually, I should thank you. Being with your family opened my eyes to some good things I hadn't recognized about my own."

Abruptly he stood, pacing back and forth along the edge of the grass. "Can you believe I wanted you to meet them? I'm so freaking stupid."

In the space of a few minutes, dusky twilight had filled the backyard. The flickering glow from the luminarias shone against the glass of liquor he held in front of him, but his face remained hidden in shadows. "I know you don't think we're right for each other."

"Our plans and goals are so different."

"Plans change, Kendall."

"Not mine," she whispered.

He stopped pacing and stood directly in front of her. The lines of his face were hard in the murky light. "If it smells like crap and looks like crap, you can call it whatever you want. It's still going to be a load of crap." He began moving again. "The thing that pisses me off is that I bought into it. I took you up there to prove that I was worthy. Although it may not look like it, I have the background to run in the fancy circles that mean something to you."

"They don't . . . that isn't it. Ty, I need to tell you something."

He held a hand up. "What you should understand is that I chose to leave that life behind. I don't regret that decision. Almost every time I talk to my mother or my dad, they pressure me to 'return to the fold,' as they see it. Hell, I'm pretty sure there's an empty office at GoldStar just waiting for me. But I'm not going back. Not for them. Not for you."

He spoke the words with more conviction than anger. His posture was rigid, his jaw set against the dim candlelight. She knew he expected her to condemn him for that decision, the same way his mother had done earlier. "Would you please sit down?" she asked quietly. "There are some things I'd like to explain."

He didn't move for several moments, then dropped back into his chair. "What kind of things?" he asked, his voice hard and doubtful.

Kendall fidgeted. She placed her wine glass beneath her chair and squeezed her hands together, not surprised when the tips of her fingers were ice cold. She'd never told anyone, not even Sam and Chloe, the whole truth about her childhood. But she'd begun to see that she was only hurting herself and her parents, who loved her, by hiding her background.

"Those fancy social circles you mentioned," she began nervously. "I don't belong there." She picked at a loose string along the flannel shirt's hem so she wouldn't have to meet Ty's gaze. "I guess I could because of my job. Television opens a lot of doors. But I didn't grow up belonging the way you did."

"Kendall, not many people can match my dad for the money he's made over the years. You went to some prep school, right? That's not exactly the outside looking in."

"You don't understand. I attended Graves on a scholarship. I told your parents my father was involved in the automobile industry. That was true. For thirty years, he's parked cars at an exclusive country club, barely making more than minimum wage. There were a lot of times he was out of work due to his drinking, and things got pretty desperate for my mom and me. She has rheumatoid arthritis so she couldn't hold down a decent job either."

She shook her head. "One of my teachers was a Graves alum. She saw that I wasn't being challenged and arranged to have me tested at the academy. I must have done pretty well because she drove out to our place the next day and told them I could enroll at Graves for no cost."

"Your parents must have been pleased."

Kendall blinked back tears and gave a short laugh. "Hardly. They couldn't see why going to some uppity school in a fancy neighborhood was so important when I was getting a fine education right there in Grady. But I knew," she added quietly. "I knew that Graves was my ticket out of that town. So I convinced them. It was a big sacrifice. Even with the scholarship money, there was a uniform and other things to buy. The school was forty minutes from our house so someone had to drive me both ways and pay for the gas to get us there."

Kendall worried the loose string of the shirt between her fingers. "It was right around the time my dad got sober for good, and he picked up work with a local mechanic to bring in more money. So many years of that routine and they never complained. They were happy to make me happy."

"You're lucky."

She looked at him now, not caring if he saw the tears shining in her eyes. "Would you believe I didn't realize that until today? When I got to the school, I was in over my head. Not academically. But in every other way, I was clueless. All of those kids had so much and they took it for granted. The first week, I pulled a notebook out of a box sitting in one of the halls. The cover was bent, but otherwise it was unused. I figured the school provided supplies to students. Wrong."

She winced at the memory. "It was a recycling box. Somebody had thrown away a perfectly good notebook because the cover was bent. Heck, where I came from recycling was using old tires as flower beds."

Ty's white teeth gleamed in the soft light as he smiled. "Grady, Kansas, environmental hotbed of the Midwest."

She appreciated that he was trying to make this easier for her. "Yeah, right. Anyway, one of the girls in my class—she was a real brat—saw me take the notebook and told anyone who would listen. The nickname 'trash girl' stuck through my first semester."

He grimaced. "That's rough."

"There were lots of things that happened that first year to show me that I was out of my league. All I wanted was to fit in. But the way I went about it was wrong." She stopped speaking, the emotion of that time—the fear, the doubt, the insecurity—washing over her in waves.

She could almost smell the unique mix of chalk and sweat that would always remind her of the school. She wrapped her arms around her waist, leaning her head forward to breathe in his scent from the shirt collar. Needing to stay in the reality of the moment.

Ty's voice coaxed her back to the present. "What did you do?" he asked.

"I reinvented myself. Most people at the school knew I was a charity case, but you never would have guessed it by the way I acted. I watched how the other girls dressed, talked, walked, combed their hair. I became one of them. But I cut my parents off in the process. I could change myself but not my mom and dad." She shook her head. "I was so mad at them for being who they were, embarrassed about where I came from."

"You were a kid," Ty said gently. "Give yourself a break."

"That excuse doesn't fly. I knew exactly what I was doing. I wouldn't even let them come to graduation, and I was the valedictorian." She buried her face in her hands as the shame of her actions washed over her.

"They gave up so much to send me to Graves, to give me the future I wanted even though they couldn't understand it. I treated them horribly."

"Kendall—"

She waved him to silence. "The worst part is I haven't changed a bit. All through college, I did everything I could to stay away from Grady. I used any excuse I could think of—my class schedule, exams, part-time jobs, internships. You name it."

Her tears were flowing freely now but she didn't care. Talking to Ty was like going to confession. She had to get her sins off her chest before they ate away any more of her soul. "I've visited my parents twice in the past eight years. I have two real friends in the world. That's it. Two. I don't let anyone get too close. It's easier than dealing with my feelings about the past."

Stabbing one hand in the air, she yelled into the night, "I grew up poor. Big flipping deal!" More quietly, she continued, "My parents live in a double-wide trailer. Why does that embarrass me? They're good people. I'm the one with the problem, not them."

She wiped her nose on the sleeve of his shirt and pushed her hair behind her ears. "I'm sorry I made you feel like I thought I was better than you. That you had to prove something to me. It was never really about that. It's me and my insecurities."

He reached over and covered her hand with his. "Come here," he said gently. She looked into his eyes and let herself be tugged off the seat.

When he pulled her into his lap and wrapped his arms around her, Kendall sank against the warmth of his chest. "I never break down like this," she sniffed into his shirt. "You're a bad influence."

She felt his smile as he pressed his mouth into her hair. "You knew that from the beginning, Princess. That's why you ran so hard."

"I'll probably keep running," she said, snuggling deeper into his embrace.

"Then it's a good thing my legs are longer than yours."

"A good thing," she agreed. Her breathing was finally returning to normal and she noticed how right Ty's arms felt holding her tight to him. She thought about all the words that had spilled out of her tonight. She'd bared her soul to him in a way she never had before to anyone.

Hell, not even to herself.

She could imagine what he must think of her. But she didn't regret telling him about how she'd acted. She needed, for once in her life, to be honest with someone.

She inhaled the combination of crisp night air and Ty's warm scent. She was glad he didn't speak right away. Her body and mind were drained after everything that had happened today. Her eyes drifted shut. A few more moments of peace then she would listen to whatever he had to say.

CHAPTER TWELVE

Ty felt Kendall's body grow limp in his arms. The candles flickered along the path, illuminating the small circle that enclosed the chairs. Everything beyond was shrouded in darkness. It didn't matter. Ty knew his backyard like the back of his hand. He concentrated on the sound of water warbling over the stones in the fountain. He needed the noise to help him relax, as it had on so many previous nights.

All he could think about was the woman he held and what she'd shared with him. He didn't understand the insecurities that came from growing up as she had. How could he? Thanks to his family's wealth and power, he'd never had to struggle that way. He'd had everything he needed, except his parents' unconditional love. There was no amount of money that could make up for the dysfunction in his family, but he was tired of letting his past have power over his future.

He'd taken a stand against his father six years ago and been firmly slapped down. In the world according to Eric Bishop, a son's first responsibility was to protect the family name and bank account, no matter the cost.

Kendall had called herself a coward. To Ty's way of thinking, he was the real chickenshit. When the going got tough with his family, he'd run like hell. At the time, it seemed like the best way to deal with his anger. Now he felt like a coward.

Is that how he wanted to live, as someone who took the easy way out? He'd made a good life for himself. Was that enough?

His arms tightened reflexively and he felt Kendall stir. Damn. He remained motionless, hoping he hadn't woken her. She sighed and shifted in his lap.

"Did I fall asleep?" she asked drowsily.

Ty kissed the top of her head. "For a few minutes. I didn't mean to wake you."

She tilted her head, looking embarrassed as she met his gaze. "I'm glad you did. It wasn't exactly fair of me to dump all that stuff on you then nod off."

"Does what you told me change things?"

"What do you mean?" Her bottom pressed against his lap as she stretched. If she didn't quit moving, Ty was going to have a hell of a time forming a coherent thought.

"Be still," he said, holding her steady. "You told me about your childhood, about the choices you've made as an adult, so I would under-stand why you pushed me away."

She nodded. "I spent a lot of years feeling judged for where I came from and measuring my own worth by it. It's probably why I've dated guys who cared more about my image than really getting to know me. Even my so-called serious boyfriend wasn't interested in my family or how I'd grown up."

"Then he didn't deserve you."

"At the time, I thought it was for the best. But from the start of what-ever this is between us, I knew you were different." Her gaze dropped as she traced one finger along the edge of his jaw. "It scares the hell out of me," she whispered.

"Join the club," he said with a strained laugh, her gentle touch driv-ing him crazy. He reached for her hand and laced their fingers together. "A big part of who you are today is because of where you came from, Kendall. Your determination and drive, the master plan I'm starting to hate. But there's more to life than getting ahead."

She bit down on her lip, as if she was unsure if she wanted to believe him or argue the point. "I became a journalist because I wanted to change the world through my reporting, the way my world was changed by the women I watched on TV. Even if my connection to them was just a little girl's fantasy, those female journalists gave me hope. The master plan is important to me, Ty. I'm not giving it up for anyone."

"Does it sound like I'm asking you to give up your dreams?"

When she shook her head, loose strands of hair tickled his chin. Her hair smelled clean like rain. For a woman who professed to hate the outdoors, she radiated a freshness that couldn't be bought at a cos-metics counter. He lifted her off his lap and climbed out of the chair, setting her back down against the wood seat. He couldn't concentrate with her perched against him.

When she spoke, he wished his arms were still wrapped around her so he could shake some sense into that gorgeous skull.

"What we have is fun, but it's not forever," she said, her voice quiet and sure. "I'm building a career and I need to stay focused on that."

Ty felt despair wash through him. He was falling for a woman who flat-out said she had more important priorities than him in her life. He'd spent most of his childhood feeling like he wasn't important to his narcissistic parents and he wasn't going to sign on for more of that brand of rejection. While he understood the reason Kendall clung so tightly to her plan, it didn't give him much hope for a future with her. Which is what he wanted . . . more than he was willing to admit. It would be best for both of them to end this now.

He looked into her moss green eyes and a voice inside him shouted *no*. All the words that would allow him to let her go slipped from his mind.

He wanted her. Wanted her in his life. Wanted her in his bed.

So much for doing the smart thing.

He lifted his hands to either side of her face and traced the supple lines of her mouth with his thumbs.

Confusion danced across her face. Her breath came out in short, shallow puffs of air. "What are you doing?"

He smiled and leaned his head even closer, until his lips moved against hers when he spoke. "Showing you that I can do a lot more for you than any damn job."

She groaned. "I can't think when you touch me."

"Good. I've told you before, you think too much."

"But . . ."

When her mouth opened to protest, he took the opportunity to kiss her. Her skin was cool from the night air, but her mouth was so hot. The temperature in his backyard rose about thirty degrees. His tongue circled hers, coaxing her to respond.

Her response nearly sent him to his knees.

She wrapped her arms around him, grazing his back with her fingernails, pressing her breasts into the hammering wall of his chest.

Out of nowhere, guilt wound itself in a tight little knot in his stomach. He wished he could blast his conscience to the moon.

With an effort of will he didn't know he possessed, he lifted his head. "If this isn't what you want . . ."

She fixed her mouth on the exposed flesh above his shirt collar. "You're kidding, right?" The words hummed along his skin.

Just about every one of his brain cells took the fast train south. Way south. "I don't want you to hate me in the morning. Shit, I don't want to hate myself."

She met his gaze, her eyes shimmering with desire. "Cold feet?" she asked with a seductive smile.

"Hell, no." He was about as hot as the surface of the sun.

The smile turned challenging. "To repeat some advice a wise man once gave me, you talk too much. Shut up and kiss me."

He grinned before stepping away from her.

"Hey!" she protested.

With practiced efficiency, he blew out the four candles, plunging the backyard into total darkness. "Ty?" Kendall's voice was small in the night when she said his name. Returning silently to her side, he bent and lifted her in his arms. She gave a small gasp, then threw her head back and laughed. He raced along the path toward the house.

Kendall twisted her fingers in the material of his shirt and hung on for dear life. "Slow down." She giggled when they rounded a corner. "You'll run us into a tree."

Ty kept his gaze focused on the darkness ahead. "No trees. I know the path."

"In that case . . ." She tilted her head up and licked along the base of his throat. She laughed again when Ty groaned and nearly tripped up the deck stairs.

"Paybacks are hell," he warned, pushing open the back door with one hip and maneuvering her into the house.

"I can't wait," she whispered. He carried her up the stairs and down the hall, careful not to bump her head as he turned into one of the upstairs rooms. Soft moonlight slipped through the large window on one wall and she could just make out a bed, dresser, and a chair.

Then his weight was on top of her, pressing her against the soft covers. He was lean and strong above her.

When he crushed his mouth to hers, it was easy to forget that he was not the right guy for her.

Easy to think about how right it felt for his tongue to slip inside her parted lips. Easy to lose herself in the whirling pleasure of his kiss.

For his hand to stroke up her thigh, nudging the hem of her dress until it bunched around her hips.

He broke the kiss and stared down at her. "Is there a zipper on this thing?" he asked, his voice harsh and raspy. His eyes were clouded with emotion and desire. "You look great in my shirt, but I need to see you, Kendall. Now."

One end of her mouth curved. "You first."

Like a shot, he was off the bed. "Whatever you say."

She liked the way he made her feel. Reckless. Sexy. A little wild.

Her eyes had adjusted to the dim light, and she could clearly see him standing next to the bed. Raising herself onto her elbows, she watched as he hastily undressed. He kicked off his sandals, shrugged out of his shirt, and dragged the gray T-shirt over his head.

Kendall knew he looked good bare chested, but seeing him standing there, all smooth muscles and honey-warm skin, her head started to spin. He undid his jeans and stepped out of them, then pulled off his boxers. When he straightened, her mouth went dry. He was beautiful. Every part of him, from his wide, muscled chest to his flat stomach to the hard erection jutting out from between his legs.

He watched her watching him, then let out a strangled laugh. "If you keep looking at me like that, this is going to be over before we get to the good stuff." He moved to the edge of the bed, trailing a finger along her ankle. "Your turn."

He was watching her with such unabashed adoration that she forgot to be shy. The only thought she could focus on was getting undressed as soon as possible. She wanted him. "The zipper's in the back," she said softly. "I may need a little help."

He leaned toward her, kissing her as his fingers found the small clasp at the base of her neck and he tugged at the zipper. When it reached the swell of her hip, he moved away to the corner of the bed with a harsh exhale.

He was waiting for her. Kendall peeled the loose fabric off her shoulders. She lifted her hips to push the dress down her legs, tossing it off the bed.

"Almost there," he murmured and again the look in his eyes bolstered her confidence.

Straightening, she reached behind her back and unfastened her bra, flinging the lacy material over the side of the bed with her dress. Her underpants followed and she raised herself onto her knees, leaning forward to crush her mouth against Ty's. At the same time, she caught him in her hand.

"Sweet Jesus," he rasped, grabbing her wrist. "Not helping to make the moment last."

"I need you," she said against his mouth.

"You've got me." He lifted her, and pressing her back down against the soft covers.

He took control of the kiss, driving her crazy with his lips and his tongue while his hands found their way to the most sensitive places on her body. When she felt herself spiraling out of control, she let the sensations take her, crying out her pleasure against his throat.

She felt free.

For the first time, she let her desire rule her unfettered. She answered his need with her own enthusiastic response. Wrapping her arms around him, she pulled him to her.

"I want you inside me, Ty. More than anything else."

His voice was shaky when he replied. "There isn't any place in the world I'd rather be." He reached toward the nightstand and pulled a condom out of the drawer.

Thank heavens he was prepared. She was so crazy with wanting him, she wouldn't have even remembered protection.

A moment later his mouth was on hers again, and she forgot about preparing for anything but opening her body to him. Then he was there, inside her, making her soar to heights she didn't know she could reach. She held on to him tightly, pressing him against her, wanting to feel all of him touching all of her.

The words he spoke were low against her throat. "This is more than fun, Kendall. This is right."

"Why are you talking?" she asked, digging her nails into his back. "It's sex. It doesn't mean . . ."

Her voice choked off as he changed the rhythm of his movement.

"Yes, it does," he said firmly, and then pressed his mouth over hers.

Suddenly, this was like no experience she'd ever had. The excitement, the sensation, the pure pleasure of it drove her wild with need.

She forgot about arguing with him. Forgot about what this could mean.

She let passion wash over her, riding the crest of the wave until she fell off the end of the earth and was lost to everything except the moment.

When she finally landed back on the bed, it was several minutes before she could form a coherent thought. Ty was still on top of her, somehow cradling her in his arms without crushing her with his weight.

She felt his heart beat against her chest. Or was it hers? Their bodies were slick and hot and it felt so right to be with him like this.

It felt good. Fantastic, even. But not right. Because if this was right, she was afraid that made her master plan wrong.

She'd worked too long and hard to get sidetracked now. She wasn't going to confuse mind-blowing sex with something more. Something that could turn her dreams, her plan, her whole world upside down.

Her skin cooled when Ty rolled off her. He kept his arm across her, tucking her hair behind one ear as he turned her face toward him. "Whatever you're thinking, stop."

"How do you know . . . ?"

"Trust me, I know. No more thinking tonight. Or talking." He kissed her and pushed down the duvet and sheets.

Kendall scooted up until she was able to stretch her legs under the clean white sheets. "Um, do you have a T-shirt or something I could borrow?"

He smiled at her as he stretched out his legs. "No."

Even though they weren't touching, she could still feel the heat pouring off him. She pulled the sheet higher until it brushed against her chin. "Really, no joking. I need something to sleep in."

He leaned back against the headboard and stretched his arms wide. "I'm all ready for you."

She rolled her eyes.

"You're putting a major chink in my ego. I've barely caught my breath from the best sex of my life and you're ready to sleep. What about round two?"

Kendall shot him a glance. "The best sex of your life? Really?"

"Without a doubt." His eyes narrowed. "You disagree?"

"No, no," she answered quickly. "It was amazing."

"Damn right."

"But I figured that had more to do with your performance than mine. I'm not exactly known for my sexual prowess."

He framed her face in his big palms and drew her close. "Listen, carefully, because I'm only going to say this once and I'm not going to argue. It's not me. It's not you. It's the combination of us. Whether or not you want to admit it, we fit."

"We do," she agreed with some hesitation, "in bed."

One end of his mouth quirked. "I guess that'll do for now."

"About that T-shirt?"

"No clothes for you," he said in a mock dictator tone.

"Pleee-aa-sse."

"I like it when you beg."

She punched his arm.

He released her face to rub his shoulder. "Ouch. I'll make you a deal, slugger. You give me another hour," he said, leaning forward to kiss her, "and I'll give you my favorite T-shirt."

She ran a finger along her tingling lower lip. "Hmmm. What would I get for two hours?"

He grabbed her around the waist and pulled her on top of him. "Anything you want."

♦ ♦ ♦

Kendall woke up to the morning sun slanting across the patterned rug at the foot of the bed. Slowly, she turned. Ty was fast asleep next to her, one arm thrown back above his head. She watched his chest rise and fall, the pale light casting shadows across his chiseled features. Even asleep, with tumbled hair and a blanket of stubble across his chin, he screamed rich boy.

Why hadn't she seen it in the first place? The easy confidence, the sense of belonging in any circumstance. Kendall should have recognized those as the traits of someone who came from privilege. Weren't they the very characteristics she'd been trying to imitate for most of her life? And she was good at it.

But it was work for her. Not for someone like Ty. For him, it was second nature. Did it really matter? It didn't change anything between them. She had her life, her plans, her future. And Ty Bishop didn't fit into that future.

If she kept repeating those words to herself, maybe she'd eventually believe them.

Trying not to disturb him, she climbed off the bed. She glanced back as she tugged on the hem of the T-shirt he'd finally given her. He was still asleep. Good. She collected her bra, underpants, and dress from the wrinkled heap near the foot of the bed and silently padded down the hall to the bathroom. Flipping on the light, she glanced at herself in the beveled mirror above the sink.

Who was the woman staring back at her? The one with hair flying in a hundred different directions, dark smudges of dried makeup under her eyes, and a faint pink shadow on her jaw that looked suspiciously like beard burn.

It sure wasn't anyone Kendall recognized. It wasn't the Kendall Clark who each night religiously removed her makeup, washed her face, flossed and brushed her teeth before she combed her hair, put in her night guard, and went to bed in matching pajamas. This woman looked like she'd been on an all-night bender.

Kendall leaned closer to the mirror, using her finger to wipe crusty mascara out of the fine lines at the corner of her eyes. Great. She hadn't forgotten to wash her face since she'd hit puberty. Now she was probably going to end up with premature wrinkles and a big pimple for the evening newscast.

Did she really want a life where she couldn't go a little crazy now and then?

Sighing, she turned on the water.

She emerged from the bathroom ten minutes later feeling slightly more normal, although it was doubtful any amount of dry cleaning would get all the creases out of her silk dress.

She followed her nose to the kitchen, where Ty stood, his back to her, in front of the stove. He wore only a pair of old khaki shorts, the muscles on his back flexing as he dipped a ladle into a bowl and transferred a scoop full of batter into a sizzling pan.

Suddenly, Kendall remembered why she'd forgotten her priorities. A pimple was a small price to pay for the pleasure of last night.

"You cook, too?" She stepped into the bright room.

Ty glanced over his shoulder and winked. "With a little help from Mrs. Butterworth."

"Pancakes?" She groaned with pleasure. "You're really pulling out all the stops."

To her surprise, he looked embarrassed. "It's not a big deal. Just breakfast. Do you want juice or coffee?"

"Coffee, please." Just when she thought she had him pegged—confident rich boy posing as cocky everyman—he switched things around on her.

"Here you go." He held a steaming mug in front of her, smiling as she took it. "You look lovely this morning," he added and leaned forward for a quick kiss.

"Liar."

He rocked back on his heels, crossing his arms across his bare chest as he examined her. "It's true. You don't need makeup. You're a natural beauty."

Kendall tried to stifle a disbelieving cough. The only thing natural on her were her roots. And only until tomorrow's monthly appointment for highlights. "Sorry, I wasn't fishing for a compliment."

"I'm happy to give one anyway. More than one, if you're lucky. But first let's eat." He leaned forward again and she expected another kiss but he stopped an inch from her nose. "You have freckles." His grin was ear to ear.

She grimaced and covered her nose with her fingers. "The bane of my existence. My foundation usually covers them."

"Aww, Princess," he crooned, peeling her hand away from her face, "you're hiding all the good stuff." He dropped a kiss on the tip of her nose and turned back toward the stove. "Have a seat. I'll get these cakes on the table."

Kendall set her mug on the butcher-block table that sat in front of a large window and sank into a chair. She pulled at the corners of her mouth, trying to wipe off the stupid smile she knew gave her emotions away.

She couldn't quite block out the words he'd whispered to her last night. Being with Ty might feel right, but only *right now*. She had to keep her feelings in check, especially the ones that made her want to spend every morning until eternity in this warm, bright kitchen with the gorgeous man making her breakfast.

She lifted her coffee cup to her mouth when Ty brought the food to the table, willing herself to get a grip. He placed a plate in front of her. Kendall dropped her gaze to the colorful arrangement and stopped trying to hide her grin.

Two fluffy round pancakes sat in the middle of the plate, surrounded by a ring of cut strawberry wedges that looked like rays of the sun. Dark splotches of maple syrup sank into the pancakes, forming two eyes and a wide smile. "It's a work of art."

Ty sat down across from her, his own plate a carbon copy of hers. "This is how Jenny's mom always made them. I thought it was the best part."

Kendall stabbed a strawberry with her fork. "I didn't think I could like pancakes more than I already did. But this is something else." She poured a scant amount of syrup across her plate. "It sounds like Jenny's mom took care of more than just the house."

Ty scooped up a large bite. "She was housekeeper, cook, part-time nanny. Mrs. Castelli kept the whole show running."

"And your mother?"

He finished chewing. "Couldn't be bothered with her children. She had too many civic responsibilities. Our job was to stay out of trouble and out of her way."

They ate in silence for several minutes. Finally, Kendall said, "I know you don't want to talk about GoldStar."

"So is it too much to hope you won't bring it up again?"

Kendall set her mouth in a firm line. "It's important."

"Make me dinner."

She tried to read his expression, but his eyes never left the stack of pancakes on his plate. "Excuse me?"

"Bribe me. Invite me over for a home-cooked meal and I'll tell you what you want to know." He paused, a forkful of pancakes halfway to his mouth. "You can cook?"

"Of course I can cook. That doesn't mean I'm going to cook for you." She stabbed at her last strawberry. "We're talking about business. This isn't a game."

"I know that better than anyone," he said, his tone as serious as she'd ever heard. "But I'm more inclined to spill my guts when my stomach is full. One meal. How much is the story worth to you?"

She couldn't remember the last time someone got under her skin the way Ty did. "Wednesday. Seven o'clock," she said without inflection. "Bring a bottle of red."

"Gladly. I'm curious. Would you have invited me over on your own?"

"If you hadn't tried to blackmail me?" She gave him a smile as warm as the north wind. "I guess you'll never know." She didn't want to admit how nervous the thought of having him over made her. At the same time, she couldn't wait to see him again. She was quickly heading down a path that could lead to heartbreak if she wasn't careful. She stood, carrying her plate and mug to the counter. "Thanks for breakfast. I do need to go. Should I call a cab?"

"Of course not," he said, clearing his own plate and glass. "I'll grab a shirt and drive you." He flashed his charming smile. "Don't be mad about dinner. I was hedging my bets."

"You should stick to the sort of hedges that need trimmers," she muttered under her breath.

"Nice comeback." He stacked his plate on top of hers and turned to face her, staring for several long moments. "God, you are gorgeous when you're mad. Add to that how good you look in the morning and it's enough to bring a man to his knees."

Despite herself, Kendall smiled at the compliment and didn't resist when he leaned forward to kiss her, tasting the sweetness of the syrup on his mouth. It would be far too easy to stay. "I need to go," she said.

Ty sighed as if he could read her thoughts and didn't like them. "Be back in a minute," he said and headed for the stairs.

Kendall stared at the kitchen's hardwood floor until he returned. She refused to look around at his home, afraid she could fall in love with it if she let herself. Refused to think about falling in love with anything.

CHAPTER THIRTEEN

There was plenty to keep Kendall busy until Wednesday night. Not so much that she didn't think about seeing Ty again. But enough that she resisted the urge to sit and stare, cow-eyed, into space and daydream about his touch.

Thank heavens for small favors.

Late Monday morning, she drove down to Silver Creek to meet with Helen Bradley again. After an hour of sun, the morning had turned gray. As she neared the Bradley property, a light mist enveloped her car. She cracked the windows, both to prevent them from fogging and to enjoy the tangy scent of the wet forest surrounding her.

Only in the past month had she begun to appreciate the true beauty of the Rocky Mountain landscape. When she was far away from Ty and Denver, she would still treasure the gift he'd given her in opening her eyes to how special this place was. It was becoming more difficult to think about leaving both the place and the man, and that scared her more than she wanted to admit.

Helen Bradley had spiced tea and homemade shortbread cookies waiting when Kendall arrived. They talked about the history of the valley, about the changes the fire had brought, and the changes that would come from development.

"I know I've got my neighbors up in arms," Helen told her sadly. "But I want to provide for the future of my grandkids and great grandkids. This land has been in my family for generations, but until recently it hasn't been worth much. When I was growing up, Silver Creek was a world away from Denver. But with how fast the city's expanding, now we're more like a distant suburb."

"But it still feels like you're deep in the mountains once you're up here."

"That's why they want to develop it now," Helen said with a nod. "My late husband and I couldn't afford to send our kids to college, but they made us proud." She fingered the thin gold band on her left hand. Helen's husband had passed away a decade ago, and the older woman often mentioned him. "We didn't have much in the way of material things, but there was a lot of love in the house. Now I have a chance to make up for the things I couldn't give them."

Kendall cleared her throat as emotion clogged it. With a new perspective on her family, the impact of Helen's words was deeper than she expected. She hit pause on the voice recorder that sat on the table between them. "It sounds like you gave your children your unconditional love, which is what's most important."

"Thank you for saying that. We certainly tried. But I want more for them, and the land company made me a lucrative offer. My lawyer's looked at the contract. He says it meets my stipulations and the plan for the building site is a good one. Still there's more value to this place than money." She broke off, and then asked, "Am I doing the right thing?"

Kendall wrapped her fingers around the paper-thin skin on the woman's hands. "You love this land as much as a person could. But you want to take care of your family. No one can fault you for that."

"You're a good girl," Helen said with a watery smile. "I'm glad that TV station sent you down here to see me."

Gently, Kendall squeezed the woman's hands. "I am, too."

As she drove back to the station, she sent up a silent plea that Ty would share what he knew about his father's company. She'd made calls and interviewed people connected to both GoldStar and the holding company but couldn't find a whiff of the scandal to which Ty had alluded. That didn't mean it wasn't there, and she wouldn't stop until she was sure the Silver Creek community was in good hands with GoldStar.

When she'd brought her concerns to Liz, the news director had dismissed them, telling Kendall to focus on the human-interest side of the piece. But she needed to know the truth about the development company and not just because it was important to her story. She couldn't stand the thought of Helen Bradley making the wrong decision about her land. It would break the heart of a woman about whom Kendall had quickly come to care.

Thoughts of the Silver Creek story and Helen Bradley were quickly overshadowed by her more irritating assignment when she returned to the station.

Liz knocked on the door to her office almost as soon as Kendall sat down in front of the computer.

"Mary told me you were here."

Kendall didn't bother to turn around. She tapped at a couple of keys, bringing up information onto the computer screen. "I need to get ready for tonight's broadcast. What's up?"

"The *It's Raining Men* results are in. I thought you might be interested, but if you're too busy . . ."

Kendall spun around in her chair in time to see Liz exiting into the hall. "Don't go," she called.

Liz leaned back into the room. "Do you want the good news or the bad news first?"

"Bad news. No. Good news."

"The good news is the viewers love you," Liz said, her smile widening.

A whoosh of breath she didn't know she'd been holding escaped Kendall's lips. "Really? They like me?"

"Read my lips, Ken," Liz said slowly, "they l-o-v-e you. According to the feedback we've received, you're the best thing to hit Denver since Peyton Manning."

"What's the bad news?"

Liz hesitated only briefly before saying, with a laugh, "They also love Scott Jenkins."

"You're kidding." Kendall choked. "The lounge lizard?"

"They liked your chemistry."

"There was no chemistry." Kendall's eyes widened. "Don't tell me . . ."

Liz shook her head. "They love him in the same way a mother loves her ugly baby—because she can't help it. They voted for Owen Dalton."

Kendall breathed a sigh of relief. Owen Dalton was the CEO of a Fortune 500 software company headquartered in the Denver Tech Center, the technology hub on the south end of town. Kendall and her cameraman had met him for coffee one afternoon last week. He'd been nice, normal, and cute in a geeky sort of way. Kendall liked him immediately but hadn't felt one ounce of spark or interest beyond platonic friendship.

"No kidding. Because you're going on another date with the techie tomorrow."

Kendall gripped the handles of her desk chair. "I'm not sure that's such a good idea."

Liz crossed her arms over her chest. "You know the rules, Kendall. Dates with two men and a second date and on-camera interview with the one the viewers picked as your best match."

"I know. But I may have met someone." She gulped.

Quicker than she could say *breaking story*, Liz scooted a chair in front of Kendall's. "Tell me."

Kendall tucked her hair behind her ears. "It's no big deal. Of course I'll go on the date. I liked Owen."

"Spill it, Clark."

"I shouldn't have said anything. He knows it will end when I leave for New York."

Liz stared at her for several moments. "You're not going to talk about it."

"It's not important."

"Wow." Liz stood and pushed aside her chair. "You're really serious about this guy, whoever he is. Be careful, Kendall. Remember your priorities."

Kendall nodded but didn't meet Liz's gaze. "What kind of date is it?"

"Breakfast and the art museum."

"Sounds nice. And don't worry, Liz. I'm always careful."

Her boss sighed, almost as if she'd hoped Kendall would put up more of a fight, and backed out of the room. "I'll get the details about tomorrow and brief you after the five o'clock broadcast."

Kendall pasted a smile on her face until Liz disappeared through the door. Then she spun back to the computer and stared blankly at the screen.

Of course she knew what her priorities were. Why had she hinted at a potential relationship to Liz? No matter how much her pulse raced when she thought of Ty, she'd finally found the courage to take a stand for the future she'd always wanted. She was about to achieve the dream she'd been working toward, and nothing was going to screw it up. Especially not her heart.

◆ ◆ ◆

A few minutes before nine the next morning, she waited outside the Denver Art Museum for Owen Dalton. Steve was behind her with the camera. They'd have breakfast at the small restaurant attached to the museum and then take a tour of the latest exhibit.

She smiled when Owen came around the corner and walked toward her. No one would guess the unassuming man in the crisp button-down shirt, sweater vest, and olive green slacks ran one of the most powerful software companies west of the Mississippi. With his damp hair combed over from a severe side part and his wire-rimmed glasses, he looked more like a geeky computer programmer than a captain of industry.

He should be her perfect man—nice but also powerful. She knew he sat on several nonprofit boards and moved in the elite circles of Denver society. The fact that he didn't set her heart racing should only endear him to her more. She didn't need any more trouble in that area than she already had.

Out of the corner of her eye, she saw the camera's green light blink on as Owen approached. He glanced nervously in Steve's direction and she gave him what she hoped was a reassuring smile.

"Hi, Kendall."

"Good morning, Owen." She lifted the wireless microphone she held in her hand. "I know it's a drag, but let me just get this mic in place and we'll be all set."

"No problem." He held still as she pinned the small device to the V-neck of his sweater. "Honestly, I can't believe I'm the guy the viewers picked for a second date."

She glanced up to see him searching her face. Ever aware of the camera, she smiled again. "I'm glad they did. I had a lot of fun the first time we went out."

"Me, too. I was hoping I wasn't the only one."

"Definitely not. Should we head over to get some breakfast?"

"Okie-dokie. I'm starved."

Okie-dokie. Owen said *okie-dokie* with a straight face. He was like Richie Cunningham from the 70s sitcom *Happy Days* all grown up. The perfect all-American guy. But she knew in her gut he wasn't the guy for her.

They entered the cozy restaurant next to the art museum and chose a table in front of the window. Steve set up the camera nearby. To Kendall's surprise, a woman seated at the table next to them leaned over and whispered, "I'm glad you didn't end up with the sleazeball."

Unfortunately, she whispered her comment directly into the microphone pinned to the lapel of Kendall's lavender jacket. Just in case the producers didn't edit the offhand remark out of the program, Kendall flashed a smile and whispered back, "I think the Channel 8 viewers made the right choice." The woman nodded and returned to her own meal as the waitress came to stand by the table.

"I've heard the pancakes are good here," Kendall said to Owen, then inwardly rolled her eyes. No thoughts of pancakes or the man who'd made them for her or she'd never make it through breakfast.

Owen shrugged. "I'm not a big fan of pancakes—too sweet. I'll try the ham and cheese omelet and coffee, please."

The waitress nodded at Kendall. "And for you?"

Not a fan of pancakes? The all-American man lost some big points there. Who didn't like pancakes? It was akin to disliking apple pie. *No, don't go there*, she told herself. Pancakes were *not* a big deal. "I'll have the fruit and yogurt plate," Kendall said. "Coffee, as well, please."

"Sure thing." The waitress smiled at the camera then disappeared back toward the kitchen.

Owen nodded. "I would have guessed you for a yogurt type."

"You know me so well already," Kendall said. But he didn't know her at all.

"I have a knack for reading people."

This wasn't fair to either of them, and she didn't want to imagine Ty watching the news tonight.

"You really are even prettier in person than on TV. I wanted to tell you that when we first met, but I was too nervous." Owen's smile was so sweet it made her teeth ache.

He was sincere and truly seemed like a good guy. Why couldn't she fall in love with him instead?

Instead.

Her brain whirled. Was she in love with Ty?

Her heart answered before her mind had time to deny it.

Head over heels in love. The kind that would hurt like hell when she left. Because she was going to leave. She had to leave.

She realized Owen was staring at her. "Sorry," she said quickly. "I'm a little out of it until I have coffee."

He smiled that Richie Cunningham smile again. "Understandable. Your work hours are crazy, I guess."

The conversation veered from work to what they did for fun and a host of other benign topics. Then they walked back to the art museum. They spent an hour touring the contemporary art exhibit, during which Kendall struggled to keep track of the conversation as she absorbed the realization that she'd fallen in love with Ty Bishop. Love was not part of her plan right now.

As they neared the exit, he asked, "Would you like to get together some time off camera?"

Because the camera was still running and because she didn't know what else to say, Kendall answered, "That would be great."

"Super-duper." Owen grinned. "I'll give you a call."

Kendall smiled so wide she thought her mouth might split open. "Great."

He leaned forward and kissed her on the cheek then walked out of the museum. She turned to Steve and said with a smile, "Turn it off. Now." He did and she ripped the microphone from her jacket.

"What's wrong?" the cameraman asked. "I thought things went well."

"Nothing's wrong," Kendall said, trying to keep her voice steady. "Everything is great. Just great. I'll see you back at the station."

Without waiting for a reply, she turned and walked away. She didn't stop until she was behind the wheel of her car. Then she reached into her purse and pulled out her emergency pack of M&Ms. She ripped open the bag and poured half of the colorful chocolates into her mouth. She chewed and swallowed the candy and leaned her head against the seat.

She couldn't be in love. She'd only known Ty for a few weeks. It was the sex. It had been so good it was messing with her mind. She felt lust, not love. She downed a few more M&Ms.

Lust. That was it. Lust she could handle.

She folded the pack of candy and put it back into her purse. How did anyone manage real problem solving without chocolate?

She thumped her head against the steering wheel a few times. It hurt but didn't clear her mind. Eyes on the prize, she reminded herself. She put the key in the ignition and eased into late morning traffic.

◆ ◆ ◆

Later that morning her head more than hurt, it was pounding like the thumping heavy metal music from Ray's Body Shop. She'd finished the recap interview from her date with Owen, talking about what a nice guy he was, how much they'd had in common, and the fact that she was looking forward to seeing him again. Two of those things were true.

Somehow she made it through the evening broadcast, and after excerpts from the date footage aired, her Twitter feed exploded with #itsrainingmen tweets. Both Chloe and Sam called and texted, but Kendall ignored the texts and sent the calls to voice mail. She wasn't ready to analyze her non-relationship with Owen, even with her best friends.

Not when she had another man on her mind.

◆ ◆ ◆

Rain drizzled against the back of Ty's Gore-Tex jacket as he stood on Kendall's front porch, where he'd been for at least five minutes without knocking. There was no question he wanted to see her. He'd been thinking of little else since she'd hopped out of his truck Monday morning.

But the information in his hand was going to open a Pandora's box of trouble he'd closed and locked six years ago. He wasn't sure if it was worth it. If anything was worth that kind of trouble.

A light flipped on behind the front door. It swung open and Kendall stood in front of him, her head tilted to one side. "My neighbor called. She thought you were a stalker."

"Sorry."

"How long have you been standing here?"

"A few minutes."

"Would you like to come in?"

"Yes." Ty didn't move.

"Tonight?"

He smiled and stepped forward. "It's good to see you." He leaned in to kiss her. She smelled sweet and felt soft and Ty knew he would do almost anything for this woman. He'd deal with the consequences later.

Kendall pushed closed the door. "What's this?" she asked, making a grab for the envelope. Ty lifted it out of reach. "Dessert."

"You don't play fair." She led the way into the living room. He still found it hard to believe that she'd lived here for more than a few weeks. There was nothing about the cold, neutral space that held any trace of the sparkle he saw in Kendall.

"As instructed," he said, lifting a bottle of wine out of the inside pocket of his jacket.

"Wonderful. Bring it into the kitchen and we can open it."

He followed her toward the small galley kitchen situated past the empty dining room but stopped short when he reached the doorway. "What's that smell?" he asked, trying to keep his lip from curling.

She smiled. "It's a new recipe. Well, not exactly new. I took a gourmet cooking class a few years ago. The chef gave the class a packet of recipes when we were through. I made one of them tonight." She gestured to a pan sitting on the stove.

Breathing through his mouth, Ty edged closer. There were several lumps of something thick and brown clinging to the bottom of the pan. Whatever it was looked like something a dog would heave up after rummaging through the garbage. "Is that beef?"

Kendall frowned and scrunched up her brow. "Yes. At least it started out that way. It's French. It's called Boeuf de Pierrelatte."

"Uh-huh." Ty wondered if that was how you said roadkill in France.

"My version didn't turn out the same way the chef served it in class," Kendall said, poking a wooden spoon at the mixture. "But I'm sure it will taste fine."

"Sure."

"It's served with homemade noodles."

Ty's interest piqued. "Homemade?"

More frowning and brow scrunching. "They're supposed to be homemade." She pointed to the far end of the counter. It was covered with a dusting of white powder. In the middle of the flour lay a large mass of raw dough. "I couldn't get the consistency right so the dough wouldn't cut. I'm boiling water for spaghetti instead."

"I love spaghetti," Ty said, trying to sound enthusiastic. He glanced at Kendall, who was glaring at him like he'd just tracked dog poop through the house. "I mean it. Spaghetti is great."

Without warning, she heaved the pan off the stove and dropped the whole mess, pan and all, into the stainless steel garbage can that sat next to the counter. A string of obscenities poured from her mouth as she slammed the lid shut.

He remained stock-still, unsure of how to respond. Somehow, he guessed a lot was riding on his response. "I really do love spaghetti," he repeated.

"Out," she commanded, pointing her finger toward the living room. "We could order a pizza."

"I can cook," she yelled, shaking her finger in front of his nose. "I spent three hundred dollars on that stupid gourmet class. And I *can* cook."

"I believe you," he said quickly.

Her eyes narrowed to angry slits. "Go watch TV or something. I'm going to cook you dinner or die trying."

"How about Chinese?"

"I mean it. Go on while I make dinner." Her voice was low and menacing. He understood it was a tone he didn't want to mess with.

He nodded and backed out of the kitchen. "I like cereal, too," he offered. The galley door swung shut in his face, and he heard something bang against it. So much for cereal.

He tried to make himself at home in her house, at least as at home as he could be in a museum. What Kendall lacked in decorative touches, she made up for in the quality of her electronic equipment. The television was large and state of the art. He picked up the remote from the coffee table, flipped on a sports channel, and settled onto the couch. He hadn't had a chance to open the wine, but he wasn't about to brave the kitchen. No sound came from that direction. He wondered if that was a good or bad thing.

Forty-five minutes later the galley door opened. Ty turned to see Kendall, her face flushed, pushing damp strands of hair off her face. "Dinner's ready. I hope you're hungry."

He smiled as he walked toward her and was relieved when she returned his smile. He framed her face in his hands. "I wasn't joking when I said I don't care what we eat. Dinner was just an excuse to see you again."

"I appreciate that," she said and planted a long kiss on his mouth.

He pulled her closer. "Maybe we could wait on dinner." Her finger jabbed into his chest. "Ouch. What was that for?"

"We're not waiting. I made my best dish for you."

"You mean European mystery meat wasn't your best dish?"

"No." She walked toward the small table in the corner of the kitchen, currently set for two. "The most impressive sounding, but not the best. Would you pour the wine?"

He followed, relieved when the smell that greeted him as he neared was good. Damn good. He peered over her shoulder at the casserole dish that sat in the middle of the table. "Is that—?"

"Macaroni and cheese," she said in a tone that dared him to comment. "We're going vegetarian tonight. "Mac and cheese and salad. My mom made it almost once a week when I was a kid so there is no way I screwed up this recipe."

He bent closer to the table. "This smells too good to be from a box."

"Of course it's not from a box. Well, the noodles are, but the rest is homemade." She held up her hand. "I sliced my thumb grating the cheese."

He took her hand in his and lightly kissed the small scratch on the fleshy pad of her thumb. "Does that help?"

"Actually, it does." She laughed.

She looked so perfect standing there with her kitchen destroyed in the background that Ty could have easily made a meal of her.

Even though he'd bribed her into inviting him for dinner, he knew it meant something that she'd gone to so much trouble. He couldn't have cared less how the food tasted. It made him feel ridiculously happy that she'd fussed over it.

He was over the moon for this woman.

"What are you smiling about?" she asked, eyeing him suspiciously.

"I'm a fan of mac and cheese. That's all." He held out her chair. "Let's eat before it gets cold."

Still watching him, she sat down. He reached for the bottle of wine and uncorked it, pouring each of them a glass before sitting down himself.

"I guess red wine's a little fancy for the meal," Kendall said, raising her glass. "We should probably have juice boxes or milk."

"The wine is perfect. The meal is perfect." He raised his own glass and clinked it against hers. "To finding perfection in the unlikeliest of places."

He thought he saw her blush but all she said was, "I'll drink to that." She served them both and watched as he took his first bite. "Well?"

"Not that I ever doubted it, but you were right. You can cook."

This time she couldn't hide the color that rose to her cheeks. "That's not exactly the truth. I sort of know how to cook. But only the recipes from when I was a kid. Good old Midwestern staples—mac and cheese, potato salad, Jell-O done fifteen different ways. Nothing you'd want to serve to guests."

Ty scooped another forkful of macaroni. "I don't know. This stuff might be award-winning. There's nothing wrong with the basics."

"You shouldn't be so understanding." Kendall picked up her wine glass. "I'll end up taking advantage of you. I don't want to do that."

"I'll take my chances." He smiled at her. "While we're on the subject of understanding, tell me about Owen Dalton."

CHAPTER FOURTEEN

He'd been dying to ask the question since he'd arrived. Unfortunately, Kendall had just taken a drink of wine, which she promptly spit across the table.

"Didn't see that one coming, I guess," he said as he wiped the front of his shirt with a napkin.

She coughed then wiped at her mouth. "Not exactly. Sorry about the wine. If you take off your shirt, I'll soak it."

"I like that idea. First, let's talk about Owen. Things getting serious with the two of you?"

"You know how the promotion went. The viewers decided he would be the one I went out with a second time."

"I watched the show last night. You agreed to a third, off-camera date."

She stood and began clearing the table. Dishes clattered as she hurriedly stacked them. So he'd struck a nerve.

"He caught me off guard, too," she said after a moment.

Ty leaned back in his chair and tried to make his voice sound casual. "He's your type, rich and respectable. Probably some kind of pillar of the community. Not much in the looks department unless you like the pocket-protector set. That might actually appeal to you."

He could tell by her rigid back that she was getting pissed. But so was he. Their relationship was new, but after Sunday night, Kendall was his.

For now, anyway.

He didn't want to share her with some geeky executive. It drove him crazy to think about any other man putting his hands on Kendall.

"Are you jealous?"

Her voice was so close. She'd left the dishes at the sink and was standing directly in front of him.

"Hell, yeah, I'm jealous." He put his hands on her waist and pulled her to him. "I almost kicked in the TV when he kissed you on the cheek."

Her fingers tickled the back of his neck. "The fact that your jealousy makes me ridiculously happy is sick and wrong. Despite being a great guy, Owen does nothing for me."

"My turn for ridiculous happiness."

Her voice was soft. "Don't get too attached. I'm going to New York tomorrow for an interview."

He struggled to match her tone. "That sucks." He still couldn't wrap his mind around the reality of her leaving, especially when she was in his arms.

"You knew my plans when this started." She tried to pull away but he held on tight.

"Right. The running shoes."

"It's not just that, Ty. A shot at New York is my dream. I refuse to feel guilty for trying to make it come true."

"Who's talking about guilt?" He stood and kissed the corner of her mouth. Either the light was especially good in her kitchen or she was wearing less makeup because he could clearly see the dusting of freckles across the bridge of her nose. He didn't think it was the light. He was getting to her. "I want your dreams to come true. I think I can help with at least one of them."

"Really?" The look she gave him was so priceless he laughed out loud. He stepped around her and retrieved the envelope he'd placed on the wire baker's rack, safe from the devastation of the kitchen.

"Despite my better judgment, here is the untold story of ERB Holdings and GoldStar." He held the envelope out to her.

She bit down on her lower lip as she stared at the envelope. If she looked at him with that sort of longing, he'd be the happiest guy on earth. But she didn't grab for the information. "Don't pretend you're not dying to have this."

"I do want it." She pushed her hair behind her ears. "But even if you don't share what you know about GoldStar," she said, her voice unsure, "I'll still like you. I just want you to understand that."

He stepped forward and pressed the envelope against her palm until her fingers closed around it. "I'm glad you told me, but I'm doing this as much for me as you. Now take your dessert and say thank you."

She flashed a smile. "Thank you."

"That's better. You have a look. I'll make coffee."

He found filters and a bag of ground coffee after opening several of her meticulously organized cabinets. Based on the order in the kitchen, tonight's dinner was a real departure for her. Again, the fact that the change was for him gave him a spike of pleasure that quickly turned into something sharp as he thought about her trip to New York. He purposely didn't turn around until the coffee machine began to percolate.

He glanced over to find her staring at him, her brows furrowed in confusion. "They're nice pictures but I don't understand the significance."

He put two mugs on the counter. He could see the photographs spread in a line across the table. He'd taken those shots six years ago. This afternoon had been the first time he'd looked at them since then.

"I should start at the beginning," he told her, leaning against the counter. "When I finished my doctorate, it was expected I would come to work for GoldStar. Use my expertise and connections within the environmental community to pave the way for bigger and better land deals. I had an idea of how my father was running the business, and I wanted no part of it.

"I went to work for the state, reviewing proposals for development sites. The first case I was assigned was a proposal to build on twenty-five acres of prime real estate in the foothills northwest of Boulder. GoldStar was slated to get the contract."

"How did your dad feel about having you involved?"

"To say he went through the roof is putting it mildly. I think he would have disowned me if my mom had let him. She wouldn't stand for the scandal." Ty poured the coffee into two mugs and carried them to the table. He sat across from Kendall and picked up one of the photos.

"It seemed like a straightforward deal so I wasn't too worried about family strife. I figured it would be the usual red tape for GoldStar. Then I made this discovery." He held up the photo to Kendall, pointing to something small near the bottom of the picture.

She leaned forward to take a closer look. "You found an eagle?" Her expression was doubtful. "I'd expect to see birds like this in a woodland area."

Ty smiled. "Not this eagle. In cataloging the wildlife in the area, my team discovered a nest of golden eagles. An endangered species, to be precise."

"I guess that complicated things."

"To say the least. The review team's findings were public record. I knew that when the die-hard environmental groups got ahold of the information, it would be a cold day in hell before they'd let the land be developed. The family who owned it was uncertain about how it was going to be developed even before my discovery. They would have been easily swayed to shut it down."

Kendall sipped her coffee and studied him. "That couldn't have made your dad any happier about your involvement."

Ty plucked another picture from the table. "This is those twenty-five acres today."

He handed her a photo of rows of tract houses. There wasn't a tree more than four years old in sight. "I don't understand," she said.

He shrugged. "I had a moment of misplaced familial loyalty. Thought I'd save my father the trouble of fighting a battle he couldn't win. I took the information about the eagles to him before the findings were released. Figured I could save him some bad publicity if he backed out early."

"He didn't back out."

"I underestimated him. By the time the findings were made public a week later, you would have been hard pressed to find a robin on that land, let alone a golden eagle."

Kendall's eyes widened. "He got rid of them? How?"

"I don't know. My boss and most of the team members assumed I'd been working for GoldStar all along. My father did nothing to discourage that assumption."

"You got fired?"

"More than fired. I was publicly ridiculed, blacklisted in the environmental community, and pretty much run out of Boulder by a gang of angry ornithologists. I deserved it. I knew my dad was a bastard. It was my fault those birds were gone. I was holed up in my apartment a week later, licking my wounds, when he came and offered to bail me out with a job at GoldStar."

Ty didn't realize he gripped the coffee mug so hard it was liable to burst until Kendall pried his fingers loose. "What did you do?"

"Told him to shove his crooked business up his ass, packed my bags, and moved down to Denver. Started the landscaping business. You know the rest." She ran her thumbs along the back of his hands. Her touch eased his tension. "It took two years before I could stand to be in the same room as him."

"Thank you for sharing this," Kendall said gently, her words as soothing as her touch. "It helps me understand more about GoldStar." She dropped one of her hands to touch the edge of a photograph. "No one ever proved that your dad's company was behind the disappearance of those birds, right?"

A muscle in Ty's jaw ticked. He knew where she was going. "You'll have a difficult time finding proof," he said tightly. "He covered his tracks well."

"Then I'm sorry to say that this doesn't help me much with the Silver Creek story. I can't take a family squabble that happened six years ago to my producer."

Ty slammed his palm down on the table. It felt like a vise was clamped around his chest. "This is more than a family squabble. I'd bet my entire business that GoldStar has run a scam on every deal they've ever made. My father is just too powerful and too slimy to be caught."

Kendall shrugged. "Hearsay."

He shot up from the table, pacing from one end of the kitchen to the other. "The lady who owns the land near Silver Creek. You've talked to her about the offer that's been made for her property?"

"Mrs. Bradley? Of course. She wants to make sure she takes care of her family and the community. I don't have specific numbers, but she's happy with how the land is going to be developed."

"How happy is she going to be when her pristine forest looks like this?" he asked, stabbing his finger against the photo of the tract houses.

Kendall blinked several times, as if processing his message. "Ty, you don't know that."

How could he make her understand what his father was capable of doing?

"I know exactly what GoldStar will do. It's their business—bait and switch. My father has perfected the move. Believe me, you'll be lucky to find a lone stick on that sweet old lady's land when he's done."

"I'll talk to her. She's got a good lawyer. She'll have him go over the contract again."

"Who's her lawyer?" Ty asked, eyes narrowing.

"His name is Lester Benson. I checked him out. He's a senior partner at one of the big Denver firms."

"And my father's tennis partner," Ty finished, sinking back into the chair. He rubbed his hands over his eyes. His dad was going to get away with it again. Why had Ty believed he could stop him?

Kendall picked up several of the pictures and studied them. "If what you're saying is true, we can't let him do that, not to Mrs. Bradley's land or any of the other properties. You've been up there. It's too precious to be ruined that way. I need to make sure Helen's all right when this is over."

Ty sighed. "Since you've just told me all my information is garbage, I'm open to suggestions."

She took a pen and paper out of one of the cabinet drawers. "I'll dig deeper into GoldStar's previous deals," she said as she scribbled notes. "There must be someone in Colorado who will talk to me about your father."

"Don't waste your time."

She didn't take her eyes off the paper. "I've got to try. This is the most important story of my life."

He moved to the other side of the table and plucked the pen out of her hand. "We're in this together. You work on your end, I'll see what else I can pull up on mine."

She nodded. "We can stop GoldStar, right?"

"Right." He flashed what he hoped was a reassuring smile. He wanted her to believe him, to believe in him. "First things first. Let's get this disaster of a kitchen cleaned up."

He didn't wait for an answer, just dove into the mess. Kendall watched as he rinsed dishes and placed them in the dishwasher. He did housework, too. How was she supposed to resist this man?

She knew he didn't want to get involved with the Silver Creek story any more than he already was. But he was going to help her despite the connection to his father. He wanted her to succeed. She'd spent so long fighting her way up the career ladder alone, she'd forgotten what it was like to have someone at her side.

It felt uncomfortably good. The kind of good she could get used to, come to depend on if she let down her guard. That wasn't going to happen.

"I can finish up in here," she said, walking toward the sink. "The mess is mine."

He picked up a kitchen towel to dry his hands. "It'll be quicker with two of us." He turned to the garbage can, lifting the bag and twisting it closed. "Is your trash out back? The fancy French fiasco is starting to stink."

She wanted to argue, to order him out of her kitchen. Hell, she wanted to order him out of her life before he complicated things even more, but she couldn't bear the thought of being without him.

Bad sign.

"It's in the garage." She pointed to a door on the far side of the kitchen.

She wiped down the counter, surprised to see how easy it was to regain control over the mess in her kitchen. If only she could avert the potential disaster with the Silver Creek land development deal so easily. She wanted to expose GoldStar for more than just the ratings the story would bring.

"Thanks again for dinner," Ty said, wrapping his arms around her as she stood facing the sink.

Kendall turned, placing her hands against the solid muscle of his arms. "I want to use what you told me, but I need more proof." Sighing, she rested her forehead against his chest. "I didn't think I would care so much about what happens to that community."

His kiss was soft against the top of her head. "Unfortunately, everything involving my father is complicated. Of course you care. Even though you try to hide behind your all-business mask, you've got a big heart underneath those designer duds."

"You don't like my clothes?" she asked, digging her nails, ever so slightly, into his shirtsleeves.

"I like everything about you." He grinned, pulling her arms away. "It scares the hell out of me." His voice was light, but his brilliant blue eyes were dark and serious.

"Me, too," she admitted.

Their gazes held for several moments before he spoke. "I should go. You have a big day tomorrow and long flight ahead of you."

He was right, but she didn't care about *right* at the moment. She wanted one more night in his arms before she stepped into the future that would take her away. "Stay." The word came out a whisper.

He eyed her suspiciously. "Are you sure? I don't want to distract you on the eve of your big interview."

"Too late," she smiled then leaned up to kiss him. "Stay, *please*." His mouth molded perfectly against hers. A hint of stubble scratched her cheek. Again her head was filled with the smell of the outdoors mixed with his soap. It made her knees weak.

"You don't have to ask twice," he murmured against her lips, pressing her hard against his body. They stayed that way for several minutes, feasting on each other until she couldn't see straight, couldn't think of anything beyond this absolute bliss.

She led him to her bedroom, trying not to be embarrassed by the utilitarian décor. She'd never thought much about how boring it was, with her streamlined wood furniture, white bedspread, and lack of homey touches. Especially compared to the warmth and charm of Ty's house. He didn't seem to notice.

They made love on her white sheets, each taking time to discover what the other one liked, creating a rhythm all their own. When they were both too tired to move, Ty scooped her into his arms. Instead of falling asleep, they spent the next several hours talking.

Not about the future, that was too uncertain.

They laughed over childhood escapades, delved deeper into the mixed-up feelings each had about their families, and quizzed the other on the insignificant details of life—favorite color, first pet, preferred pizza toppings. Kendall tucked away every kernel of information, knowing that these were the memories she would take with her when she began her next journey. She wouldn't admit how depressed it made her to think of embarking on that journey without Ty in her life.

He left in the middle of the night, insistent that she get a few hours of sleep before flying to New York. She thought she'd be too nervous to sleep, but she crashed as soon as her head hit the pillow and was shocked when her alarm went off at five a.m.

It was good that he was gone, she reasoned, as she applied makeup in her bathroom mirror. The morning light helped bring her focus back onto her real goals. She was ready to secure the place she'd earned in the big city. This was her chance.

Nothing was going to throw her off track.

◆ ◆ ◆

Kendall met Sam and Chloe for happy hour the following night, after she returned from New York. She'd had a text waiting from Ty when she landed at DIA, but she ignored it, summoning her two friends to a popular downtown bar instead. Since the *It's Raining Men* broadcast, she'd been recognized even more often, so she tried not to make eye contact as she scanned the crowded room, afraid she'd be given another dose of unsolicited advice.

Two arms waved in her direction and she made a beeline for the back.

"This place is a meat market," she muttered as she slipped into the booth. "You should see the way some of the men in here were looking at me."

"You start dating on television and it's open season for losers," Sam said, lifting her glass of mineral water in a mock toast.

Kendall rolled her eyes. "Tell me about it. Three different guys hit on me at the airport yesterday. Didn't they watch the last show? I picked Owen."

"They don't buy you and the geek," Sam said.

"Are men with as much money as Owen Dalton still considered geeks?" Chloe asked, licking salt off the rim of her margarita glass.

"Oh, yeah." Sam nodded. "They're just geeks who can land hot chicks."

"You have a way with words." Kendall tapped the rim of the white wine glass in front of her. "Is this for me?"

"Yes," the other two women chorused. Chloe leaned forward across the table. "Enough with the small talk. We're dying here. What happened in New York?"

Kendall sipped at the wine, trying hard to make her smile seem real. "I got it. They offered me the position before I left." She was thrilled with the offer, which didn't explain the queasiness in her stomach that had started the minute the plane touched down in Denver. "Believe it or not, *It's Raining Men* helped. Gave them more insight into my glowing personality and ability to think on my feet."

Chloe scrambled out of the booth and crushed Kendall in a big hug. "I knew they'd love you."

"I can't believe it's finally happening. You should have seen the studio. In the middle of Manhattan. Everything state of the art. One of the execs gave me a tour." She bit her lip, a genuine smile finally tugging the corner of her mouth. "We passed Savannah Guthrie's office."

"Yeah, baby," Sam said. "Our girl is going to be rubbing elbows with the big-time players."

"The thing is," Kendall said, "the position is open earlier than they expected. They want someone to start June first."

Chloe's gray eyes widened. "That's less than a month from now."

Kendall nodded. "I'd have just enough time to wrap up the Silver Creek story before moving. The network will help me find housing in the city."

Chloe rested her dark curls against Kendall's shoulder. "You're really leaving. It won't be the same without you."

"What am I, chopped liver?" Sam asked. She held up her hand when Chloe started to protest. "I'm kidding. You're right, it won't be the same. I think this calls for some major celebrating, spa style. Let's head up to the mountains for a girls' retreat."

"That sounds perfect."

"I can't." Kendall took a big drink of wine. "I've got the station's gala tomorrow night."

"Skip it," the other women said in unison.

She shook her head. "There are other things I need to take care of sooner rather than later."

"Is McDirt, PhD, one of them?" Sam leaned forward. "Have you been holding out on us?"

Kendall saw several people turn and stare. "Keep your voice down," she whispered. "I haven't been holding out. Things with Ty are complicated. It didn't seem smart to discuss them until I had it straightened out in my mind."

"And now you do?" Chloe asked.

"Not exactly." Kendall picked at the corner of a napkin. "But I like him. A lot."

"Are you sure *like* is the L-word you're looking for?" Sam asked.

"Well, *leaving* is an L-word," Kendall said, tearing more fiercely at the napkin. "That's what I'll be doing in a few weeks. Does it really matter how I feel?"

"Of course it does," Chloe said. "You can Skype, text, visit, e-mail. Long distance relationships can be good."

"No. This is my big break. I promised myself I wouldn't be distracted by anything or anyone, especially not a man. I'm going to meet someone in New York once I'm settled."

Chloe's brow wrinkled. "I don't think that's how love works. You can't decide when or where or with whom it's going to happen. It sort of finds you."

"Not if I don't want to be found," Kendall muttered.

Sam reached across the table and pulled the shredded napkin out of her hands. "It may be too late for that. You should think twice before throwing away a real shot at happiness."

Chloe placed her hand on top of Sam's. "Following your heart doesn't mean you have to give up your dream."

Kendall shook her head. "But what if it does?"

"Whatever you choose, we'll support you." Sam told her. "But it's your decision to make."

◆ ◆ ◆

She detoured to Ty's house on her way home. It was like the Jeep's GPS was programmed with his address. Her feelings for him raced through her mind as she idled at the curb.

As much as she wanted it, the two of them together weren't meant to be. Better to devote herself to the future. She walked to his front door and pressed the bell twice for good measure.

When he opened the door, need and desire rushed through her. Desire she could handle, need not so much. She wanted to launch herself into his arms. But if she did that, there was no way she'd ever leave.

"I'm moving to New York City and I can't see you anymore," she blurted, before her brain could process how good he looked in his faded jeans and worn Broncos T-shirt.

He cocked his head to one side and studied her. "Congratulations on the job. I was worried when you didn't text me back. Have you been drinking?"

"Of course not. One glass of wine. That has nothing to do with this."

"Who's there?" a voice called. Ty stepped back to reveal a young boy standing in the hallway.

"This is Kendall," Ty told the boy. "A friend of mine."

The kid's brown eyes widened as big as saucers. He pointed a finger at Kendall. "You're that lady who goes out with all the guys on TV. Mom says you wear too much makeup and have a stick up your butt."

An audible gasp could be heard from the back of the house.

"Cooper Castelli, you get back to the kitchen this instant." Jenny peered around a doorway, her eyes narrowed. "We are leaving. Now."

"But, Mom," Cooper whined, "Ty said we could watch *Top Gear*. It's not fair."

"Now, Cooper," Jenny repeated.

Ty stepped toward him and ruffled his shaggy hair. "Do what your mom says, Coop. I'll DVR tonight's *Top Gear*."

"Can you record the series?"

"Sure."

"Cool." He turned to Kendall. "I hope you get that stick out of your butt. It must hurt real bad."

She nodded dumbly and watched him walk past his mother. Jenny sighed and moved into the hall. She looked like she wanted to drop through the floorboards.

"Sorry about that. Ty is a friend and he's been hurt before by people he—"

"I'll call you tomorrow, Jen," Ty interrupted.

"Fine. We'll let ourselves out the back."

When she disappeared again, Ty turned to Kendall. "Would you like to come in?"

She hadn't realized she was still standing on the porch. "I don't think that's a great idea. Jenny's right and I've said—"

He grabbed her by both arms and pulled her across the threshold, slamming the door shut with his heel. "Sit down."

She perched on the edge of the couch. "I'm sorry I interrupted you while you had guests."

Ty stood in front of the fireplace, arms crossed across his chest. "You should be sorry. Not for stopping by—you're welcome here anytime. But your little bombshell is a hell of a greeting."

She crossed and uncrossed her legs, picked at the fabric of the couch. All to avoid his gaze. She felt uncomfortable and guilty at being called on the carpet. "I got my dream job. The rest shouldn't come as a surprise."

"I meant it when I said congratulations." He closed his eyes for a moment. It killed her to see the pain on his face, to know that she'd caused it. It was an obvious struggle for him to remain calm. "I should probably uncork a bottle of champagne, but I'm not in a festive mood."

"Me neither." She stood, her emotions too jumbled to remain sitting. "This is my fault."

His hand slammed against the brick fireplace. "Are you seriously using the 'it's not you, it's me' line?"

She thought about that for a moment. "No. I'm not. Because it *is* you. I told you from the beginning what I could give. You screwed it all up by being so strong and sweet and sexy and . . . you. You made me want more." She poked him in the chest with one finger, holding onto her anger like a lifeline. Anger was better than the heartache ripping through her chest. "I'm leaving, Ty."

"So what? This is the twenty-first century. You've heard of phones, texting, e-mail, airplanes. We can make it work."

She wrapped her arms around herself. She wanted to wrap her arms around him instead, sink into his warmth so that the sadness that threatened to split her in two would melt away.

"I can't. I forget my priorities when I'm with you, and I forget the plan that's guided me through every challenge I've ever faced. I don't know how to live my life without it."

"I want us to be one of your priorities." He took a step toward her, gentled his voice. "I love you, Kendall."

She hadn't known until that moment it was possible for a heart to literally break, but there was no other explanation for the stabbing pain in her chest.

She nodded. "I'm sorry. I wish I could make this easier. You have to understand, this is my dream and I can't devote everything to it and still give you what you deserve. It's twisting me up inside. I told you I couldn't handle complications. Now my life is full of them and it isn't fair to you or me. Love isn't part of my plan yet."

"Screw the plan."

She ignored him. "The list goes: school, career, and then personal life. I can handle only one thing at a time."

He gave a disgusted snort. "You've handled me fine so far."

"Sex is different."

He reached for her, pulled her hard against him, then gave her the softest, most romantic kiss she'd ever experienced. It left her reeling and hating herself for wanting more. "This is more than sex, even if you won't admit it."

"I can't do this," she whispered.

"We can do anything, sweetheart. I'm willing to do whatever it takes to be together."

The heartache she felt was reflected in his eyes. "I'm not."

She knew her words struck harder than any physical blow. For an instant, she saw raw misery in his expression. Then his features hardened, his voice grew cool and distant. "If you leave now, it's over. No second chances."

She forced herself to move away from him. "Good-bye, Ty," she whispered.

CHAPTER FIFTEEN

When Kendall walked into the restaurant where she'd agreed to meet Owen for a drink before the Channel 8 anniversary gala, she didn't imagine the hush in conversation that fell over the room. She'd returned from New York the conquering heroine of the newsroom and already her job offer was public news. Tonight was her moment to shine in front of the coworkers who'd written her off as nothing but broadcasting eye candy. She should be walking on air.

But all she felt was tired. Tired of checking boxes off a list but never feeling satisfied. Tired of allowing the outside world to define who she was.

She wanted to curl up and sleep, preferably in Ty's arms.

Not a chance of that anymore.

Nausea churned in her stomach as she'd replayed the scene at his house. The look on his face said she'd wounded him to his core. And as much as she told herself she'd done the right thing, the words sounded as hollow as her heart felt. She had hurt Ty because she was afraid. Afraid of what she felt for him. Afraid that it was too much and would change her, make her weak and willing to give up on her dreams.

He'd said they could make things work, but she knew a long-distance relationship would never be enough. Every minute she was away from him, she craved his touch. A complete break was the best option, but believing that didn't lessen the pain.

She dabbed at the skin under her eyes. She wondered if it was obvious how much concealer she was wearing to cover the dark circles that marred her face.

The evening air held a hint of warmth, the signal that spring finally had pushed away the long winter for good. The temperature wasn't mild enough to account for the beads of sweat gathering at the nape of her neck.

She would have liked to cool off by removing her lightweight jacket but could feel half moons of sweat darkening the fabric of her pale-blue cocktail dress.

Owen rose from his chair as she approached the table. "Hello, there. You look lovely, as always."

"Thanks, Owen. It's nice to see you." She stuck out her hand as he leaned forward to hug her. Her fingers jabbed into the surprisingly firm wall of his stomach. "Oops, sorry."

They did an awkward little dance, trying to figure out how to greet each other.

Finally, Owen patted her on the shoulder and pulled out her chair. "Have a seat."

A flash of light caught her eye. Next to the table sat a shiny silver bucket complete with ice and a bottle of what looked like champagne. She peered closer. *Dom Perignon.*

He met her questioning gaze with an embarrassed smile. "I hope it's not too presumptuous. I thought a celebratory toast might be nice."

"Could we order a bottle of something a little less . . . expensive?"

He raised a finger and a waiter appeared instantly. "Why settle for less than the best? I won't." An emotion she didn't recognize flashed in his eyes. "Tell me about your new job."

The waiter uncorked the champagne bottle and poured two glasses. The golden liquid fizzed as it bubbled near the rim. "It's everything I dreamed it would be. The network, the city. They've started talking about assignments already. There are so many opportunities there."

Owen picked up his glass. "A toast to opportunities." They clinked glasses and sipped the crisp champagne.

She set her glass on the table. "Actually, I wanted to talk to you about an opportunity of a different kind."

He nodded, his smile slipping a little. "As a matter of fact, that's something I wanted to talk to you about as well." He tucked two fingers into his shirt collar, adjusting it. "Do you mind if I go first?"

She nodded. The fact that he looked nervous was making her feel edgy. "Is something wrong, Owen?"

He shook his head. "I've enjoyed getting to know you. The whole on-camera dating experience was bizarre, but you have a gift for making people comfortable."

"Thanks." She watched him tip back his flute of champagne and drain the glass.

"The thing is, I've met someone . . ."

Kendall blinked several times.

The waiter appeared and poured more champagne. She took the moment to study Owen. His face was flushed, almost mottled, and she guessed it wasn't from one glass of champagne. He mopped his napkin across his brow.

"I'm sorry," he added when the waiter was gone. "I know we agreed to another date."

Every single cell in Kendall's body relaxed. She leaned across the table and patted his hand. "Please don't apologize. I'm happy for you."

He looked suspicious and maybe a little disappointed. "Are you sure?"

She choked back a laugh. "You're a great guy. Any woman would be lucky to have you."

"You mean lucky to have access to my bank account."

She shook her head. "That's not true. And I hope this woman, whoever she is, knows it."

He couldn't hide his smile. "The thing is, I think she's turned off by my money. It's crazy and makes me like her all the more."

Kendall returned his grin. "You're an interesting guy."

"You know," he said, looking embarrassed, "I have you to thank for meeting her."

"Me?"

"Do you remember the landscaper you told me about?"

"Ty Bishop?"

"Right. One of his associates did most of the work on my garden project."

Ty had associates? Kendall's eyes widened. "Are you talking about Jenny Castelli?"

His smile stretched ear to ear. "She's fantastic."

Kendall quirked her head to one side. "Forgive me for saying this, but . . ."

"You don't see us together," Owen finished.

"Not exactly."

"Neither does she. I'm going to change that. I'm crazy about her. She argues with me about everything, and it makes me feel more alive than I have in years." His serious gaze pierced through Kendall. "I've been so focused on being successful, proving wrong all the people who doubted me, who looked at me and saw nothing more than a nerd who was good with numbers. I forgot all about creating a life beyond my ambition."

His words hit home. Hard. "I can relate to that."

"I sensed we were connected in that way."

She lifted her glass. "May you find all the happiness you deserve."

He tipped his champagne glass toward her. "What is it you wanted to talk to me about?"

She took a moment to gather her thoughts. "I did some research on your foundation, Owen. The mission is to promote the well-being of people in Colorado."

He nodded.

"Are you familiar with the community near the site of the Silver Creek fire?"

"Only what I saw on the news right after the fire."

"I'm doing a story on the area and how the residents are rebuilding their lives. We've uncovered some . . . unsettling information about the company that wants to redevelop the land. I can't talk about the details until the piece runs, but when it does I want to make sure the people who live in that community aren't part of the fallout."

"And you think the foundation can help?"

"There's a huge opportunity for conservation and restoration programs if they're handled the right way. The potential devastation from wildfire is something that affects everyone in the state. If you knew—"

Owen held up a hand, smiling. "I'll text you the name of our senior program officer. This could be exactly the type of initiative we're looking to fund."

"Thanks, Owen."

They talked for a few more minutes before going their separate ways. As Kendall walked the few blocks to the gala, she thought about what she'd accomplished. As proud as she was of getting the job in New York, it didn't satisfy her in the way she'd expected. Owen's words about creating a life that was more than ambition rang in her ears.

Suddenly her mind cleared.

She'd spent so much time planning her life, she'd forgotten to live it.

Her entire body tingled as she saw New York City for what it truly was—one step on her career ladder but only a small piece of the life she wanted to create.

Ty had said no second chances, but he'd also told her he loved her. That couldn't change in a matter of days.

She moved through the crowded reception area, not stopping even though many of her coworkers shouted out congratulations to her. She wanted to find a quiet corner to call Ty. She needed to get out of this place as quickly as possible so she could see him, be with him. She would do whatever it took to convince him to forgive her.

Just as she turned down a hallway, a hand fell across her shoulders. "Kendall." Bob Cunningham smiled as he pulled her to him. "So good to see our own future network star. I have some people I want you to meet."

Of all times for the station's owner to notice her, it had to be this moment? Kendall turned and stifled a gasp as Eric and Libby Bishop stared back at her.

What were Ty's parents doing here?

"We've already had the pleasure," Eric said, as he took Kendall's hand. Libby's lips thinned into a line that might have passed for a smile.

"I hope you don't mind, Kendall," Bob said with a wink, "but I gave the Bishops an advance showing of your piece on Silver Creek."

"Oh." Kendall nodded and tried to think of something to say that didn't involve defending Ty. She waited for someone to begin screaming or for Libby to reach out and slap her.

Eric said, "We were thrilled to see the work you put into it. Nothing like a little extra publicity to rev up interest before the lots go on the market."

Before she could reply, the lights in the lobby blinked several times, indicating that the dinner portion of the event was about to start.

"We'd better take our seats," Bob said. He gave Kendall a pat on the back. "I'm proud of you, Clark. You showed what you're made of on this one. We're going to miss you when you leave for New York City."

The three of them turned as the crowd began inching toward the main room. Kendall stood rooted to the spot, confusion and unease clashing in her stomach.

"You showed exactly what you're made of."

She whirled around to see Ty standing in the shadow of the hallway. Her body quivered with yearning. "You're here. I have so much to tell you . . ."

She took a step forward, but he leveled a look at her that brought her to a dead stop.

"You told me you'd do anything for your career. I should have believed you." His voice sounded as hard as granite.

"What are you talking about?" She tried to understand what he was insinuating. "Why are your parents happy about the story?"

For the first time she noticed he was wearing a tux. In the formal clothes, with his hair cropped and his face freshly shaven, he looked every inch the scion of his powerful family.

"Don't play dumb, Princess." There was an odd, dark note in his tone. "It doesn't suit you. I get to be the fool in this scene. I watched the piece with them."

"What did I do? Would you please tell me what the hell is going on?" She sounded hysterical but didn't care.

"You turned our hard work into a promotional video for GoldStar. That's what the hell is going on. All your talk about Helen Bradley and the community. About wanting to preserve the forest. Christ, if you ever get bored with reporting, you could win an Oscar with your acting skills." He laughed, but there was no humor in it. "Of course, your brand of journalism is acting—just like your dating. Save the good stuff for on camera."

"I don't understand," she whispered, dazed by what he was telling her.

"That makes two of us." He stared at her and for a moment she caught a glimpse of pain in his eyes so bleak it made her step back.

"Ty—"

"I came here tonight to show you I could fit into your world. No matter your doubts, I believed our connection was stronger. My love for you was stronger." He shrugged off his jacket. "I even pulled out the damn monkey suit. But you were right. We don't fit because I would never be with someone willing to sell out the people around her. You're just like my parents. And as far as I'm concerned, you can have their world all to yourself."

He started past her, but she grabbed his arm. "Ty, wait. Whatever the problem is with the story, I can fix it. You have to give me a chance. This is not how it's supposed to end."

He pried her fingers off his shirt, his gaze scathing as it raked over her. "Some things are too broken to fix." He strode through the lobby without looking back.

Kendall's mind buzzed. She had to find Liz and figure out what had gone wrong. As if on cue, the door to the ladies room opened and Liz walked out. "God, I need a cigarette," she drawled. "For a scientist, that man has a flair for the dramatic."

Her tone was light, but Kendall could read the guilt in her boss's eyes. "What did you do to my story?"

"You didn't expect the piece you submitted to be broadcast, did you? I threw you a bone with Silver Creek so you'd agree to *It's Raining Men*. Ratings have been dropping and we needed the boost the promotion gave us. *I* needed it. You were supposed to take a few shots of the new trees, get a couple people to talk about rebuilding their lives after the fire. All that business about the GoldStar development wasn't part of the deal, so we took it out."

"But it's the real story. The truth. GoldStar has done a lot of damage over the years, Liz. I worked hard to gain the trust of the people involved in those previous land deals and to convince them to share their stories on camera."

"Don't be naïve," Liz snapped. "Bob and Eric Bishop have been friends since college. He was never going to let it run unedited. What does it matter? You've got the New York job. Denver's just one more notch on your belt. Along with the scientist, I gather."

"Shut up," Kendall hissed. "Don't bring Ty into this. Not like that. He risked his reputation to help me expose GoldStar and his father. We can't ignore the way they have duped innocent people all these years."

Liz shook her head. "Let it go. It's old news, Kendall, and not part of your assignment." She stepped forward and took Kendall by the shoulder, her nails digging hard through layers of fabric until they pinched skin. "You may not see it now, but no story and no man are worth risking everything you've worked for. This story will ruin you if you let it."

Kendall shook free from the other woman's grasp as the tears she'd been fighting finally fell. "You don't get it, Liz. It already has."

♦ ♦ ♦

Ty heard the door to his outer office open and shut. He sprang to his feet and took one step around the desk before slouching back down in his chair. He knew it wasn't Kendall. After what she'd done, he shouldn't want to see her anyway.

But he did. The way she'd smiled at him last night hurt the most. Even though she'd stuck a knife deep in his back, to see her eyes light up and a grin spread across her face when she first saw him had almost made him forget the betrayal.

Almost.

He closed his eyes while his fingers massaged his temples. His head had been throbbing from the time he'd left Kendall to the moment he woke this morning. The fact that he'd slept like shit hadn't helped.

The smell of hot coffee coaxed his eyes open.

"Morning, boss," Jenny said as she put a steaming cup and a brown paper sack on his desk. She slid into her usual chair and sipped at her own cup. "So how'd it go with your girlfriend and all the rich and wanna-be-famous people last night? I've been watching her on television lately. The stick up her ass seems to be dislodging a bit."

He reached for the bag. "She's not my girlfriend," he muttered around a mouthful of breakfast burrito.

"Trouble in paradise?"

He wiped his mouth across the back of his sleeve. "She sold me out to my dad and flushed the work we were doing to expose GoldStar down the toilet."

Her eyes widened. "That's plain evil."

He took a drink of coffee and tried to make his voice casual. "Other than looking like an idiot again in front of my parents, it's no big deal. Better I found out what she was like now before things got serious."

"Not serious. Right. That reminds me. We got a call Friday from Sally Hendricks. You were there in the morning?"

"I planted her front garden bed. It felt good to do the work myself. What's the problem?"

"She wants to know who Ken is."

"What are you talking about?"

"The petunias you planted spell out the name Ken. Poor thing was sick with worry that she was outing you. You know anyone named Ken?"

"Shit."

"About sums it up." Jenny smiled sweetly. "So save that crap about *no big deal* for someone else."

"It's over, Jenny." He pushed a stack of papers across the desk. "And just when it was about to get interesting."

"What are those?"

"The real plans for Silver Creek, not the crap GoldStar is pitching to Kendall's sweet old lady."

Jenny almost fell off her chair as she scrambled forward to get a better look. "Where did you get them?"

"His office. My sister let me in over the weekend."

"Did she know what you were looking for?"

He nodded. "I promised her she wouldn't be implicated. I think Clare saw a scandal as her best chance to escape from under the family's thumb. Channel 8 wasn't willing to run the story, but someone has to be interested in the truth. Now that I have proof, I won't stop until I expose GoldStar."

"What happens when your dad finds out? He'll know it was you."

"It doesn't matter."

Jenny whistled low. "This is going to start an epic battle within your family. I thought you were trying to avoid fighting with him again. Isn't that what you keep telling me and anyone else who will listen?"

He saw the concern in her eyes. From decades of being friends and years of working together, she knew him all too well. He turned to the window, staring at the view of the small park behind the building.

He'd renovated the small scrap of land shortly after purchasing the office. During that time he'd worked sunrise to nightfall to keep his body so exhausted that his mind couldn't analyze just how his life had gone so wrong. He was back in that same place, but this time he wasn't going to run.

"I guess it's about time I pull my head out of the sand."

Jenny laughed softly. "Is that where it's been? I kind of thought you had it lodged—"

"I get your point." He chuckled. Jenny always knew how to lighten his mood. "And you're right. I've stood by for too long and let GoldStar get away with destroying land that people care about. I don't know if the woman with the Silver Creek acreage will find another buyer willing to pay as much, but she deserves to know the truth about the plan for her property."

"What happens when your dad comes after you?"

"Let him. I'm not going to roll over and play dead this time around."

"Hallelujah!" Jenny's whoop of delight split the air. "I knew you wouldn't be a wuss all your life," she said as she grabbed him in a bear hug.

"Is that a compliment?"

"As close to one as you're going to get." She stepped back and looked up at him. "Are you sure you don't want to take the plans to Kendall?"

His smile vanished. "Positive."

She nodded and plucked the papers off the desk and rolled them into a small cylinder, sliding them into one of the canvas totes leaning against the wall.

"Thanks, Jen."

She chucked him lightly on the arm. "That's what friends are for, buddy."

He watched her disappear through the door of his office and listened until the front door shut. Then he sank back into his chair and clicked the mouse until the computer screen flashed on. He pulled up a proposal he'd be presenting later in the week. He'd learned the hard way that life goes on even when you want to stop the world and get off.

◆ ◆ ◆

Kendall looked up at the soft knock on the office door. "Jenny, come on in."

The redhead's willowy frame filled the entrance. "I hope it's ok I stopped by without calling."

"It's fine." Kendall smiled, trying not to look as shocked as she felt. She'd almost fallen off her chair when Mary buzzed her and said Jenny Castelli was in the lobby asking to see her. She glanced at her watch. "I've got about a half hour before I need to start working on the early broadcast."

"I brought a friend along."

Kendall's heart shot to her throat at the same time her stomach took a nosedive toward her toes.

Jenny reached into the hallway and tugged. Owen Dalton gave a weak smile as he appeared in the entrance to the office. "Hi, Kendall," he said with an apologetic wave.

"Owen," she said, her heart still hammering in her chest. "Uh, nice to see you."

Jenny smiled sweetly. "Expecting someone else?"

"Not at all." So the claws were coming out. Well, she was due for a manicure so figured she could deal with a couple of chips.

Jenny approached her desk. "I have something for you. It's from Ty." Without waiting for a response, she pulled a roll of paper out of a plastic tube and threw it on the desk.

Kendall looked down at the blue markings that dotted the top sheet. "Are these plans?"

Jenny nodded. "For Silver Creek. The real deal. Not what Eric Bishop has been peddling to those people."

Kendall waved to two chairs in front of her desk. "Maybe you should sit down." She leafed through the pages, her breath catching. "How did he get these?" she whispered.

"It doesn't matter," Jenny said. "The important part is you have them now. What are you going to do about it?"

Kendall's mouth opened and closed several times as she stared back and forth between Jenny and the plans. "I need time to think," she stammered. The plans that were on her desk held no resemblance to the idyllic community GoldStar Development had laid out in its proposal to Helen Bradley. The neighborhood depicted in these sketches looked like the Silver Creek community's worst nightmare. Houses were crammed on top of each other in plots no bigger than a quarter acre. There wasn't a tree anywhere. It looked like one of the cookie-cutter subdivisions that could be built anywhere in America, not the rustic retreat detailed in the plans Helen had shown her.

"What's there to think about?" Jenny's voice was curt. "You can't possibly go forward with the fluff piece on GoldStar in light of this." She paused then added, "Although fluff is your specialty."

Kendall narrowed her eyes at the redhead's challenge. "Despite what Ty thinks, I didn't know about the changes to the Silver Creek story." She tried not to sound too guilty as she added, "But it's set to air tomorrow night."

"You're going to give up? What the hell is wrong with you? Do you know what this will cost Ty? He risked everything to get these plans."

Kendall's head snapped up. "I never asked him . . . I never expected him to go this far to bring down his father."

"Well, he did. And it's likely his parents will never forgive him for it."

"I'm sorry," Kendall replied. "He deserves better."

"He deserves better in a lot of areas," the other woman agreed. She grabbed the stack of papers and tried to pull them from Kendall's grasp. "If you're not going to use this information to stop GoldStar, I'll find somebody who will."

Kendall thought about Helen Bradley and the other residents of Silver Creek, who loved their land. She thought about Ty, who had finally found the courage to fight his father to win. "If I mess with this story, my boss will ruin me."

"Then let go of the damn plans," Jenny spat out.

Owen straightened, looking like the last thing he wanted to do was mediate a scuffle between Jenny and Kendall. "If we could just take a minute."

Jenny glared at him. "I told you she wouldn't have the balls—"

"We'll find another way," Owen said gently.

Kendall held tight to the papers. "I can't let this happen," she whispered.

Jenny tugged harder. "Don't make me fight you for them. I'm a lot tougher."

Kendall released the papers so fast that Jenny's hand flew up and the papers scattered across the floor on either side of the desk.

Kendall didn't notice. She picked up her phone and hit several buttons. "Hi, Tom, it's Kendall," she said into the receiver. "Liz asked me to go over the Silver Creek story one last time before tomorrow's broadcast." She paused, then smiled. "Yes, I'm sure she knows about it—just a few continuity things to tweak. Could you book one of the editing rooms for me tonight? And tell Steve I need to borrow a camera this afternoon. Great, thanks."

Her hand trembled as she hung up. What she was about to do amounted to career suicide. She thought about the years she'd worked to get to this point, the hours she'd devoted to her job, the life she'd sacrificed in the process. An image of Ty leading her through the forest drifted into her mind. Nothing was worth the pain she'd caused him.

Her ambition might have cost her his love, but she'd do anything to make sure that the work he'd done wasn't in vain. She owed him at least that. Owed it to herself and to Helen Bradley and to the viewers who trusted her.

She turned to where Jenny and Owen were picking the papers up off the floor. "I don't have much time."

Jenny straightened. "You lost me."

Kendall sighed. "I lost myself, too. Give me the plans, Jenny. I need to take back what's left of me."

The redhead clutched the papers tightly to her chest.

"Trust me," Kendall said. "I'm going to drive down to see Helen Bradley. I want her reaction on camera when she first sees them. That should have the viewers up in arms against Eric Bishop."

Jenny looked stunned. "You're going to use these plans in the broadcast?"

"I'm going to do my best. If I can't, I'll make sure I get the information to someone who can expose GoldStar and help Helen."

Owen sat back in his seat. "I think that's where I come in."

Kendall's attention shifted to him. She'd wondered why he'd tagged along with Jenny. "You have an alternative solution?" she questioned, her smile hopeful.

He returned her smile with a self-deprecating grin. "What's the use of having all this money, if you can't use it to do the right thing?"

She glanced at Jenny, who, to her surprise, was watching Owen with what could only be described as a goofy grin. The redhead's gaze switched to Kendall. Her eyes narrowed before she shrugged and shook her head. "What are you looking at?"

Kendall grinned. "Nothing. Owen, are you busy this afternoon?"

"I thought I might take a short ride into the mountains."

She nodded. "Let's get going."

CHAPTER SIXTEEN

Kendall wrapped newspaper around the glass and tucked it into the box with the others in the set. "That's the last of them," she announced. She closed the box and taped it.

Sam's blond head appeared around the corner of the living room. "Since you're a devoted minimalist when it comes to decorating, I think we have things taken care of out here."

"Very funny."

"Chloe has double and triple wrapped the few things you do have so there's nothing to worry about."

Kendall checked her watch. "The movers are scheduled to come in two hours." She looked at the open cabinet doors and empty shelves. Her life was packed into a couple dozen boxes scattered around her bare condominium.

Tomorrow she'd drive to Grady, Kansas, to visit her parents for a week before continuing to New York City. It was time to begin her new life. The life she'd wanted and worked so hard to achieve. She should be thrilled to her toes. She knew that. But Denver had begun to feel like home to her, especially in the past few months. She hadn't expected it would be so hard to leave.

"Have you talked to him?"

She glanced up at Sam, pushed the cardboard box against the wall and stood. She didn't pretend to misunderstand who her friend meant, though she wanted to. "No," she said simply, bending down to retrieve the tape dispenser.

"Things have to be tense with his family," Chloe said with a sigh. "I feel bad for him."

Sam snorted. "'Tense' might be the understatement of the year."

It had been two weeks since Kendall and Owen had met with Helen Bradley. That eighty-year-old woman was one tough cookie. She'd been dead set on bringing down GoldStar when she'd found out what they had planned for her beloved forest. In private, she had a backbone of steel. On camera, she played the role of the pitiable, frail, and innocent old lady to perfection.

Kendall had taken her reworked story directly to Bob Cunningham. The station's owner may have been a college buddy of Eric Bishop, but he was also a seasoned newshound. He saw the potential in ratings and publicity that breaking a story like Silver Creek would produce.

Through his private foundation, Owen had signed a deal to purchase the land around Silver Creek. Working with several state organizations, a conservation plan had been agreed upon that would integrate wildlife habitats with trail restoration and ranching interests in the area. Once the paperwork had been signed, Channel 8 aired the first of a three-part special on the Silver Creek community.

The initial segment covered the forest rejuvenation and included excerpts from the time Kendall and Ty had spent together in the burn area. Seeing his face on camera, watching the respect he had for the land reflected in his expression, had felt like a punch to her stomach.

One she probably deserved.

She worried that his father would find a way to ruin the landscaping business as punishment for Ty's leaking the plans. What would Ty do then? Colorado was his home. She couldn't imagine him starting over someplace else. There was no doubt Eric Bishop would be out for revenge.

The second part of the series had focused on Mrs. Bradley's story—the reasons she needed to sell the land, GoldStar's "too good to be true" proposal, and how the community would have been devastated if they'd learned the truth too late.

The final segment, which had aired two nights ago, included interviews with residents of other communities developed by GoldStar and the bogus promises that had been made in almost every instance. The station had been flooded with calls and e-mails from angry viewers eager to add their stories to the mix.

The other news outlets in Denver had picked up the exposé, and this morning a short piece had run on CNN. Lawsuits were already being filed in courthouses in several Colorado counties to stop construction on other GoldStar developments.

The elation she'd expected to feel never materialized. She was proud of the work she'd done on the story, and she was relieved that Silver Creek was safe from GoldStar.

Mainly, though, she wanted to cry.

"Honey, are you sure you don't want one of us to drive you to your parents' house?" Chloe had joined Sam inside the kitchen doorway. "I can take a couple days off work."

Kendall took a long sip from the mug on the counter. "Of course not. I'll be fine."

Her friends didn't look convinced. "You need to eat something on the road," Sam ordered. "You can't live on coffee and diet soda."

"I'm eating. You were here when the pizza came for lunch. You saw me eat."

Sam didn't back down. "I saw you take two half-hearted bites before tossing your plate in the trash. How much weight have you lost in the past three weeks?"

Kendall didn't have the energy to argue. "I don't know," she answered truthfully, slumping against the counter. "My jeans are loose but I haven't stepped on the scale."

Sam's voice was soft when she said, "Call him before you go."

The tenderness in her friend's tone was Kendall's undoing. She blinked back tears. "I can't. I made my choice. I can't turn back now."

Ty had left her a message the night the first segment aired. He'd apologized for doubting her, then wished her good luck in New York. But he hadn't asked her to call him or given any indication that he wanted to speak with her again.

As much as it hurt, Kendall told herself that a clean break would be the easiest for both of them.

Chloe squeezed Kendall's arm. "But can you move forward like this?"

"I have to." Kendall's voice trembled. "I have to," she repeated and rested her head against Chloe's shoulder.

"Oh, sweetie, we want you to be happy." Chloe wrapped her arms around Kendall's back.

"I'll have to add happy to the plan. Right after I cross out romance with a permanent marker."

"Men," Sam whispered as she joined the small circle. "Can't live with 'em, go to jail if you kill 'em."

"I'm going to miss you two so much." Kendall laughed through her tears.

"We're here when you need us," Sam assured her.

◆ ◆ ◆

She never thought she'd miss the drone of the window AC unit in her parents' trailer, but it was better than baking in the Midwestern heat. She'd spent the past week with her mom and dad, although her father was gone for long hours most days. It was the height of the summer season at Elmwood Country Club, and he spent early mornings and evenings mowing the lawns at the homes of some of the club's wealthy members.

Her mom's RA had flared shortly after Kendall arrived, so they'd stayed indoors for most of the visit. They both loved Jane Austen and there had been several movie marathons with Elizabeth Bennet, Mr. Darcy, Anne Elliot, and Captain Wentworth. And although her hands were swollen and red, Marianne Clark still loved a manicure.

"Do you ever regret it?" Kendall tried to be gentle as she held her mother's stiff fingers between hers and painted the nails a bright shade of pink.

"Regret what?"

Kendall could feel her mom watching her, but kept her eyes focused on her task. "Everything you gave up for Daddy."

"What do you think I gave up?"

"School. A career. Your future."

"Sweetie." The nail polish brush jerked as Marianne moved her hand under Kendall's chin, tipping it up. "Those things weren't meant to be for me."

"Because you gave—"

"Because I made a choice. A choice to love your father for better or worse. The same commitment he gave to me."

"But—"

"I know this life wasn't enough for you." Her mother's smile was sad. "We weren't enough for you."

"That's not true." Kendall shook her head and her mother gently tucked a stray piece of hair behind her ear.

"It's ok for you to want something different, but I'm happy. You need to stop blaming your father. Don't be afraid that loving someone is going to make you weak. Real love doesn't tear you down. It builds you up so that you can get through the hard stuff. I want you to be happy. You deserve that. And not because of what you do or where you live. You deserve to be happy and loved for who you are. That's how your father and I love you."

"I love you, Mom."

"And . . ."

Kendall closed her eyes. "And Dad, too."

"That means the world to me, sweetie."

When Marianne went to her bedroom for a nap, Kendall spent a few moments alone before she packed a cooler and headed toward Kansas City. She grabbed her water bottle and the cooler from the backseat and walked toward the front entrance of the Elmwood Country Club.

"Hey, baby doll." Her dad smiled as he glanced up from the valet stand. Mike Clark was only in his early fifties, but the years of pre-sobriety drinking had taken their toll. He was still lean and muscled from the handyman jobs he took over the winter when his valet hours decreased, but lines bracketed his eyes and mouth, and the skin around his jaw was sagging.

She knew it wasn't only alcohol that had aged him. Her father worked harder than any man she knew, doing whatever necessary to bring home money to cover his wife's medical expenses. They didn't talk about the fact that Kendall supplemented the family finances when insurance and his paycheck weren't enough to cover the prescriptions and doctor visits she needed. When Kendall was younger, it had been one more source of embarrassment that her family couldn't afford the lavish vacations her friends bragged about, let alone a weekend away. Now she saw the truth . . . that her father's work ethic was a testament to his love and dedication to his family.

"Hi, Daddy." She leaned forward to kiss his tanned cheek.

"What are you doing here?" he asked, giving her shoulder an awkward squeeze. "Is your mom ok?"

She and her father had never related well without her mother as a go-between. Although they were family, it was as if neither of them knew how to talk to the other. But Kendall had amended her master plan to include addressing things in her life that needed fixing before she moved to New York. Her relationship with her dad was one of the most important.

"She's fine." Kendall lifted the small cooler. "I heard noon is your break and thought I'd bring lunch."

Her dad's eyes widened for a moment and she held her breath, wondering how he'd take her gesture after all these years of their strained connection.

Then he smiled. "That's nice of you, baby girl. I sure do appreciate it."

He introduced her to the two young men working with him, explaining that she was visiting Kansas before moving to New York for an important network job.

It was the most she'd ever heard her quiet father say in one breath. She shook hands with both of the guys before one of them dashed away as a Mercedes pulled under the awning that shaded the club's main entrance.

"Your dad brags about you all the time," the other one, a stocky teenager with shaggy brown hair, told her.

She glanced at her father, who shrugged. "You're a good girl, Ken," he said simply. "I'm real proud."

Tears pricked the back of her eyes. Her parents had shown their support in so many ways over the years, but this was the first time her father had said those words to her. She hadn't realized how much she wanted to hear them until now.

"There's a picnic table outside the kitchen where we can sit." He wiped a hand across his brow. "But it's dang hot today. I get it if you want to leave the lunch and head back to your mom."

She sniffed and dabbed at the corner of one eye. "I made egg salad sandwiches."

"My favorite."

He led her across the driveway just as a thin, blond woman in a printed sundress stepped out of the sports car. "Kendall Clark?" she breathed, bringing her fingers up to delicately touch her lips. Kendall was almost blinded by the huge diamond sparkling from her left hand.

"Remmie Carmichael." Kendall recognized her at once. Remmie had been the ringleader of the popular clique at Graves and one of Kendall's biggest tormenters during her first year.

"What are you doing in Kansas?" Remmie asked, her shrewd gaze sweeping over Kendall, head to foot.

Kendall was wearing a shapeless T-shirt and denim shorts, flip-flops on her feet, and not a stitch of makeup. She'd showered earlier but tied her hair back in a messy ponytail, knowing it was pointless to style it when the humidity would cause it to frizz in minutes. She had clear memories of Remmie's assessing stare from years ago, but found it didn't have the same effect now.

"I'm visiting my parents." Her dad had taken a step away, but she pulled him forward. "You know my father."

"Of course," Remmie answered but didn't bother to flick him a glance. "We saw you on the national news last week and heard you're going to be working on *Wake Up Weekend!*"

Kendall nodded.

"It's one of my favorite shows. After the *Real Housewives*, of course." Remmie smiled. "I fly up to New York several times a year to go shopping. I'd love a tour of the studio."

Kendall felt her mouth drop open then snapped it shut. Remmie seemed to take her silence for agreement and continued, "I'm meeting some of the Graves girls for lunch. You're welcome to join us." She scrunched up her pert nose. Kendall hadn't remembered it resembling a ski slope quite so much when they'd been teenagers. "I'm sure the club office has something *appropriate* for you to wear."

She gripped her father's hand harder when he tried to pull away. "No, thanks. I'm having lunch with my dad today. If any of the *girls* want to say hello, we'll be sitting outside the kitchen."

"The kitchen? In this heat?" Remmie's eyes filled with disbelief. "Are you sure?"

"Positive." Kendall took a step away then turned back. "And if you want to visit the studio, call the station's front desk. Tours for the general public are scheduled through the marketing department."

She didn't wait for Remmie to answer, but followed her father quickly around the side of the building. When they were out of sight, she clapped a hand over her mouth to stifle a giggle.

Her dad raised a brow.

"It's probably wrong of me to say this, but that felt *really* good."

Her father threw back his head and laughed, then grabbed her into a tight hug that lasted almost a full minute. When he finally let her go, he was still smiling. "So proud," he whispered.

CHAPTER SEVENTEEN

Three weeks later, Kendall hefted her suitcase into the back of the ancient Land Cruiser, slammed the cargo door shut, and climbed into the passenger seat. "I bet this isn't what you had in mind when you said you were only a phone call away," she said, her smile wry.

Sam studied her over the rims of her Jackie O sunglasses. "You look like hell."

"You would, too, if you'd just flushed your life down the toilet." Kendall cracked the window an inch and leaned back against the headrest. The air in Colorado, even in the congested parking lot at the airport, smelled like the mountains. Like home.

"It's still true." Sam shifted into gear and sped away from the bottleneck of traffic at Denver International Airport.

As they rounded the corner of the massive circus tent that housed the main terminal, Kendall caught her first glimpse of the Front Range, rising out of the distant landscape. Even in early June, there was still a light dusting of snow on the highest peaks. The mountains looked solid and steadfast. Her gaze held tight to their constancy like a life preserver.

When they pulled onto the interstate, the downtown Denver skyline came into view. A cloud of light brown smog hung over the buildings this morning, but to her the city had never looked so beautiful.

She was grateful for Sam's companionable silence. How was she supposed to explain what had happened in the past few days when she barely understood it?

The soft whir of the tires against the asphalt lulled her and her eyes drifted close. She blinked them open when the Land Cruiser stopped. "Are we at your house?" she asked drowsily, stretching her neck from side to side. Sam only lived about twenty minutes from DIA, so she couldn't have slept that long.

"We're here. Rise and shine." Sam opened the door and hopped out. Kendall squinted through the front window to where Sam greeted a large, black dog in front of a Victorian-style house. The animal seemed to be doing its best to knock Sam over with all of its jumping and wiggling. Kendall climbed out of the truck and closed the door as quietly as she could manage.

It didn't matter. The dog's floppy ears perked at the sound of the click. He turned, spotted Kendall, and thundered across the yard toward her. She pressed herself flat against the side of the Land Cruiser and watched Sam walk up the steps. Based on Kendall's previous experiences with animals, there was no telling what a big dog might do to her. Teeth, claws, misplaced bodily functions. Was it any wonder she expected the worst?

From the front porch Sam called with a laugh, "Frank, sit."

Mere inches in front of her, Frank dug his paws into the yard and plopped his wide rear on the ground. His long tail swished the grass back and forth and he panted hard.

"Good dog," Kendall breathed, reaching out to pet his head. His tail thumped harder and she smiled.

It seemed like almost everyone in Colorado had a dog. If she planned on making this her home, she should think about adopting one. Frank's sloppy tongue licked her outstretched hand, leaving behind a slimy coating of slobber. On second thought, maybe she'd start with a cat.

Wiping her hand on her jeans, she eased around the dog and hurried up the walk. Her suitcase could wait until later. When she got to the front porch, she heard a whistle from inside. Frank rose from his spot near the curb and lumbered to the middle of the front yard. He rolled onto his back to soak up the morning sun.

"He's well trained," she said to Sam, who held the screen door open.

Sam smiled. "And as gentle as they come. Don't let his size fool you. Animals can sense your fear."

"Who can't?" Kendall mumbled as she stepped into the house.

To her surprise, Sam didn't make a snide comment. Kendall figured that meant she was too pathetic to joke about. How sad was that?

"Do you want something to drink?"

Kendall made a face. "Got any rat poison?"

"Fresh out. But there's some iced green tea in the refrigerator. Have a seat in the living room and I'll pour a couple glasses."

"Any chocolate?" Kendall questioned hopefully.

Sam grinned. "I'll see what I can do."

When Sam disappeared down the hall, Kendall turned back to where the dog still lay stretched in the grass. If only life were that easy. She went back outside. It was too beautiful a day to be in the house. And she needed whatever calm the fresh spring air could bring.

Frank lifted his head when the screen door banged shut but didn't get up. She sank into one of the wicker rocking chairs that sat on the large porch. A few minutes later, Sam emerged from the house carrying a tray with two glasses and a wooden bowl.

"No chocolate," she announced. "But I've got carob covered almonds."

Kendall grimaced but took both the glass of tea and the bowl of nuts.

"Get used to it," Sam warned. "It's all organic in this house."

Kendall popped an almond into her mouth. It was no M&M, but it would do for now. "Thanks again for letting me stay. I know camp preparations start soon. I'll try to keep out of the way."

"Stick around long enough and I'll put you to work." Sam sipped her tea. When Kendall met her sideways glance Sam asked, "Do you want to talk about it?"

"Yes. But I don't know where to begin. Everything happened so fast."

"Start with the visit to your folks."

Kendall stared toward the street where a young boy on a bike sped past. "I hadn't been back there in almost four years. All this time I believed my mom had made the wrong choice. But I talked to her this time, to both of them." She looked over. "They're happy. She's happy. They struggle sometimes, but who doesn't in a marriage?"

"Who doesn't in life?"

"Right. But I can't believe it took me so long to appreciate the parts of my childhood that helped make me the person I am today." Kendall took of sip of tea. Her hand shook so hard the ice rattled in the tall glass. She tried to laugh it off. "I should have invested in some therapy long ago. It would have saved me a lot of shame and guilt."

"I'm glad you finally figured out what the rest of us already know. You're pretty great just the way you are."

Kendall sighed. "Then I got to New York. Feeling comfortable in Kansas and making it in the Big Apple are two different things. Talk about a Dorothy Gale complex. I might as well have landed in Oz. New York City has been part of my plan forever, but all I could think when I got there was that it wasn't home for me. Everything was overwhelming—the city, the network, all the new people."

"Seems normal. You didn't want to give it some time?"

"That would've been prudent."

"You're always prudent."

"I used to be. I don't know who I am anymore." Kendall took another drink, her hands steadier this time. "Even if I had stayed longer, it would have ended the same. Did you ever have a gut feeling so strong that you didn't doubt it for an instant?"

Sam nodded.

"That's how it was in New York. I knew in my heart that it wasn't what I wanted. I could never be happy there, no matter how many times I wrote the word on my priority list."

"What do you want?"

Kendall dragged her fingers through her hair. "That's the million dollar question. The news director at the network asked me the same thing yesterday when I resigned. He looked at me like I was crazy and suggested I think about my decision for a few days."

"And you told him . . . ?"

"That I didn't want to waste any more of his time. I won't change my mind, Sam." Kendall bit her lip. "Do you think I'm crazy?"

"Stop it." Sam pursed her lips. "Crazy isn't part of your equation."

"You sure about that? I've got no job, my condo's sublet for the next six months." Kendall counted her screw-ups on her fingers. "I ruined a relationship with the man I'm pretty sure was the love of my life. I guess things can only get better from here."

"Let's hope so." A smile tugged at the corner of Sam's mouth.

Kendall pushed out of the rocking chair and leaned against the front porch rail, stretching her hands out as if to catch some of the sun's warmth. For someone who had avoided the outdoors as much as possible most of her life, now all she wanted was to soak up the sights and smells of nature. She needed the fresh air to remind her why she'd given up everything she'd ever worked for, everything she'd thought she always wanted.

"I want to belong," she whispered, watching the light and shadow make patterns across her arms. "I want to be part of a community, to have a home." She glanced over her shoulder. "How corny is that?"

Sam's expression was unreadable. If Kendall was looking for unquestioning acceptance of her decision, this wasn't the place to find it. "Why here?" Sam asked. "Is it because of Ty?"

Kendall turned back to the yard. "I hope so, but I don't know if he'll give me a second chance. I hurt him pretty badly. No matter what happens, I'm home. When I was working on the Silver Creek piece, I felt alive. The story's impact on my career wasn't as important as its impact on people who lived there. I made a difference for that community. Maybe New York City would have been as fulfilling, but I know now that it's not where I am that makes me a damn good reporter. It's who I am. I found my voice in Colorado, and this is where I want to use it."

"Welcome back." Sam pulled her in for a hug. "Let's call Chloe and figure out how we're going to clean up the royal mess you've made of your life."

Kendall looked up. "Do you think I can?"

Sam shook her head in mock horror. "You'd better. I can't have you mooching off me forever, babe. What if I find some stud I want to bring home? You'll cramp my style."

Kendall took a step back and let her eyes wander from Sam's braided hair to her oversized sweatshirt and baggy cargo pants. Sam did her best to hide the million-dollar body under those frumpy clothes. "What style?"

Sam's ice-blue eyes narrowed. "Real funny." She gave Kendall a small shove toward the front door.

◆ ◆ ◆

Ty placed the keys in Jenny's outstretched hand. "Are you sure you don't want me to come with you to get everyone settled?"

She gave him a look like he had a horn growing out of his forehead. "I'm sure."

He shoved his hands in his pockets to keep from snatching back the key ring. "The guys don't like working on Saturdays. They can be really pissy first thing in the morning."

"Are you talking to someone here I can't see?" Jenny glanced from side to side. "Because I'm the one who's been overseeing weekend crews for six years. What is your problem?"

"It's not that I doubt your competence," he explained. "I've always been—that is—you've never been . . ."

He stopped, unsure of how to verbalize his thoughts.

"I've never been the *real boss*," she finished for him, tossing her long red ponytail, clearly annoyed.

"You'll be great," he said quickly.

"Hell, yeah, I will." She took a deep breath. "Ty, I love the business. Probably more than you do. I'll take good care of the clients, the staff, everything."

He nodded and mopped the back of his hand across his brow. The early morning air was pleasantly cool, but he was sweating as if it were summer in the Sahara. "I know." He looked past Jenny. "What if I suck?"

She smiled gently. "You've never sucked at anything in your life. Owen wouldn't have hired you if he didn't think you could do the job." Her voice held a hint of pride when she added, "He's an excellent judge of people."

"So you keep telling me. But what do I know about land management?"

She rolled her eyes. "For one thing, you've grown up around it your whole life. Osmosis has to count for something. And you're a damn good biologist. You know more about the land in this state than anyone I've ever met."

He flashed a sheepish grin. "Was it obvious I was fishing for a compliment?"

"I'm not blowing sunshine up your ass," Jenny said with her usual candor.

He was going to miss working with her every day.

"Thanks, Jen." He slapped his hand lightly against the truck's ancient side. "Take care of my baby here. She's almost as perfect as you."

Jenny opened the door of the truck and winked. "Then we'll be a great pair. You'd better haul ass. You don't want to be late for your first day on the new job."

He watched her drive away until the taillights turned the corner, then glanced at his watch. Shit. A crew of volunteers was scheduled to meet him near the San Isabel trailhead in forty-five minutes. He climbed into his truck and hit the gas hard.

When he finally reached the small mountain road that led to Silver Creek, he began to relax. Almost six weeks had passed since the GoldStar headlines had exploded in the local and national news. As expected, his father had barged into Ty's office, breathing fire about how he was going to make his son's life a living hell for dragging the family name through the mud.

It hadn't mattered. Ty was long past the point where his father could hurt him, either emotionally or professionally. He knew he'd made the right decision in exposing GoldStar.

He'd felt more alive than he had in years.

And more alone.

When Owen had approached him about heading up an environmental group to buy parcels of wilderness area for conservation purposes, he'd jumped at the chance. Resurrecting his professional reputation and working with the land would allow him to reclaim the life he'd walked away from eight years ago.

The only thing missing was someone to share it.

Suddenly the air in the truck's cab was stifling. He rolled down the window to let in the fresh scent of pine trees.

He'd checked voice mail a thousand times since he'd left Kendall that last message. But she hadn't called back. Finally, he'd thrown the damn phone at the television, unable to stand watching her on the news bits that continued to replay the GoldStar scandal. Anger was easier to stomach than the pain of a broken heart.

It drove him crazy, but not a day went past that he didn't think of Kendall. No doubt she was already firmly entrenched in big-city life. She probably hadn't thought of him once after how he'd treated her, and he couldn't blame her. He'd been a jerk, and, he realized too late, a total fool.

He'd thought about calling her again but never picked up the phone. What was the point? Their lives were going in different directions.

All he could do to get through each day was make the most of his new opportunities. His work so far had been on paper, but today he would supervise a crew clearing out a dozen acres of overgrown forest.

He turned the truck down the dirt road. Half a dozen cars were parked on either side. A small group huddled near the trailhead that led up the mountain. Most held shovels, rakes, or other tools.

After parking, he walked toward the group, shading his eyes from the sun's harsh glare. "Good morning," he called. The bright light made the crowd of faces blend together. "Thanks for giving up a Saturday to help with the clean up. I'm Ty Bishop from the Dalton Land Trust. The area we'll be working on is about a mile and a half up the trail. Let's start hiking. We'll do introductions and talk about what needs to get done on the way."

The group turned toward the mountain. Out of the corner of his eye, Ty caught a glimpse of golden brown hair and a green plaid shirt. His gut clenched and he felt as dizzy as if he was on the top of a high mountain peak. What was she doing here?

He started toward her, but a man he recognized from his earlier work with the Forest Service blocked his path. "Hey, Bill," Ty said. "Nice to see you again."

The man nodded. "You, too, Bishop. 'Bout time you came back to the woods. It's where you belong."

"Thanks." Ty tried to keep his voice casual. "I left a few things in the back of the truck. Keep an eye on the group until I catch up, will you?"

Bill nodded again. "You bet." He trotted to join the others.

Ty approached Kendall slowly—afraid she might disappear. His heart was about to beat out of his chest. It was several minutes before he could speak. "That's my shirt," he said, thinking about how lame he sounded.

Her smile was tentative, but to him it felt like the sun breaking through the clouds after a month of rain. "I thought you'd want it back."

"You flew all the way from New York and tracked me down on a Saturday morning to return my shirt?"

She took a step closer. "No. I'm here because . . ."

The breeze kicked up and her clean perfume mingled with the scent of the pine trees. Suddenly this was too much. Seeing her, aching to reach out and touch her. The pain was too fresh, too real.

"It doesn't matter," he told her, pulling tools out of the truck's rear bed. "Keep the shirt. I don't have time for games." She was beside him a moment later, reaching for a shovel. "Kendall, what the hell are you doing?"

"I'm here to volunteer. I talked to Owen yesterday. He told me about the work you were managing on the trail. I want to help."

Less than twenty-four hours on the job and his new boss had sold him out. All the anger he'd felt when she left came flooding back. He looked over her shoulder, "Where's the cameraman? Should I expect to see myself on the evening news?"

He tried to ignore the look of pain that flashed in her eyes.

"I'm not doing this for the publicity, Ty. I want to *help*." She kicked the ground with the toe of one hiking boot. They looked new, but at least she was wearing sensible shoes today. "I'd also like to talk about us."

Jesus, he had to get away from her. As much as he shared the blame for what had gone wrong between them, she'd left him behind. After the hell of these last few weeks, he couldn't risk that heartache again. "You want to work, I'll put you to work." He stalked toward the trailhead. "But there is no *us*. Got me? This isn't the shopping mall, Princess. I've got a lot to do and no time to worry about you chipping a nail."

Rocks crunched as she jogged to keep up with him. "I can hold my own."

He shot her a disbelieving look over his shoulder and saw her chin hitch up a notch. "Tell you what, you make it to the end of the day and then we'll talk."

"Fine," she shot back, her voice breathless. He prayed the altitude would stop her if the prospect of a day of toiling in the dirt didn't.

They continued up the trail in silence. He heard her curse under her breath when she tripped over a tree root. He didn't turn around to help. For his own survival, he had to keep moving. He didn't know what the hell she was doing here. He wasn't sure his heart could afford to find out.

The way he saw it, nothing had changed. He was still the same guy, maybe with a slightly more illustrious title, but not fancy enough to meet Kendall's requirements.

The group of volunteers waited near the small stream that ran alongside the trail. Ty should have expected Kendall to be recognized when introductions were made. Several people congratulated her on the Silver Creek story and her new job. He noticed she was vague when answering questions about what she was doing back in Colorado.

She's here to drive me crazy, he wanted to shout. Instead, he gave a short introduction on the Dalton Land Trust, the regeneration efforts in this part of the forest, and what he hoped to accomplish today. After answering a few questions, he broke the group down into pairs of two and began assigning tasks.

He put Kendall with Bill and gave them the job of shoring up the sides of the creek bed near the trail and building a walkway across. Bill Mason was a no-nonsense retired marine. Ty had met him on one of the burn teams right after the big fire. Bill was hard working and not afraid to get dirty. He wouldn't cut Kendall any slack.

Ty left to lead a group of college students into the burned-out forest. When he returned to the trail three hours later, he expected Bill to be working alone.

His mouth almost hit the ground. Kendall's back was to him. As he watched, she drove a shovel into the embankment as Bill shouted instructions. Her jeans were wet up to her knees and her boots covered with mud. She'd tossed his flannel onto a dry rock and wore a thin white T-shirt that was splattered with flecks of dirt.

"Ty," Bill called. "How's it look?"

For the first time, Ty noticed the fallen log that spanned the width of the stream. The side facing up had been cut flat so hikers could walk across it. His gaze flicked to Kendall, who'd turned to watch him through narrowed eyes. Tendrils of damp hair clung to the sides of her face as she ran the back of one gloved hand across her forehead. Her brows rose in silent challenge.

"Looks great, Bill. If you're almost done, the crew could use some help shifting the fallen trunk over the top of the rise. I'm taking a group with me to check out the conditions about a mile deeper in." He smiled at Kendall. "If you'd like to take a break, feel free. I know this isn't your usual work."

She opened her mouth to respond, but Bill shouted, "No way, man. Kendall's with me. I haven't seen anyone work so hard since I was in boot camp."

She flashed Bill a brilliantly sincere smile.

"Lead on, my captain." She grinned then saluted. Ty felt like he'd taken a hard right to the jaw.

For the first time, he admitted that he wanted to see her smile like that at him again, real or not. Maybe he should have talked to her earlier. She could have said her piece and been gone. Now he was stuck until the work was through.

"Fine, but don't go near the edge, Kendall. The ground is rocky up there and can shift at a moment's notice. Bill, keep an eye on her." He ignored the look she gave him and stalked away, pissed that he'd acted like he cared. He told himself it was because she was so inexperienced and for today, he was responsible for her. Nothing more.

Yeah, right.

Around noon, the group headed back down the trail. Ty unloaded a cooler full of sandwiches, chips, and water from the back of his truck. He skipped lunch, preferring to keep moving, keep busy, and keep away from the woman who made him feel like he was losing his mind. For the rest of the day, he stayed as far away as possible, if for no other reason than to preserve his sanity.

The sun had almost dipped behind the mountain when he brought his crew back toward the trailhead. He hoped Kendall had given up and gone home already. She had no right to come here in the first place, making him feel so out of control again.

He rounded a bend when one of the volunteers from the other group almost knocked him over as he barreled up the trail. Ty's first aid kit was clutched in his arms.

He grabbed the man before he could pass. "What happened?"

The volunteer pulled away. "I gotta get this up there," he panted. "Could be bad . . . I don't know . . . Kendall needs help."

Ty wasn't sure if the guy said anything more because something roared to life inside him, blocking out any other sound. He ripped the first aid kit from the volunteer's hands and raced up the mountain.

The anger he'd felt moments earlier disappeared as quickly as acres of underbrush consumed in a wildfire.

Three words filled his mind. *Kendall. Needs. Help.*

He tripped over a rock jutting out from the ground, cursing as he scrambled up again.

His lungs burned as he came to the top of the hill. The second crew stood in a group near the edge of a small cliff. Christ, what if she'd gone over? It wasn't a big drop but she could easily break a bone in the fall.

He shoved past volunteers as he pushed to the front of the small crowd. He caught sight of her bent over the ground a few feet back from the edge and fell to his knees beside her.

"What the hell were you thinking?" he yelled. "I told you to be careful. Why couldn't you stay away?"

He moved his shaking hands along the length of her body, wanting so badly to pull her against his chest and bury his face in her hair. Since he didn't know the extent of her injuries, he couldn't risk hurting her.

"Ty, what are you doing?" She gripped his hands when they moved to her hips. She sat back, looking at him like he had two heads.

Only then did he notice Bill lying on his back in front of her, his head propped on a balled-up jacket and a bloody T-shirt wrapped around his thigh.

The older man gave him a tight smile. "You wanna feel me up for injuries, too?"

Ty's mind reeled.

"What the—" He looked over his shoulder to where the volunteer crew watched him. He searched Kendall's face. "The guy with the first aid kit said you needed help."

She stared at him.

Finally Bill answered, "She does need help. Patching me up."

Ty's gaze switched to the older man.

"You screwed up who should keep an eye on whom." Bill laughed then winced. He gestured to his leg. "I got caught on a branch from one of the trees, almost went over the side. Kendall's a helluva lot stronger than she looks. Pulled my fool ass up before I went too far."

As Ty tried to reign in his emotions, Kendall's cool fingers slid over his wrist. "Are you ok?"

"I thought you were hurt," he answered woodenly, refusing to meet her eyes. Afraid his gaze would reveal too much.

She tugged the first aid kit out of his stiff fingers. "We need a better bandage around Bill's leg."

He still couldn't look at her.

"I'll take care of this," she continued. "You find something to use as a walking stick. He's going to need support going down the hill."

He stood, grateful for the distraction. He was thankful to his core that she hadn't been hurt but he needed to get away from her before he made an even bigger fool of himself.

The volunteers still watched him. "Ok, people," he said, struggling to keep his voice steady. "Let's gather up the tools and move out. We need a couple of big guys to help Bill. Everyone else, head for the parking lot."

His legs felt like rubber as he searched the surrounding area for a branch large enough to make a walking stick. He handed what he'd found to one of the volunteers standing near Kendall.

"I'm going ahead," he said, "to make sure the trail is clear of rocks and debris." Mainly, he needed space away from her. To regain his control before the conversation he knew was coming.

Kendall didn't look up, but Bill nodded. "Don't worry 'bout me. I've had mosquito bites that hurt worse than this. Although I'll never complain about being tended to by a beautiful lady."

Kendall smiled. Pain ripped across Ty's chest. "I'll see you down there," he managed to choke out before he turned and walked away.

◆ ◆ ◆

Kendall took a long drink from the water bottle and waved to one of the other volunteers. "Nice to meet you, too. Maybe I'll see you another weekend." The woman smiled and nodded, then pulled out onto the mountain road.

Kendall wasn't sure when she'd be able to lift her arms above her head again, let alone do more of this type of work. She hurt in places she hadn't even known she'd had muscles.

"You did great today."

She spun around at the sound of Ty's voice.

He looked way too good in his dusty jeans and faded gray T-shirt with a hole below the collar. She brushed her fingers self-consciously through her hair. She felt out of her element away from the city. If she looked as worn out as she felt, she was one scary sight.

"About what happened on the mountain," she began, untying the flannel shirt from around her waist.

"Sorry I grabbed you like that." He stared at her hard, his gaze unreadable. "I don't know what got me so worked up."

Worked up was good. This morning she'd been worried he'd want to push her off the cliff himself.

He shook his head when she tried to hand him the shirt. "Keep it. It looks better on you anyway."

Her heart fluttered as delicate tendrils of hope trickled out from its edges. "Thanks." She tried for neutral ground. "How are things going with your family since the GoldStar story broke?"

The smile he gave her was brittle. "What family?"

She cringed. "I'm sorry."

"I'm not. Actually, it's my parents and Charlie who've disowned me again. Clare and I had dinner last week. For the first time in years, we had a conversation that didn't end in a fight."

"I'm glad," Kendall said, wishing she could reach out and brush the sadness from his face. "The rest of them will come around eventually."

"I doubt it. Did you come here to talk about my dysfunctional family? I think an e-mail would have worked." He tilted his head and studied her. "Or even a phone call."

"Would you have talked to me?"

"That would've been difficult. My phone had a little accident after you left. You made your choice clear."

"Great choice." She smiled sadly. "I threw away everything that mattered to me for a dream that I was too headstrong to realize I didn't want anymore."

He went still. "What does that mean?"

She dragged in a deep breath. Now was the moment of truth. "I quit my network job. I moved back to Denver a few weeks ago. I'm staying with Sam until I find a new place."

His gaze shifted as if he couldn't stand to look at her.

Her stomach clenched, but she rushed on, "I told you I'd worked most of my life for an opportunity like the one in New York. That was true. The problem was I never stopped to reevaluate if my childhood dream was right for the woman I've become. Once I got there I was homesick for a place that was only supposed to be a stepping stone on my—"

He held up a hand. "If you say the word *plan* I'm going to do something I might regret later."

She tried to smile. "Not going to say the word. I've got enough regrets for both us. I realized it wasn't *the place* I missed, it was *the life* I created here. My friends . . . the community . . . you." She toed the dirt. "Mainly you."

Tears stung the back of her eyes, and she hoped her voice would hold out. "I got everything I ever wanted." She smiled through the tears that clogged her throat. "It turns out I wanted all the wrong things."

"What do you want now?" He turned back to her. His eyes scanned her face. His voice was low, no more than a whisper.

She wiped her hand across her cheeks. "To belong somewhere. I want a home, work I care about, maybe a cat." She paused and met his gaze. "I want another chance."

When he said nothing, just continued to stare at her, she felt her chest begin to deflate. The cool breeze tickled her wet cheeks. In the distance, a woodpecker tapped out a rhythmic beat against a tree trunk.

Kendall wanted to jump into Sam's Land Cruiser and speed away before she could be humiliated. But she'd committed to trying to make things right with Ty, and she couldn't quit now.

She didn't care if she sounded desperate. "I know you said no second chances. I don't blame you. I was stupid, selfish, and I probably don't deserve another shot." Now the tears were coming fast and furious and she hiccuped before continuing, "I need you to know how sorry I am. You're best man I've ever met. You deserve to fall in love with someone wonderful, someone who deserves you and—"

"I already have."

Kendall's mouth gaped open as her heart wrenched. Her legs threatened to buckle. It had only been six weeks since she'd last seen him.

"Oh."

She reached into the pocket of her jeans for a tissue. Finding none, she wiped her nose on the back of her hand. Her dignity was lying in a pathetic pile on the ground. One more soft kick at it wasn't going to hurt. "I hope you'll be happy," she whispered, looking everywhere else but into his eyes.

His hand reached out and tugged at the front of her shirt, pulling her to him. "There's a boarding pass in the glove compartment of my truck." He tipped her chin up so she couldn't avoid his gaze. "I was flying to New York in the morning."

She swallowed. "For a visit?"

He leaned forward and placed his mouth on the fluttering pulse at the base of her neck. "For as long as you would have me," he said against her skin. "I was coming to fight for you. For us. You made me realize that I never want to give up on the things that matter." He kissed his way up her neck, then took her face between his hands. "You matter, Kendall. You were waiting for the plan to make you into who you wanted to be. But you're already that person. You had the power all along."

"Another Dorothy Gale moment," she said with a smile, "and you're Glinda."

He frowned at her.

"The good witch," she explained. "Except in flannel, not a pink gown."

His brows drew together. "Are you sure you didn't hit your head on the mountain?"

"Positive," she said and wrapped her arms around his neck. "You were saying . . ."

He laughed. "I was saying that you're smart, determined, dedicated, and loyal."

"Loyal?" She sniffed. "Dogs are loyal."

"And beautiful and sexy. Dogs aren't sexy."

"Agreed."

He kissed the corner of her mouth. "I love how you challenge me every step of the way. I love who I am with you and what we are together." He tightened his grip on her, nipping at her earlobe before whispering, "I've been working on my own plan."

"Is that so?" she asked, her knees going weak as his breath tickled her skin.

"It involves you and me—"

"And a second chance?"

"And a third, fourth, or fiftieth chance, if that's what it takes." The pads of his callused thumbs brushed across her cheeks. "I love you, Kendall. Now that I've got ahold of you again, I'm never letting go."

"I love you, Ty. You are the man I want to spend the rest of my life with, dirt and all."

"What do you know?" He grinned as he spun her around in a crazy circle. "Chicks dig flannel *and* dirt."

She kissed him again. "This chick digs you." When he finally put her down, she held her hands in front of his face. "It must be love because I broke all but one of my nails to impress you."

With exquisite tenderness, he kissed the tip of each finger. "Everything about you impresses me." He leaned forward and placed another lingering kiss on the side of her neck. "Let's go home and I'll work on soothing some of your other aches," he said against her ear, his voice a sexy rumble.

A shiver ran down her spine that had nothing to do with the cool mountain air. "Wherever you are, Ty Bishop, that's where my home is."

"Forever?" he asked.

She laced her fingers in his. "Forever."

EPILOGUE

"Are you sure you have to head home so early?" Sam asked. "There's a new martini bar downtown I thought we could check out."

Kendall scrunched up her nose. "We don't drink martinis."

Sam grinned. "True. But it seems like the sort of trendy spot where Denver's newest morning anchor might enjoy being seen."

Kendall returned her smile. "Well, this morning anchor has to be to work at four a.m., so a late night is not in my future."

She glanced around at the casual Mexican restaurant where they'd met for her celebratory dinner. Strings of lights in the shape of *jalapeños* lined the walls, papier-mâché piñatas fluttered from the ceiling, and the Formica booth top was clean but chipped in several places.

"Besides, what could compete with this atmosphere? There's no place I'd rather be."

"The chips are to die for," Chloe added, popping one with a generous scoop of salsa into her mouth. "We're so happy you're back."

Thanks to the Silver Creek story, Kendall had been in hot demand once word got out that she'd returned to Denver. She ignored the calls from Bob Cunningham and Channel 8, even though he left numerous messages about how Liz Blessen was now working in the Albuquerque market.

Instead Kendall had weighed her options and what *she* wanted from her career. She received offers for investigative reporting positions, but decided she liked the mix of news, politics, and lifestyle pieces the morning show format provided. The wide demographic she had access to as host appealed to her, as did the input she had on features and special reports. It might not be as fast-paced or glamorous as New York City, but it was a perfect fit for her.

Just like Ty.

A young woman approached the table. "Aren't you Kendall Clark?"

Kendall nodded.

"Can I get your autograph?"

She felt Ty and her two friends smiling at her. "Do you watch the news?" she asked as she took the pen and paper from the woman.

"Not really," she said, shaking her head. "Any chance you're going to do another series like *It's Raining Men?*"

"No chance," Ty answered for her.

She scribbled a message and her name then handed the paper back to the woman, whose gaze remained on Ty.

"I guess things didn't work out with the computer geek?"

Kendall laughed. "Things worked out exactly as they were supposed to."

The woman nodded quickly. "Hot guy. Nice choice," she whispered then walked away.

Sam burst out laughing and even Chloe couldn't keep a straight face. "Do you regret doing *It's Raining Men*?" Chloe asked. "It seems like you'll never be able to leave it behind."

"I don't want to," Kendall said. "Owen is now a friend, and the promotion was the catalyst that took my life to where it is right now. It helped me understand that it's who I am on the inside that counts, not the woman I thought I was supposed to be."

"Because you're perfect just the way you are," Ty whispered and placed a soft kiss on the top of her head.

"Damn, he's good," Sam muttered. "If we can't convince you to come to the martini bar, can we borrow the eye candy?"

Kendall snuggled into Ty. "If you take him, who will tuck me in?"

He reached his hand around the back of the booth to run his fingers across her bare shoulder. "Sorry, ladies," he said to Sam and Chloe. "Looks like I'm booked."

Kendall's gaze dropped to the diamond that glittered on her left hand. "You're booked for the rest of your life, buddy."

"Fine by me," he said and pressed his mouth to hers.

"Ugh," Sam groaned. "Get a room."

Chloe punched Sam on the shoulder. "Don't be such a buzzkill. They're cute."

"Cute like chicken pox."

Kendall smiled at Ty as her two friends bickered. She couldn't remember ever feeling so happy.

She'd burned her list in the fire pit on Ty's patio the first night she'd moved in with him. It felt good to finally trust her instincts and her heart. The more she gave herself over to the possibilities her life could hold, the more they seemed to unfold before her. Even her parents had agreed to visit and were flying into Denver from Kansas City for the Fourth of July weekend.

At first she'd been nervous about what Ty would think of them, but he'd already had several sweet phone conversations with her mom

and had been following the Kansas City Royals since the start of baseball season so he'd have something in common with her dad. They were
hosting a barbeque, and while she doubted his parents would attend,
Clare would be there and even Charlie had agreed to stop by.

They left the restaurant hand in hand. A full moon lit up the night
as they walked the few short blocks to his truck. Her future was as
bright as the glow from that moon, and she planned to savor every
moment of it.

ABOUT THE AUTHOR

Michelle Major grew up in Ohio but dreamed of living in the mountains. Over twenty years ago, she pointed her car west and settled in Colorado. Now her house is filled with one great husband, two beautiful kids, several furry pets, and a couple of well-behaved reptiles. She's grateful to have found her passion writing stories with happy endings. Michelle loves hearing from readers, so find her on Facebook or Twitter or at www.michellemajor.com.